'A real cracker … Steph Broadribb kicks ass, as does her ace protagonist' Mark Billingham

'Pacey, emotive and captivating, this is kick-ass thriller writing of the highest order' Rod Reynolds

'A relentless page-turner with twists and turns that left me breathless' J.S. Law

'Fast paced, engaging and hugely entertaining' Simon Toyne

'Brilliant and pacey' Steve Cavanagh

'Excitement and exhilaration flies off every page' David Young

'An explosive, exciting debut' David Mark

'A hell of a thriller' Mason Cross

'A setting that zings with authenticity' Anya Lipska

'Fast, furious and thrilling' Graeme Cameron

'A series that will run and run' Howard Linskey

'A blistering debut' Neil Broadfoot

'If you love romantic suspense, you'll love this ride' Alexandra Sokoloff

'A stunning debut from a major new talent' Zoë Sharp

'Perfect for fans of Lee Child and Janet Evanovich' Alex Caan

'Another adrenaline-fuelled, brilliant thriller from Steph Broadribb. Trouble has never been so attractive' A.K. Benedict

'Powerful, passionate and packs a real punch' Fergus McNeill

'Delivers thrills at breakneck pace' Marnie Riches

'Assured and emotionally moving' Daniel Pembrey

'Crying out to be a Hollywood movie' Louise Voss

'High-octane and breathlessly paced' Ava Marsh

'One of my favourite debut novels for a long, long time' Luca Veste

'A fast-talking, gun-toting heroine with a heart of gold'
Claire Seeber

'A top crime talent! Unputdownable' Helen Cadbury

'Relentless, breathtaking and emotionally charged' Jane Isaac

'A gritty debut that will appeal to Sue Grafton fans'
Caroline Green

'Great action scenes and great atmosphere' C.J. Carver

'Crazy good ... full-tilt action and a brilliant cast of characters'
Yrsa Sigurðardóttir

'Broadribb's writing is fresh and vivid, crackling with life ... an
impressive thriller, the kind of book that comfortably sits alongside
seasoned pros' Craig Sisterson

'Fast paced, zipping around the south-eastern US with chases,
fights, ambushes and desperate escapes ... All the action is well
described, with the right amount of bone crunching, gunfire and
gore. It feels realistic and not over the top ... there's a sensitivity in
the telling of Lori's struggle to save her daughter that gives *Deep
Down Dead* a bit more depth than other action thrillers'
Crime Fiction Lover

'A thrilling, assertive and energetic read, go on I dare you, grab
yourself a copy' LoveReading

'Yet again, Steph Broadribb has written a great, engaging
novel' Segnalibro

'I absolutely loved this book. Just everything is right – from the
plot to the characterisation to the setting as we weave in and out of
the southern states, including the ominous gator country. The
authenticity of Steph's language is, as always, impressive' Joy Kluver

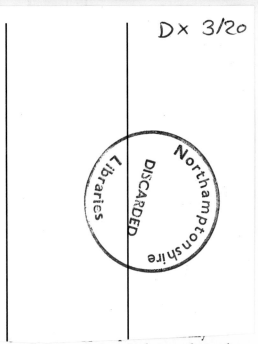
addictive thriller in which our heroine Lori Anderson takes on her most unforgiving adversary yet – darkness itself' Liz Loves Books

'*Die Hard* on speed'! A brilliant, fun, one-sitting read that will push your adrenaline levels sky high!' Off-the-Shelf Books

'This is Broadribb firing fast and furiously on all cylinders as we take a massive thrill ride into Chicago's criminal elements. An electrifying read that will have you on the edge of your seat, praying for Lori to succeed … a fresh and exciting take on the quintessential locked-room mystery' Live & Deadly

'An extremely tense, action-packed thrill of a ride with a relentless pace that had my heart pounding and pulse racing throughout' Novel Deelights

'A fast-paced and exhilarating read that I managed to finish in just two days. I know, without a doubt, that I'll be hopping on board to find out what happens next. Breathtaking and brilliant' Hooked from Page One

'Broadribb is at the top her game, keeping this pacey, relentless novel rattling along at almost breathtaking speed and building tension on tension as the body count increases ... a superb addition to the Lori canon' Blue Book Balloon

'A gutsy, relentless and substantial book with a heart of gold – rather like Lori herself. And I hope she comes storming back in another adventure very soon' My Chestnut Reading Tree

'Brimming with tension, high-stakes jeopardy and high-voltage action, and a deep, emotional core, *Deep Dirty Truth* is an unmissable thriller by one of the freshest and most exciting voices in crime fiction' Steph's Book Blog

'This book is a real firecracker and takes off from the first page ... Broadribb's writing style is full on and unrelenting' The Library Door

'This is a very tightly written book, the action relentless, the characters unforgiving. But don't just take my word for it: read it' The Literary Shed

'Explosive, emotional and full of the usual wicked humour, this is another sure-fire Lori Anderson hit. This is a series that could run and run ... and I can't get enough' Jen Med's Book Reviews

'A compelling and thrilling read with a kick-ass protagonist readers are going to love' By the Letter Book Reviews

'The story is so sharp, so well written that I felt like I'd been following all along' Tales before Bedtime

'It is tense, exciting and surprising but is also packed with perceptive characterisation, an atmospheric sense of place, some witty touches of black humour and real emotional depth' Hair Past a Freckle

ABOUT THE AUTHOR

Steph Broadribb was born in Birmingham and grew up in Buckinghamshire. Most of her working life has been spent between the UK and USA. As her alter ego – Crime Thriller Girl – she indulges her love of all things crime fiction by blogging at crimethrillergirl.com, where she interviews authors and reviews the latest releases. She is also a member of the crime-themed girl band The Splice Girls. Steph is an alumni of the MA in Creative Writing (Crime Fiction) at City University London, and she trained as a bounty hunter in California, which inspired her Lori Anderson thrillers. She lives in Buckinghamshire surrounded by horses, cows and chickens.

Her debut thriller, *Deep Down Dead*, was shortlisted for the Dead Good Reader Awards in two categories, was a finalist in the ITW Awards, and hit number one on the UK and AU kindle charts. The sequels, *Deep Blue Trouble* and *Deep Dirty Truth,* soon followed suit. *My Little Eye* (2018) and *You Die Next* (2019), written under her pseudonym, Stephanie Marland, were then published by Trapeze Books.

Follow Steph on Twitter @CrimeThrillGirl and on Facebook at facebook.com/CrimeThrillerGirl or visit her website and sign up for her readers' club: crimethrillergirl.com.

Other titles in the Lori Anderson Series
Deep Down Dead
Deep Blue Trouble
Deep Dirty Truth

DEEP DARK NIGHT

Lori Anderson Book Four

Steph Broadribb

**ORENDA
BOOKS**

Orenda Books
16 Carson Road
West Dulwich
London SE21 8HU
www.orendabooks.co.uk

First published in the United Kingdom by Orenda Books, 2020
Copyright © Steph Broadribb, 2020

Steph Broadribb has asserted her moral right to be identified as the author of this
work in accordance with the Copyright, Designs and Patents Act, 1988.

*This is a work of fiction. Names, characters, places and incidents are either products of
the author's imagination or are used fictitiously. Any resemblance to actual events,
locales or persons, living or dead, is entirely coincidental.*

A catalogue record for this book is available from the British Library.

ISBN 978-1-913193-17-1
eISBN 978-1-913193-18-8

Typeset in Garamond by typesetter.org.uk

Printed and bound by CPI Group (UK) Ltd, Croydon CR0 4YY

For Nanna,
with love x

PROLOGUE

Sure they knew they shouldn't go down to the basement.

It was damp, unsafe, their parents said. And there were rats – a whole bunch of rats. They knew for sure about the rats because they'd seen them with their own eyes. But they'd lived in the neighbourhood their whole lives, and the warnings didn't make no difference – the place being off limits that way made them want to go down there even more.

Danger was cool, they thought. They were young and wanted adventure and fun is all – something to give them a break from school and studying and exams. And the tension at home – the anger and the resentment, the frustration and fights.

And it was huge down there in the basement – a dark space that stretched out the whole way under their apartment building, maybe a whole lot further. They wanted to explore it all, see what was hidden down there in the far corners, inside the mouldy cardboard boxes and shielded underneath those thick plastic-covered stacks. They broke in all the time. Picked the lock if they had to. It was all a part of the thrill.

This one time, though, something was different.

They smelled it first.

Sometimes when they opened the door to the basement and stepped inside, it just smelled of damp cardboard and old, stale air. Every now and again there'd be something else – bleach or some kind of chemicals, a dead rat, a garbage sack forgotten and left to fester rather than getting put out with the rest of the trash. From time to time, when they left they'd leave behind the aroma of the mellow smoke from their joints, or the smell of young bodies experimenting with sex for the first time.

But on that day, the smell was different. And instinctively, a primal sense within them told them it was bad.

Still, they didn't turn back. Because, well, curiosity, you know.

The five of them huddled closer together; the one with the nickname Hawk in the front, and the one they called Lookie at the back. And they kept on going, scanning the dark void of the basement with their flashlights. No one wanted to be the one to suggest they turn back.

Every step further, the smell got stronger. Acrid. It clogged in their throats and made their eyes water. And as it did, they figured it was more than one smell – it was like skidding tyres and bonfires and bacon, all mixed up together, but not in a good way.

They found him a few steps later.

He was on his knees. Hands roped behind his back.

His blackened lips were wide. His contorted face twisted mid-scream.

An old tyre had been hung around his neck. It had gotten damaged by the fire, but it was still intact. The man hadn't fared so well. He was dead – they could tell that much for sure – nobody could have survived. But who he was once, beneath the burnt, blackened flesh, that they couldn't tell, at least not right then, anyways.

Lookie vomited. One of the girls started crying. The rest of them just stood and stared and didn't know what to do. Hawk – always the bravest of the group – took a few steps closer. Said they needed to call the cops. Give a description. Do the right thing.

The others were just about to agree.

Then Hawk began to scream.

1

CLOUD GATE, MILLENNIUM PARK, CHICAGO

Chicago isn't a one-mob kind of a place. There's a whole bunch of them, all vying for the top spot, but the Cabressa crime family – for whom FBI Special Agent Alex Monroe has a major hard-on – has its history written in blood among the bricks and bridges of this windy city.

But right now there's no sign of blood or the infamous wind. Here in Millennium Park the sun's out and the breeze is a gentle whisper. Still, I shiver. In spite of the cloudless sky, fall in Chicago just doesn't come close to matching the intensity of the Florida heat.

Beside me the gigantic metal 'Bean' sculpture, so called because it's shaped like a kidney bean laying on its side, towers upwards. It's way taller than me, many times over, but compared to the size and scale of the buildings in this city it seems kind of like a doll-house miniature.

Turning, I scan my surroundings, double-checking I've gotten into the right position. Huge skyscrapers rise like glass-and-steel mountains behind me and on both flanks of the park. Ahead of me, dwarfed by the giant buildings all around but determined not to be upstaged, the trees look real fancy in their fall colours of burnt gold, bronze and red. I gaze past them, across the great lawn, to the edge of the park and South Lakeshore Drive. I can't see it from here, but I know from the map I committed to memory on the way here that just beyond the street lies the shimmering water of Lake Michigan. I exhale. I'm in the right place.

In the distance, I hear a clock chime. It's noon. This is the rendezvous point. They were very clear: Millennium Park, twelve o'clock, in front of the Bean, facing towards the lake. The person I'm meeting should be wearing a Chicago Bulls ballcap and carrying a go-cup from Starbucks, but that's all the intel I have. I scan the people around me – three ladies, clad in bright Lycra shorts and crop tops, jogging, a bald guy walking five dogs of assorted sizes, a couple of families – obvious vacationers from the way they're pointing at things and stopping to look, and a load of folks walking along the pathways or sitting at the wooden benches eating lunch. At least five of them are wearing Bulls caps, but none is carrying a Starbucks.

Damn. I need to meet the contact. I have to get this job done.

I check my watch: near on five after twelve. Turning, I glance at my reflection in the huge mirrored surface of the Bean. Flick my gaze to the right. The reflections of people further from the sculpture are more distorted because of the curving sides, but JT is still easy to pick out – tall and athletic with dirty-blond hair – he's a little ways across the grass, joining in with a park yoga class. He's the only one wearing Levi's.

You won't be alone. I'll be hiding in plain sight, JT had said. And I'm glad he's here. Because even though I guess there's more safety in meeting in a busy public place like this, you can never really be safe when you're waiting on a meeting with a mobster. A mobster who, right now, is late.

I wonder if they came and didn't like what they saw. I know how these old crime families tend to be real patriarchal. Could be they took a look at me and decided they didn't want to do business with a woman. I've had that before – a female bounty hunter just isn't macho enough. It's dumb-as-a-stump talk, obviously, but you get burned that way a few times and it sure does begin to irritate.

Or maybe they won't show. Could be that calling them up cold and telling them I had something Cabressa wants didn't pique their interest enough. I think of the debt I owe to FBI Special

Agent Alex Monroe for helping me out on my last job in Miami, and the fact I'd do just about anything right now to be free of that debt and back home with my daughter, Dakota. I glance again at JT, who's clumsily attempting a downward-dog yoga pose, and wish that we could have stayed home in Florida, away from the mob, with more time to work through the past decisions that've recently come back to haunt us.

I adjust my weight from foot to foot. Press my palm against the outside of my purse and check that the contents are safe. I feel the curves of the metal object inside and exhale. Hope to hell our plan works out. After what happened just a couple of weeks ago in Miami – me getting caught in the middle of a three-way shoot-out between law enforcement and two fractions of the Miami Mob – I'm not sure I have the stomach for much more violence. But I'm no quitter. This isn't my first rodeo, and I'm damn sure that it won't be my last.

'Miss Anderson?'

Turning as I hear my name, I see a man approaching me from the other side of the Bean. He's almost as wide as he is high, and in all truth he's not that short. His Popeye arm muscles look like they're about to bust clean out of his shirt sleeves, and his thighs are stretching his pants to the max. There's a red Chicago Bulls ballcap propped on top of his mop of curly black hair. He's wearing shades, and I'd reckon on him being in his mid-forties. He's swigging an iced coffee from a Starbucks plastic go-cup.

My stomach lurches but I keep my voice strong, professional. 'Yes?'

'I'm Critten.' He takes off his shades. 'I hear you got something you want to tell my boss?'

His cold blue eyes take a predatory sweep of me, like a shark does a free diver. I hold my ground, square my shoulders and straighten my spine. 'Sure do.'

He jerks his head towards the path leading out across the park to the water. 'Let's take a walk.'

I do as he says, and once we reach the pathway I start talking. 'Like I said on the phone, I've got the gold chess pieces from the 1986 Vegas Legends game. Word is your boss is in the market for a set of pieces like that.'

Critten says nothing, but there's a muscle pulsing in his neck.

'It's the full set, all one point three five million dollars' worth.' I glance at Critten again – he's staring straight ahead, giving nothing away. 'I'll take eight hundred thousand, and your boss will think you've brokered him a real bargain.'

'How do we know you're for real?' Critten says. He's still looking along the path, not making eye contact.

I scan the people near us, figuring there must be more mob guys around. But there's no one real obvious, just some parents hand-in-hand with young kids, a couple of joggers with their dogs trotting alongside them, tongues lolling out, and a group of college kids in #NotMyPresident T-shirts, chattering loudly. None of them looks like a threat. Critten, on the other hand, moves his hand to his belt, and as his jacket flaps open, I see the gun at his hip.

Sliding my hand into my purse I feel the cool, hard metal inside and pull out the proof that I'm not bluffing. I hand it to him. 'Here, this should convince you.'

He stops walking and examines the pawn. It looks tiny in the middle of his meaty palm.

Stopping beside him, I wait. Feel my heart punching faster against my ribs. Trying not to think about his gun, just inches from me, I calculate how long it'd take for me to grab the Taser from my purse and fire it into him, if things turn bad.

Ten seconds pass, then another twenty, as Critten examines every bit of the pawn. Suddenly there seem to be fewer people around. I notice a man in a sport coat a little ways from us, taking pictures on his cellphone; there are bulges beneath the coat, exactly where a double shoulder holster would hold a pair of guns. As our eyes meet, I look away. Then I see another guy, sitting on a bench, watching us. There's a gun at his hip, same as Critten. He sees me looking, but he doesn't glance away. Nor do I. I might be in these boys' city, but I'm not a woman to back down easy. Let them watch us; I've got a job to do.

A full minute goes by and still Critten doesn't speak. Like a girl all dressed for prom and standing on the front porch looking out for her date, I'm getting real sick of waiting. My mouth's as dry as gator hide in the sunshine. Everything hinges on this. I need for Critten to take the bait.

Finally, he looks at me. 'Tell me how'd you get this?'

I act coy. 'Let's say I procured it.'

'How?'

I glance away. Not sure how much to tell, or how much I want to tell. I decide to stay as close to the truth as I can without giving away my involvement with the Feds. 'I took them from Marcus Searle – the man who butchered your employee and stole them.'

Critten shrugs. 'What employee?'

'Patrick Walker, your accountant. I know what happened to him and his family on board the yacht *Sunsearcher*. I saw the pictures on the news. And I know Searle was behind it and took the pieces.'

'How the hell you know about that?'

I don't tell him that I made the discovery when I was on an off-the-books job for the FBI – tracking down the escaped convict, Gibson 'The Fish' Fletcher, before he crossed the border into Mexico. And I stay silent on the fact that Gibson had been working for Special Agent Alex Monroe – stealing the chess pieces to facilitate an elaborate sting operation in Chicago – and that messed-up situation, and the one I'm now in, was all due to Monroe's hard-on for Cabressa. Instead I smile real sweet and say, 'Word travels fast, especially when the items are high value and blood gets spilled.'

Critten frowns. 'Way I heard it, the man who took them ended up dead. You do that?'

I shake my head. 'He was already dead when I found him, but the pieces were no place to be seen. I figured if I could find them there'd still be people interested in buying. Your boss is top of that list.'

'We haven't seen you in our city before.' Critten narrows his eyes. His fist clenches around the pawn like he's trying to choke it. 'Are you with Herron?'

I shake my head. 'Herron? I've no idea what the hell that is.'

Critten looks unconvinced. 'So you just a thief then?'

I stare into his cold, hard eyes. Force myself not to look away. I try not to think how many people have already paid for these chess pieces with their blood, that I must be outside my head to do this job. 'I don't work for anyone. I'm more of an opportunist.'

We stare at each other for a long moment. I hold my breath. The tension makes my stomach flip.

'Okay then,' says Critten. He thrusts the pawn back into my hand.

I frown. Confused. 'Okay?'

Critten doesn't reply. Instead he leaves me standing on the path, watching him walk away. For the first time in a long while, I don't know what to do next.

They haven't taken the bait. I've blown it.

I can't pay my debt to FBI Special Agent Alex Monroe.

How the hell am I going to get myself free?

2

Back at the hotel things are going to hell in a handbasket. JT sits on the narrow desk beside the coffee maker. I remain standing. I've filled JT and Monroe in on what happened at the park. Now JT and me are watching Monroe as he paces back and forth across the room. His black suit is crumpled, his tie crooked.

'What the hell – there isn't a plan B?' I say. 'I don't get it. This was never a dead cert anyways.'

Monroe shakes his head. Keeps pacing side to side across the room. It's a nice room in a mid-price chain hotel – big enough for JT and me to remain anonymous but small enough for us to make a quick getaway if we need one. And even though it's got a decent square footage, with a king bed and a good-sized closet, with all Monroe's frenetic energy it's suddenly feeling a whole lot smaller.

'We should go home,' says JT, running his hand over the dirty-blond stubble on his jaw. 'No sense staying if they're not going to play.'

'No.' Monroe stops mid-pace. Turns to JT. 'Not yet.'

JT frowns. 'Why not? The guy just—'

'Look, Cabressa is totally OCD about things. It's a well-known fact. Something he's made a part of his image – nothing overlooked, every issue dealt with.'

I take a step closer to JT. His muscular bulk and chilled attitude is a whole lot more appealing than Monroe's angry mania. 'Maybe he just doesn't want these chess pieces all that bad,' I say.

Monroe turns to face me. 'He wants them, believe me.'

I frown. 'A man like that, head of the top mob family, can buy anything he wants. There are other valuable chess sets out in the—'

'Not like this one,' snaps Monroe. 'Cabressa was in Vegas for the game back in eighty-six. He took his favourite son, his youngest, Roberto – a hell of a chess player himself, so I'm told, and a real fan of the game. It was the boy's seventeenth birthday.'

'So he wants it as a present for the son?'

Monroe shakes his head and runs his hand through his overlong red-brown hair, making it stick up. It makes him look like a greying rooster. 'Roberto died a few days later back in Chicago. There was a pile-up on the freeway outside the city, nine vehicles – the boy never stood a chance. Cabressa was still in Vegas when it happened. The last time he saw his son had been the night of the chess match.'

I bite my lip. Hell, losing a child, that's the kind of pain a parent can't ever recover from. 'Cabressa wants the chess pieces to remind him of that last time with his son?'

'He's been after these pieces a long time,' says Monroe. 'You gave Critten the pawn, yes?'

I nod. 'I told you that I did, but that he gave it right back.'

Monroe mutters something to himself then looks back at me. 'Then we'll have to hope it isn't all lost.'

'But the man just walked away,' says JT. 'That's a pretty clear demonstration of not being interested.'

'Sure,' I say. 'But if what Monroe's saying about Cabressa is true he'll still want this chess set.'

Monroe nods. 'We need to wait. He'll get in touch.'

JT looks from me to Monroe and lets out a long whistle. Doesn't look a whole lot convinced. 'Maybe.'

Monroe frowns. The tension between Monroe and JT hangs thick in the air. JT doesn't trust Monroe an inch, and right now they look like two stags ready to lock horns.

I move over to the bed and sit down as I change the subject. 'So who's Herron?'

Monroe looks real worried. 'Who told you about him?'

'Critten asked if I worked for him. I said no.'

'In truth, we don't know who Herron is. My sources tell me the rumours started a couple of months back, every time a shipment went missing, stashes got robbed, or a club got turned over, the word on the street was that Herron was behind it. They're saying he's the new man in the city, with a fresh crew, and that's making everyone twitchy.'

'Even Cabressa?' JT says.

'Especially Cabressa.' Monroe rubs his hand across his chin. 'And when Cabressa gets twitchy, there's usually a bloodbath.'

A wave of nausea floods through me. I swallow hard. Fix Monroe with my gaze. 'I didn't sign up for that.' I glance at JT. '*We* didn't sign up for it.'

Monroe gives me a crocodile smile. 'But you're here, and you got a job to do.'

'This is a sting, not a combat operation.' JT's expression is real serious. His tone no-shit determined. 'Things get messy, we're out.'

Monroe glares at him a beat longer than is comfortable. Then he laughs. 'Yes it's a sting, for sure, and you're not here as cannon fodder, but I don't want any mistakes, you got to make sure you do the job right.'

I can tell from the firm set of his jaw that JT's pissed. I'm feeling the same way. I catch Monroe's gaze. Raise my eyebrows. 'You doubting us now?'

Monroe sighs. 'Look, for the Bureau the pieces are the tip of the iceberg. You do your job right, and we arrest Cabressa for handling stolen goods. Taking him into custody will send a ripple through the mob's world, and word will get around fast to the other crime families here in the city. When we've arrested him before there's not been enough evidence to make things stick, but we do this right and we'll be able to hold him. That'll disrupt the power he has over the city.' Monroe's getting more passionate as he speaks. 'People will see he's in trouble and they'll want to talk, cut a deal, before they get pulled in. The crime eco-system will be in flux, and that'll give us the chance to get more dirt on Cabressa. Then we can lock him up for good.'

I've never seen Monroe so passionate about catching a criminal, and I know for a fact that he's only really interested in doing things where he personally benefits. I tilt my head to one side. 'Why this guy; why not one of the others?'

'What the hell does it matter to you?' Monroe growls.

'I'm curious why you're getting your panties in such a wad. And if I'm risking my hide for this, why don't you humour me?'

Monroe is silent for a long moment. Shakes his head. 'Look, I lost a promotion when the sting I planned last time failed ... That made this personal. If I lose again this time, my career's over.' He glares at me. 'That a good-enough reason for you?'

'Sure,' I say. But, as I watch him start to pace again, I wonder if he's told me the whole truth. It wouldn't be the first time he's lied to me. And when he does lie, things have a habit of getting real dangerous, real fast.

3

Monroe leaves a few minutes later, but the tension remains in the room. The confusing meet with Critten and the conversation afterwards with Monroe has me feeling jacked up as a junkie on crystal, and I can't work out if it's the fear of failure or the fear that the job will go ahead that's causing my adrenaline to spike.

Getting up from the bed, I cross the room to the coffee maker and start to fix a mug. I fumble with the mechanism. My hands tremble as I slot the coffee pod into the machine.

JT moves closer to me. 'What's up?'

'I'm fine,' I say, struggling until the pod clicks into place. Then I fill the water reservoir and press the button. Watch the coffee start to drip through into the mug below. Clench my hands into fists to stop them shaking.

JT looks real concerned. He puts his hand on my shoulder. 'Like I said, Lori, you don't have to do this.'

'But I really do. This whole situation has me stuck tighter than a hair in a biscuit. It's the only way I can pay the debt I owe Monroe.'

'But you know he only helped you out on that Miami job because it suited him? He wasn't doing you any favours.'

'For sure.'

'Then walk away.' JT shakes his head. 'You don't owe that man a damn thing.'

JT might be right, but things didn't work like that. 'He'll always have a hold on me if I don't do this, and you know that's the truth – if I do something he doesn't like he'll find some way to make our lives hell. Shit, he'll probably try and throw you in jail again just to spite me.'

JT looks thoughtful. He looks at me with those big old blues of his. Squeezes my shoulder. 'I guess you're right. But working for him on this? Hell, I sure don't like it any.'

'Me neither.' I lean into his hand. Hold his gaze. I can sense that there's something more he wants to say, but he's holding back. That's kind of the story of our relationship – things left unsaid, stuff left unresolved. I don't want it to be that way, and I can guess what's eating at him. I take a deep breath. 'You want to talk about Dakota and the bone-marrow donor thing?'

He lets go of my shoulder. Takes a step back. 'Jeez, Lori, you want to have that conversation right now?'

Beside me the coffee maker gurgles and hisses as the last of the coffee filters into the mug. I keep my focus on JT. 'We've been putting it off, and I can tell it's eating at you.'

'Maybe we should get this job—'

'Could be I don't survive the job. I don't want you never knowing.'

'Don't talk like that.' He looks hurt, worried.

'Talk like what? Honestly?'

JT shakes his head. 'Okay, look, while we were on the boat with Red, Dakota told me how when she was real sick and they were thinking the cancer wasn't going to respond to the treatment, they said she might need a bone-marrow donor.'

'That's right.'

'She said you got tested but you weren't a good match.'

Tears prick my eyes as I remember my sweet baby girl, just eight years old then, lying in the hospital bed. Skinny and sick, she'd looked as pale as the bed sheets. It was the worst time in both our lives. 'Yes.'

JT frowns. 'You never got in touch with me, even when our daughter was so sick she might die. I could be a match – but you never even gave me the chance to—'

'It didn't come to that. She started responding to the treatment, and the doctors stopped talking about needing a donor.'

'What if she'd died back then? I'd never have known I had a daughter.' There's hurt in his eyes, and a whole lot of it. His voice is loaded with emotion as he says, 'You would have robbed me of that, Lori.'

It's true, I would have. But back then I had no idea JT would even like the idea of having a daughter, let alone be happy to find out he'd gotten the real thing. Ten years ago, he'd been a reclusive bounty hunter and I'd been grieving the death of my best friend, who'd been shot in front of me by my good-for-nothing husband, Tommy. Tommy had evaded the cops and disappeared into the wind. JT had helped me find him. He'd taught me how to track a man and how to capture him. But when it came to me bringing him in, Tommy attacked me, and I emptied my gun into him. JT never understood why I didn't shoot to disable rather than kill, just as he'd taught me. I couldn't explain why either. That night, as JT helped me bury Tommy's body, our romance died. The next day I packed my belongings in silence and drove out of JT's life. Four months later, when I realised I was pregnant, I made the decision never to tell him – he'd let me go and he'd never once tried to make contact after the fact. He'd been the love of my life, but I'd gotten used to the idea that I'd never see him again. And it'd stayed that way until earlier this year, when a job brought us into contact, and back together. Since then we've been trying to figure things out.

'After the way things ended between us I never thought—'

JT sighs. 'I lost it. That night, with Tommy fresh under the dirt, I wasn't thinking straight.' He steps closer. Softens his tone. 'I forgave you a long time ago, Lori. But seems you couldn't bring yourself to forgive me?'

He's right. I couldn't, not for a real long time, and then, when the hurt of how he'd reacted to me in the aftermath of Tommy's death had dulled a little, it felt like it was too late to make amends. Still, a relationship goes both ways. 'If I had my time over, I'd tell you. But that's with hindsight and the knowledge that you were happy to learn about Dakota. Back then things were different. No,

I didn't tell you, and yes I am sorry about that, but you near as dammit threw my ass out on the street, and although you're saying you forgave me, you didn't come find me either.'

'I didn't. And I've regretted that for a long, long time.' He reaches out and takes my hands in his.

My mouth goes dry and my heart hammers against my ribs for a whole other reason than earlier. It's always been this way between us. His touch ignites something in me no other man ever has, but it's not just the physical stuff; it's the connection and the way I feel with him, how he is with Dakota, and the fact I know for sure that he would do anything to protect our daughter, even if it cost him his life.

JT gazes into my eyes real serious and says, 'So where does that leave us?'

'Here. Now,' I say, squeezing his hands. 'Let's start again from now.'

'Deal,' says JT.

I press my lips against his and we kiss. He wraps his arms around me and I melt my body against his. In this moment I feel calm, and secure, and happy. JT has always felt like safety.

My cell vibrates in my pocket. The maximum-volume ringtone blasting out like the horn of the Staten Island ferry. Reluctantly, I pull away from JT and take out my phone. I smile when I see the caller ID.

Pressing answer, I accept the FaceTime call. 'Hello sweetheart.'

Dakota's face fills the screen. Her long strawberry-blonde hair is pulled up in a messy bun on the top of her head. Her vivid blue eyes, just like her daddy's, are bright, and she's got a big smile on her face. 'Hey Momma. Mr Red said it would be okay to call. Is it okay? Is JT with you? What's Chicago like?'

I laugh at the barrage of questions. Turning the phone, I angle it so she can see JT on screen as well. 'Of course it's okay to call – it's great you're calling. We're both here. Chicago is nice but not as hot as where you are.'

'We're on the boat,' says Dakota. She pans her phone's camera round, giving us a glimpse of the green-and-gold livery of my good friend and trusted confidante, Red's, houseboat. 'Mr Red is teaching me how to sail. Today I was allowed to steer her all by myself.'

'That sure sounds a lot of fun,' says JT. 'What was Red doing when you were steering?'

'He was having a sleep.' Although Dakota's expression has turned serious, I can tell from the giggle in her voice she's trying hard to conceal her mischief.

I decide to play along. Gasping, I fake a shocked look. 'He was doing what?'

I hear Red chuckling in the background. He steps into the picture, crouching down beside Dakota. Silver hair, deep tan and a wicked smile, he looks relaxed and happy as he says to Dakota, 'Don't you go worrying your momma; tell her and JT the truth.'

She giggles. 'Don't worry, Momma. We're just messing with you. Mr Red was right next to me, teaching me how to steer. I was good, wasn't I?'

'That you were, Little Fish,' says Red, the chuckle still in his voice.

I raise an eyebrow at JT. 'Little Fish?'

'It's what Mr Red calls me, because I'm such a great swimmer. We're going swimming every day in the ocean. Mr Red has been teaching me how to dive too. First I had to do sitting dives but now he's said I can do standing dives off the boat.'

'I'm glad you're having fun, honey.'

Suddenly she frowns, and her tone changes. 'When are you and JT coming back?'

I look at JT. In truth we don't know. I need to get this job done, and it could be I need to do a whole lot more grafting to get closer to Cabressa. The longer he takes to take the bait, the longer we'll have to stay in Chicago.

'We're not sure,' JT says. 'Hopefully not too much longer.'

'Well good,' Dakota says. 'Because I *really* want to show you my diving.'

JT nods. 'I'm looking forward to that.'

'Me too,' I say. 'Honey, can I have a word with Red?'

She frowns. 'Why?'

'Just boring grown-up stuff.'

'Okay. But come home soon, Momma. Then we can all go swimming together.' She passes the cell to Red.

JT pours our coffee as I wait for Red to move across the boat, away from Dakota. As he walks, the camera shows the outside deck, the water lapping against the jetty, a gull pecking at something on the wooden boards. Then it swings upwards and Red reappears. 'What's on your mind, Miss Lori?'

'Is she really doing okay?' I can't disguise the worry in my voice.

'She's doing real good. You don't need to be worrying on that. Your little apple didn't fall far from the tree – she's tough, just like her momma. You just focus on doing what you need to get done, then get on back here.'

'Thank you,' I say. 'For everything.'

'You've no need to thank me, Miss Lori. It's always a pleasure helping out.'

'I'm thanking you anyhow.'

Red puts his fingers to his forehead in a mock salute. 'Appreciate that.'

In the background I hear Dakota asking if they can practise diving again. I swallow down the feeling that I should be there with her, having these new experiences with her, not stuck in another city, in another state, thousands of miles from home. I force a smile. 'You should go.'

Red nods. 'Be safe, Miss Lori.'

'You too,' I say, and then I end the call.

I stand for a moment with the cell clutched to my chest. Fighting the urge to say to JT, *Let's grab our stuff, leave this hotel and jump on a plane back to Florida.*

He passes me a mug of coffee. Frowns as he sees the expression on my face. When he speaks it's as if he can read my mind. 'Lori, we can walk away from this. Whatever you decide, I'm with you.'

The coffee is hot in my hand. The fear of failing, or worse – something bad happening to both me and JT, and our daughter getting orphaned – makes my stomach churn. There's a sour taste in my mouth, and I feel like I might vomit. I feel this, but I still know that I can't walk away. I made a deal with Monroe – a deal with a devil in federal agent's clothing: his help for mine. And I never go back on my word.

I put my coffee down on the desk and shake my head. 'I can't,' I say softly. 'Like I said, I have to finish this. We'll never be free of Monroe if I don't.'

'Then together we'll get it done, and then we'll go home.'

'Thank you,' I say, as my cell buzzes.

I check the screen. Feel my pulse accelerate as I read the message from an unknown number:

DuSable Bridge. 30 minutes. Bring the pawn. Come alone.

4

I have to get my hustle on if I'm going to make DuSable Bridge, where Michigan Avenue crosses the river, in thirty minutes. I've gotten my purse, with the pawn inside, and a can of pepper spray in the pocket of my Levi's, but that's all the preparation I had time for before I left the hotel.

I walk fast. Scanning ahead as I weave around the folks on the sidewalk, not letting them slow me down. I know JT is tailing me a little ways behind – watching my six, looking out for whatever these Chicago mobsters have in store.

And although I'm having to improvise, I'm real glad Critten made contact so fast. I've no kind of patience for Cabressa's people getting a case of the druthers. I don't have time for any messing around – I want to get this job done and get home to my baby. I check my watch. Walk faster. Just over fifteen minutes to make it to the meeting point.

The screech of tyres alongside me makes me jump. I dart away from the traffic. Glance over my shoulder and see a blue, double-cab pick-up truck mounting the curb as the driver wrestles with the wheel. It's hurtling towards me.

I think, brake failure. My breath catches in my throat, and I dive across the sidewalk. The front of the vehicle just misses smacking into me and stops inches from the wall on my right. I exhale hard, but there's no time to relax. The door of the rear passenger side swings open and, as a bearded blond guy with his expression set at a grimace grabs for my purse, I realise this isn't a damn accident.

Holding tight to my purse, I try to wrestle it away. Damn

asshole's trying to rob me. Well, I sure as shit won't be allowing that to happen.

'Let go, girlie,' growls the blond man. He yanks the purse so hard that I lose my balance and stumble forward, slamming against the side of the vehicle. All around us horns are blasting.

'You done?' calls a man from the driver's seat. I can't get a good look at him from this angle. All I see is a denim jacket stretched over broad shoulders and a glimpse of the side of his head: dark hair, a pair of shades and a navy ballcap.

'Give me a minute,' says the blond guy.

He tugs at the purse again, but I'm clinging on tight. I want to reach for my pepper spray but can't risk taking my hands off the purse.

'We gotta move,' says the driver. There's an undertone of panic in his voice now.

The blond guy cusses. It feels like he's losing his grip on the purse. I lean forward, pulling it to me. Next moment he slams the heel of his hand into my chest, shoving me backwards.

I let go of the purse. 'Asshole,' I hiss at the blond guy.

He ignores me. Yells to the driver, 'Go.'

The truck starts reversing. I grab for the shoulder strap of my purse through the still-open rear passenger door. As my fingers close round it the vehicle bumps down off the sidewalk. I grit my teeth. Can't let them take the purse, it's got the pawn I need to show Critten.

I won't let them take it.

The vehicle stops. I see the driver shoving the gear into drive. The blond asshole is trying to tug the shoulder strap from me. I've a split second to make up my mind, so I choose. As the vehicle lurches forward onto the street I leap off the sidewalk into the back seat of the pick-up.

'What the...?' says the blond asshole.

I use my momentum to power a punch into his bearded face. Capitalise on his surprise to grab the purse.

He won't let go. 'Give it up, girlie.'

'Never,' I hiss.

The car speeds down the street, throwing me back against the rear seat. The rear passenger door is still open and bashes against my feet with every bump in the road. The blond won't let go of the purse and nor will I. We punch and slap, and when he tries to grab my face between his fingers I bite him. He recoils briefly, but I'm not in a good position – half lying, half sitting across the back seat. I get an elbow jab into his ribs, but it's not as powerful as I'd like. Next moment the car races around a bend, and I'm thrown across the seat again.

When I look back at the blond asshole he smiles, his lip curling up like a rabid dog. Raising his hand, he lunges towards me.

That's when I see the knife.

5

JT's a half-block behind Lori when it happens. Tailing her at the distance they'd agreed; watching her six but not being too obvious about it.

She reaches an intersection and turns the corner onto another street. It's okay, it's part of their planned route, but JT has a few seconds without eyes on her until he reaches the corner and makes the turn too. When he's around the corner his breath catches in his throat. Up ahead Lori is having a tussle with someone in a blue pick-up that's been parked across the sidewalk.

Shit. JT's seen enough ambushes in his time. He knows that's what this is. Breaking into a run, his focus is on Lori and what's going down half a block ahead. He sprints faster. Dodges around the line at a hot-dog stand and along the sidewalk.

He doesn't see the attack coming.

One moment he's at full speed. Next a heavyset guy wearing a leather jacket and shades steps into his path.

JT moves right to scoot around him.

The guy sidesteps, blocking him. 'Steady cowboy.'

JT skids to a halt. Keeps his eyes on what's happening up ahead. Sees Lori battling whoever's inside the truck. Next moment she's yanked forward and slammed into the side of the truck. JT winces. Ducks around the heavyset guy.

The guy reaches towards him. 'Don't...'

JT ignores him. Pushes back into a sprint. Has to get to Lori.

He makes it two paces before he feels it. First a sharp pain in his back, just above his kidneys, which he barely has time to register before the volts hit him. As his knees give way, JT glances over his shoulder. Sees the Taser in the heavyset man's hand.

'Should have stopped when I told you,' says the heavyset man. 'Didn't want to have to school you this way.'

Body convulsing. Nausea rising. JT tries to keep running, but his legs won't obey him. As the volts keep pumping through him JT hits the concrete.

His vision's blurring, but he scans the street, has to know Lori is okay. The pick-up truck is reversing. Lori's still fighting. She flies back from the vehicle then, as the truck lurches forward, she leaps inside.

JT tries to call Lori's name, but he can't form the word.

The truck accelerates rapidly.

Then they're gone.

6

My situation in the truck has gone from bad to shit. With the blond asshole wielding a knife, my priority has shifted from getting the purse back to getting out of here alive. It seems like the driver wants me gone too, but his asshole associate has other ideas. He lunges the blade towards me.

'Just get her out of here,' yells the driver.

'I'm working on it,' says the blond asshole as he thrusts the blade at me again, just missing my left cheek.

I struggle, but he's got one of my wrists in an iron grip and I can't twist away unless I let go of the purse. I hang on a moment longer, mentally struggling with giving up the purse with the pawn inside for Cabressa. Slam an elbow into the asshole's ribs. He bellows and swipes the knife at me, the blade scores along my forearm. Warm blood drips into my face.

I let go of the purse and reach into the pocket of my jeans.

The driver's yelling at the asshole again, but I pay him no mind. I've got a plan to get free and clear, I just need to focus. I force myself up from the seat, and in the brief moment before the asshole pulls me down I see we're approaching an intersection. I don't have long. Timing is everything.

Shoving my boots against the offside door, I kick it open. As the asshole brings the blade down towards my belly, I yank the pepper spray from my pocket and fire it into his face. I keep spraying until he's screaming for his momma, then I grab for the purse, get a hold of the shoulder strap and push myself across the backseat.

I leap from the truck as it starts to swing left across the intersection. As I crunch and roll across the sidewalk I think I've done it – gotten free and kept the purse. But as I uncurl myself I realise that's not true. The shoulder strap is still in my hand, sure, but the purse has been severed from the strap by a clean cut.

Hot damn.

I slam my palms against the sidewalk in frustration.

The blue pick-up speeds away.

7

The sirens are getting louder. JT can't be here when the cops arrive.

He feels dazed. His body's stopped convulsing, but his limbs are leaden and unresponsive. But staying put can't happen. He needs to move.

Looking up at the crowd that's gathered around him, JT searches for the heavyset guy in the leather jacket and shades. He catches snippets of the conversations. Sees the pity in the rubberneckers' eyes.

'...poor bastard didn't stand a chance...'

'...argument or whatever...'

'...just left him flapping around and ran...'

The heavyset guy's gone – melted into the crowd and away. The sirens are coming closer.

Clenching his jaw, he rolls onto his side and forces himself up to sitting. His vision blurs, and a wave of nausea surges through him. JT clenches his fists. He can't sit here on the sidewalk – he has to get to Lori.

The memory of her disappearing into the truck replays in his mind, firing him into action. Gritting his teeth, he forces his body to move and scrambles to his feet. He stands, swaying for a moment.

'Are you okay?' says an older lady in pearls and a tweed skirt, her face creased in concern.

JT tries to answer but can't form the words. Instead he turns in the direction the truck took Lori and takes a step. Stumbles. And just manages to stay upright.

'You really should sit down,' says the lady.

JT doesn't look back. Bruised, wobbly, he focuses on putting one foot in front of the other and heads for DuSable Bridge.

8

I wait on the bridge. Alone. My chest aches from where the blond asshole punched me, and blood's smeared over my forearm from the slash of his blade. I've got no purse, no pawn to show Critten, and there's no sign of JT.

I've got a bad feeling about this.

On either side of the bridge skyscrapers tower – huge, glinting buildings of glass and chrome reflected in the water running beneath me. They say there's honour among the old-school mobsters, and that being honourable is a real good thing. I guess that's true, but the honest truth is, sometimes honour will get you killed. In this world disagreements are settled in blood, and respect and strength are king. Getting mugged and bloody sure as hell isn't the way to win the Cabressa family's respect.

I check my watch. They're late. Thirty-four minutes have passed since the message from the unknown number. The traffic continues along the bridge, a steady stream of SUVs and sedans. The foot-traffic is minimal, and I feel kind of exposed standing here, leaning against the iron railings, not doing a whole lot of anything. I glance around again. The breeze tickles against my face and makes my hair billow around my shoulders. I tuck it behind my ears.

A homeless guy ambles past me. 'Got any change?' he asks.

I dig in my pocket and pull out a few quarters. 'Sorry, it's all I got.'

He smiles, exposing blackening teeth. 'Thanks, lady.' And then sings me a couple of lines of an old Cole Porter song.

His voice is so good it makes the hairs on the back of my neck stand to attention, and for a moment I forget the pain in my chest and why I'm here on the bridge.

Then I hear tyres slowing against asphalt and turn to see a black SUV pull up alongside me. It's got Illinois plates featuring the Bulls and dark tinted windows. My heart starts hammering, and I forget about the homeless guy with the stunning voice.

The rear passenger-side window slides down. The man inside has curly black hair and wears a dark suit that's tight around the biceps – Critten. He looks at me over the top of his shades. 'Get in.'

I do as he says and climb inside. Try not to look fazed. The back seat seems too small. Critten's bulk takes up far more space than I do, and him being so close makes me feel trapped and claustrophobic. A flashback to the bearded asshole and getting mugged plays on a loop in my mind. Critten might look more gentlemanly, but the threat feels real similar. I force myself to stay calm. Clasp my hands together, attempting to disguise that they're trembling.

I've always felt an element of fear about the jobs I do. In the right dosage it can help you. It gets your adrenaline firing, makes you think clearer, faster – gets you alert and ready to tackle anything that comes your way. But if the fear builds too much, all that good stuff swings things around; the nerves make you hesitant, jumpy and too cautious. That's when you start making mistakes. And mistakes, in my world, can be fatal.

As the doors lock and we move out into the traffic I know that I'm trapped. My heart rate accelerates.

Critten leans across the leather seat and checks me for a wire. I say nothing, don't complain. Feel kind of violated, but I figure there isn't any point. He's showing me I'm his prisoner now, in this car, so I have to play by his rules. I decide to let him keep thinking that for now.

Satisfied there's no wire, he speaks. 'The boss liked your sample. He wants the rest.'

I frown. 'What sample?'

Critten smiles. 'The pawn.'

I'm confused a moment. Then I hear a cellphone ringing. Glancing down into the footwell in front of Critten I see my purse. Guess that it's JT calling me. Glare back at Critten. 'You had your people mug me?'

'You're in our city now, wanting to play with the big hitters. We needed to test how tough you are.'

I cuss under my breath. Hot anger rises inside me but I keep my tone cold and hard. 'I don't like to be treated like I ain't got a lick of sense.'

'I get that,' says Critten, adjusting his shades. 'Turns out you're real impressive for an itty bit of a girl.'

I hold his gaze. Narrow my eyes. 'I'm a woman not a girl.'

Critten nods. 'You're tougher than your back-up guy for sure.'

'What the hell did you—?'

'Cool it. He's fine.' Critten smiles, showing a set of impossibly white teeth. 'A little tickle with the Taser never hurt no one.'

The flames of anger in my belly leap higher. 'You bastard.'

Critten shrugs. 'You needed to understand the situation, Miss Anderson.'

'Understand what?'

'That you need to do as we say, or you'll regret it.'

I give a little shake of my head. Look Critten up and down. To hell with respect and getting in with these assholes. They might dress like gentlemen but the only thing these people understand is tough talk and tougher actions. My tone is granite hard as I say, 'Don't let your mouth write a cheque your ass can't cash.'

Critten stares at me a long moment. Just as the silence is getting real uncomfortable and I'm thinking I'm going to need to make a leap from another moving car today, he laughs and slaps me on the shoulder. 'You're quite a girl, Miss Anderson.' He passes me my purse. 'You've got a deal – eight hundred thousand for the chess set. Let's hope *your* ass can cash the cheque your mouth's written.'

I'm relieved Cabressa's taken the bait, but I'm still real angry. But I don't let either emotion show; instead I think fast, and start to outline my proposal for the exchange. 'No problem. Let's do this by—'

'You play poker?' Critten asks, interrupting me.

I frown. Lie. 'Sure.'

'Friday night at eleven, come to suite 6311 in the Skyland Tower.'

'And then what?'

Critten smiles. 'Then you play.'

This is not what I expected, but I say nothing. Wait for him to continue.

'Stay in the game until you're heads-up, just you two. Then bet the pieces and let him win.'

That makes no kind of sense. If I'm betting the pieces so Cabressa can win them, what about the money? My cover story is that I'm here to sell the pieces – it'll fall apart if I seem too eager. I narrow my gaze. 'No. That doesn't work for me. I need to get paid.'

Critten thinks a moment. Huffs and puffs a bit like this is a big inconvenience. Then begrudgingly says, 'Okay. Have it your way. Once you're heads-up, Cabressa will put in your fee as a bet of eight hundred thousand dollars, or something of that value, and you'll bet the chess set to match him. He'll lose the game, and you'll keep the money, but you'll let him keep the chess pieces as a gift, a mark of respect for a good player.'

I narrow my eyes. Unsure. 'What if he doesn't lose?'

'If we've agreed he'll lose then he'll lose. He'll fold a winning hand if needs be to get the pieces.'

I'm more comfortable with this plan, but I still have to wait until we're one-on-one. 'What happens if I don't make it to heads-up?'

Critten fixes me with a serious stare. 'Then he'll be pissed, and you don't want to let that happen.'

I swallow hard. Stay cool. The plan works – I'll get the fee

Monroe wants through Cabressa's eight-hundred-thousand-dollar bet, and I'll gift him the chess pieces. I nod. 'Okay, let's do this.'

Critten taps his hand against the driver's headrest and the SUV glides to a stop. The door beside me unlocks.

'Eleven p.m., Friday,' Critten says. 'Skyland Tower 6311.'

I nod and pull on the handle, opening the door – keen to escape the car and these assholes.

As I turn to get out, Critten grabs my arm, his meaty fingers pinching my bare flesh just below the wound from the bearded asshole's blade. He looks at me over the top of his shades. His cold, dead eyes bore into mine. 'The buy-in's fifty thousand dollars, Miss Anderson. Bring it in cash, and bring the pieces.'

'How am I meant to get that kind of cash?'

'That's not my concern. Just get it, or don't bother showing. It's your choice.'

'I'll get it, and I'll be there,' I say, hoping Monroe can get his hands on some FBI funds fast.

Critten squeezes my wrist tighter. 'Don't fuck it up. Don't deviate from the plan. The boss doesn't enjoy surprises.'

I pull my arm away from him. Meet his gaze with a serious glare of my own. 'Neither do I.'

Back on the sidewalk I wait until the SUV has driven away, then call JT. I tell him I'm okay, and he tells me that he's fine. We arrange to meet back at base. Ending the call I get my bearings and start walking back towards the hotel. I rub my wrist. Look at the red marks Critten left and the long tear in my skin from the bearded guy's knife. Assholes. If I didn't need to keep Critten sweet for this job I'd have gotten a whole lot of pleasure pressing my Taser against the barrel of his belly and firing both pins into his domineering flesh.

I shake my head. Paranoid gangsters are worse than the everyday kind, and from what I've heard Cabressa is plenty paranoid, with all kinds of vices. From my conversation with Critten it seems that poker is one of those.

It's too bad I've never played a game in my life.

9

'No, listen to me. You do that, you'll end up in a world of trouble.'

Cussing, I throw my cards down on the table. 'I'm never going to get the hang of this.'

'Sure you will,' JT says. His voice is steady, patient. 'You just need practice.'

I'm sick of practising. We've been at this for three hours straight and I still can't play a convincing bluff. 'I've got less than twenty-four hours to get good enough to beat players who spend thousands of dollars doing this every week.'

'We best keep on it then.' JT's tone is light, but I can tell he's as worried as I am. He pours me another two fingers of bourbon and the same for himself. We're both sore from our run-in with Critten's men, but we're trying to tough it out and stay focused on the job. JT takes a swig of his bourbon then collects up the cards, shuffles them and deals again.

I look at mine: ace of hearts, king of spades. Not a bad hand, but I try not to let my enthusiasm show. Instead I concentrate on making sure I keep the cards on the table, but angled so they're shielded from the imaginary players around the makeshift poker table we've fashioned from the desk.

JT looks at me. Raises an eyebrow.

I rap the table with my knuckles. 'Check.'

'Okay, then.' He deals the flop – three cards laid face up in the middle of the table: king of hearts, eight of diamonds, four of clubs.

With the cards in my hand, and the king on the table, I've got a pair of kings, ace high. I feel a fizz of excitement; I might be able to win this game. Remembering what JT said about bluffing, I try to keep my expression neutral.

'Lori?' JT says. 'What are you going to do?'

'Check,' I say, tapping my fingers against the table to show I'm not betting again this round.

He watches me a beat longer, then separates three fifty-dollar chips from his stack and pushes them into the centre of the table – increasing his bet. 'Raise.'

I take a sip of my bourbon, fiddle with my chips, and then stare at the board. Act cautious, like I'm dithering about making a bet. I want to bet enough to keep JT in the game but not so much he folds because he thinks I've got a winning hand.

After another glance at my cards, I pick three fifty-dollar chips from my own stack and slide to the middle of the table. 'Okay.'

JT deals the turn. It's the king of clubs.

I've got three cards of the same kind. Again, I try not to let my excitement show. Splitting off another three chips, I push them to the middle of the table. 'Raise.'

Nodding, JT matches me.

He deals the last card. It's the ace of diamonds.

I've got a full house of aces and kings – a great hand.

JT looks at me, waiting to see what I'm doing.

I pretend to debate with myself a moment then push all my chips into the middle of the table. 'I'm all in.'

He looks surprised. 'You sure about that?'

I nod. I know if he's got a flush – where all the cards are from the same suit – or a straight of five cards in numerical order he could beat me, but hell to caution, the odds just gotta be in my favour at least once tonight.

'Alright then.' He downs his bourbon in one, and then pushes his stack of chips into the middle to join mine. 'Let's see what you got.'

JT looks real sure of himself, and for a moment my confidence falters. I turn over my cards and watch his expression as he sees the hand I'm playing. He smiles, and for a moment I think he's got me beat. Then he flips over his cards – a two and a nine – and I realise he's got nothing.

I smile, feeling relieved and exhilarated all at once. 'I guess that makes me the winner.'

'Good job,' JT says. 'You used a smart strategy, getting me to keep betting. Your bluffing is getting better.'

'I'm relieved to hear it.'

'But there's this thing you do when you're concentrating, you kind of bite your lip with your bottom teeth.' He gestures towards my mouth. 'You need to stop that.'

'I wasn't aware I was doing it.'

'Yep. Thought that. It's always when you're thinking about your bet, if you've got a good hand.'

Damn. 'Okay, let's go again.'

JT shakes his head. 'It's late. We can do more in the morning. It'd be good to deal in Monroe as well – get you some practice with more players.'

'I'd rather just practise with you.'

'It's more realistic if there's three of us. And you haven't played him before – it's a good chance to have a try at reading a new player.'

'I guess.' It's hard to put any enthusiasm into my voice.

JT ignores my druthers. 'Good. And we can put the blinds into play. You'll have the big and little blinds in the game tomorrow – the forced bets that have to be made by the two people sitting to the left of the dealer at the start of each hand.'

'So you said before.'

'And they'll go up at regular intervals throughout the game. They should tell you the timings before you start playing. If they don't, then ask. That'll show them you know what you're doing. Don't let them intimidate you.'

'I'm a goddamn bounty hunter, and this isn't my first rodeo. I'm not going to let a bunch of—'

'It's just us two here, Lori.' He looks at me all intense. 'You don't need to bluff with me. What happened today wasn't good – mugging and cutting you, tasering me. These people play by a different rulebook.'

'They're assholes.'

JT nods. 'That they are.'

I exhale hard. Don't want to talk about how I'm feeling right now. It's not just the pressure of learning the game that stirs up emotion, it's that I'm playing the game that corrupted my ex-husband and turned him from a good man to a compulsive gambler, and from a gambler into a killer. I don't want to talk about that, and I don't want to talk about the fear I'm feeling about this job, and my distrust for Monroe. Instead what I need right now is a distraction.

Moving closer to JT, I run my hands up his chest and bat my lashes. 'You know you had fewer chips than I did in that last bet.'

'Is that so?'

I nod. 'For sure.'

'Seems I owe you a little more.'

'I'd say so.'

JT looks thoughtful. 'I wonder how I can make up the short-fall?'

I give him a playful smile. 'I got a few ideas.'

'Oh yes?' he says, moving closer.

We start to kiss, and the smoky, bourbon taste of him makes my stomach fizz with desire. I slide my hands back down his chest to his jeans and undo his belt. I want him. Need him. He pushes the chips from the table and lifts me onto it.

The sex is urgent. Passionate. We've always been gasoline and fire.

*

Later, we lie on the bed naked and sweaty. I trace my finger over the scars on JT's body. They're like a permanent reminder of the jobs we've done and the challenges we've faced, the bullet wounds and the stabbings he's taken – all in the line of duty. I shiver at the thought of what tomorrow will bring. We've lost each other before, but fate reunited us. Now we're taking on an old-school mobster on his own turf, and our only back-up is an FBI Special Agent who's unreliable at best, and at worst above the law. The potential for problems is high, and the outcome isn't guaranteed.

'It'll be okay,' JT murmurs in his sleep, then turns over.

I lie still, wishing I could believe him, and listening to the steady rhythm of his breathing. You think I'd be old enough to know that my wants can't hurt me; but in this life, this world, the threat of hurt is never far away.

So I don't want this night to end. I don't want to risk losing him again. Because, as I think through the job in my head, I see a multitude of ways the poker game tomorrow could play out, most of them bad.

Moving towards JT, I snuggle close against him and kiss the back of his neck. I slide my arm around his waist and entwine my fingers in his. He squeezes my hand. As I close my eyes I make a vow that I'll do everything in my power to get the job done right and us out of this goddamn city, away from Monroe and back to our baby.

10

Monroe's pounding on the door by seven. When we don't open up right away, he thumps again. 'You in there? We've got things to do.'

I open my eyes.

Getting out of bed, JT pulls on the jeans he hastily tossed last night, and goes to let Monroe in. As he does, I grab some clothes from the beaten-up leather carryall I always use as my go-bag and head for the shower.

I close the bathroom door and set the water running. Hear Monroe's voice, then JT's. I try to listen, but their words are too muffled by the walls and the water, so I give up. Stepping into the shower, I let it rain down over me, washing away the smell of sex and sleep, and helping me get my head ready for what's coming.

Fifteen minutes later I'm dressed and ready. I find JT and Monroe hunched over a stack of papers that they spread out across the desk. 'What's that?'

Monroe turns. His eyes are bloodshot. His suit looks crumpled. He looks like he hasn't slept a wink. 'Well, good morning. Nice of you to finally join us.'

I ignore him and his sarcasm, and focus on JT instead. 'What is it?'

'These are the blueprints of the Skyland Tower,' he says. 'Monroe brought them over. We're familiarising ourselves with the layout.'

Hurrying over to the desk, I take a look-see myself. The diagram on the top of the pile shows the floor plan for level sixty-three of the tower. It makes sense to be forearmed with information on the building's layout, especially if things turn bad and we need to hightail it out of there. I point to a sheaf of transparencies that are hanging down from one side of the plans. 'What are these?'

'They're the fit-out details that layer over each of the floor plans,' says Monroe, taking hold of the top transparency and smoothing it over the plan for level sixty-three. The drawings on the transparent sheet match the layout and add another level of detail. 'See, they show us the utilities, exit points and maintenance features.'

'Good.' I nod. We need as much intel on the Skyland Tower as we can get. Prior and proper preparation is key to prevent a shit show. 'So what have you found out?'

JT pulls out another sheet of blueprints and lays it alongside the one for level sixty-three. 'It's an interesting development. The Skyland Tower has sixty-three levels plus a roof terrace and heli pad on the sixty-fourth.' He moves his hand from the original sheet to the new one. On it I can see the image of a chopper landing space and a glasshouse. When he layers over the transparency I see the glasshouse has an emergency exit from the penthouse below, and there's an old-fashioned external fire escape zig-zagging down from the roof terrace.

I tap my finger against the marking on the transparency for the fire escape. 'Isn't this building too high for one of these?'

JT nods. 'Yep, it's all kinds of unusual, but having had a look at these plans it seems the architect has incorporated various, more traditional features into the building.' He shakes his head. 'Mind you, you'd have thought an external stairwell from the sixty-fourth floor would be a damn health-and-safety issue.'

'For sure.'

'You need to remember this building is all about luxury,' says Monroe. 'They'd have put things in here that you can't get in any other place in town.'

JT nods. He's never cared much for cities or buildings. 'Seems it's mainly fitted out as a luxury hotel, but the top ten floors are used as serviced residential apartments.'

'It's very expensive and very exclusive,' adds Monroe. He sounds impressed.

I cock my head to one side. 'A penthouse in this building seems an odd choice for a poker game. Wouldn't it be better run out of a club or something?'

'Not really,' says Monroe. Taking a photograph out of his jacket pocket, he places it on top of the blueprints. 'This is Carmella Davies. She runs the poker game you're going to. I met up with one of my key contacts in the city last night, and she told me this Davies woman is a real big deal. Her games are the most exclusive and have the highest stakes of all the games played here, and anyone who's anyone wants to get in on the action.'

I guess Monroe's *meeting* with his female contact has contributed to his lack of sleep and crumpled appearance. Taking the picture, I look at the woman – Carmella Davies. She's real pretty – late-twenties at the most, with black hair, olive skin and a smile that reaches all the way to her dark brown eyes. There's a genuine warmth about her that makes me want to smile back. Instead I look up at Monroe and say, 'Tell me everything you know about her?'

He runs his hand through his cockatoo hair. Nods. 'Word is she grew up in New York City. Started running games at nineteen, working for a big-shot businessman by the name of Linwood Banks. Carmella ran his weekly game for three years while waitressing on the side. Around a year ago she moved to Chicago and started up on her own. She still runs Banks's game in New York – flying back and forth – but she's built two games of her own here on Tuesdays and Thursdays: ten-grand buy-ins, no limit Texas Holdem. Three months ago she added a third game, played once a month in a moving location, but always here in the city. It's higher stakes, higher risk and the players are the cream of Chicago royalty – politicians, sport legends, mobsters, rock stars, you name it. Believe me when I say, if someone thinks they're a big deal in this city, then they're itching to get a seat at the table for her big game.'

JT frowns. 'If that's so, how did Lori get a seat so easy?'

'Because she's a guest of Cabressa, is my guessing,' Monroe says. 'The family is the ruling mob of the city, and my contact thinks there's some kind of connection between Linwood Banks and Cabressa. If that's the case, given she still works for Banks in New York, it wouldn't be smart for Carmella to turn down a request from the head of the Cabressa family.'

He's right, but the thought bothers me. Being a guest of a man like Cabressa – a man with protection and enemies – has its upsides and downsides: it can make you safer and more of a target, all at the same time. Right now neither one of those things makes me feel comfortable. 'What's the security like?'

Monroe takes the photo from me. Puts it on the desk and taps his index finger against Carmella's face. 'From what I've heard, she runs a tight operation. She has her own security to keep people in line, and, as players bring a lot of cash to the table, it's usual for them to bring along their own security too.'

'Armed security?' I ask.

'That'd be my assumption.'

I glance at JT. *Don't make assumptions* is one of our bounty-hunting rules. But here and now it seems like gossip and assumptions are all we've got to work with.

'Have there been any problems?' I ask.

Monroe shakes his head. 'Not that I've heard. Like I said, Carmella Davies runs a solid operation. You'll be safe enough in there.'

It's my turn for sarcasm now. 'Safe like how we got mugged and tasered on the street in full daylight yesterday? Yeah, that's real safe for sure.'

JT clears his throat. 'I'll go in with Lori.'

Monroe looks pained. 'You're meant to be on the outside of this, an extra layer of back-up, I don't want you—'

'This isn't a negotiation.' JT fixes Monroe with a hard stare. 'If players often have security, I'll be Lori's. She'll be walking in there with a bundle of dollars and the chess set. The pieces alone are worth one point three five million dollars. Her having security isn't going to faze them none.'

Monroe is silent a moment. Keeps glaring at JT.

'I like that idea,' I say, nodding. 'Adds authenticity, given the value of the assets I'll be carrying. Like JT says, they'll expect me to have protection.'

Monroe runs his hand through his flyaway hair. Looks pained. I can guess what he's thinking – that JT's real strong willed and doesn't like to follow orders. He's someone Monroe can't control. And if there's one thing Monroe always wants, it's to be the person in charge, the puppeteer.

JT keeps staring at the federal agent. 'This is a deal-breaker. If I don't go in, neither does Lori.'

The two men glare at each other.

I say nothing. Wait to see what happens.

Monroe looks from JT to me, and then back to JT. He shrugs. 'Fine. Just remember this is my operation.'

JT narrows his eyes. 'And *you* remember that it's Lori's life on the line.'

Monroe squares up to JT, and I feel the tension building. We don't have time for this posturing. We need to get focused. Learn all we can about the game and this penthouse.

'Enough talk,' I say, pushing between them and peering again at the blueprints. 'We need to get prepped. Monroe, tell me about the security in the Skyland Tower.'

Monroe glares at JT a moment longer, then turns to face me. 'It's part hotel and part residential, and the security is tight on both.' He removes Carmella's picture from on top of the blueprints, and then picks up the sheaf of papers, flicking through until he finds the one for the first floor. He points at the grand atrium of the kerbside entrance. 'This is the hotel lobby; it's separate from the serviced residential entrance and concierge, which is located over here.' He taps his finger on another entrance, equally grand, that's accessed from a different street.

'Is it possible to get from the hotel accommodation to the penthouse?'

Monroe shakes his head. 'Both share an underground parking garage and a state-of-the-art gym and spa complex, but except for that, the facilities are kept separate. The elevator cars either stop at residential floors or hotel floors; none stop at both. All the public spaces have security cameras.'

'So where will you be when JT and me go up to the penthouse?'

'I've booked a hotel room on level fifty-three, and a back-up SWAT team will be stationed on the street a couple of blocks away. It'd be too risky to bring them all into the building, so I'll monitor your progress from the hotel room and will alert the team if we need them to assist.'

I frown. 'Monitoring us, how?'

'I'm going to need you to wear a camera.'

'I'm not comfortable with that.' In truth the thought of it makes my stomach flip. When I met Critten he checked me for a wire before we spoke. There's no reason to imagine the poker game will be any different. If they catch me wearing one I have no doubt that they'll kill me and JT. Monroe has to know it's a fool move.

JT shakes his head. 'There's no way that's going to happen.'

'It has to,' Monroe says. 'Non-negotiable.'

'I can't do that, Monroe. It's a deal-breaker.' I keep my voice real serious. 'I won't wear a wire. If I do I'll be dead within minutes of stepping into that penthouse.'

Monroe looks pissed. 'It's not a damn wire.'

I frown. Don't believe him. 'What is it then?'

'A new generation micro camera – it's an ultra-high-tech piece of kit designed to stick onto your skin. It's camouflaged and virtually invisible, and built for covert ops. They won't pick it up in a wire sweep either – it doesn't use the usual frequencies, wi-fi or cell service – so you'll be safe.'

'And you can guarantee that?' says JT, looking sceptical.

Monroe sighs. 'I can't one hundred percent guarantee anything.

What we're doing is risky, that's the damn truth of it, but with the micro camera in place I'll be able to see and hear what you guys are seeing and hearing – it gives audio and visuals one way. It also means that whatever happens will be on camera – we'll have hard undisputable evidence – and if things go bad in that penthouse, I'll know and send in the team to pull you out.'

JT shakes his head. Looks at me. 'I don't like it, Lori, but it's your call.'

I don't like it either, but if Monroe's got eyes and ears on what's happening it does give us an extra layer of support. We won't be on our own, and if things go south then having a SWAT team storming in would be a real advantage. So I put my hand on JT's arm. 'We should take a look at the camera and see what we think.'

He looks reluctant. Frowns. 'You're sure about that?'

I nod. 'I am.'

'Good,' says Monroe. 'So there's one more thing you need to know about the penthouse where the game is taking place.'

I glance from Monroe to the blueprint. 'Okay.'

'Penthouse 6311 is one of four unique properties in the building. On the sixty-third level each penthouse has panic-room capability.'

I frown. 'Don't all penthouses have safe rooms?'

'They do,' says Monroe, tracing his finger around the perimeter of the penthouse on the schematic. 'But this penthouse doesn't have a panic room within it ... the whole penthouse can be locked down as a panic room.'

I raise an eyebrow. 'Interesting.'

JT nods. 'Before you stepped out the shower, Monroe was telling me it's the latest thing in luxury – all the new places are designed like this.'

'So what does that mean for us?' I ask.

'Nothing especially,' Monroe says. 'Just so long as things go to plan.'

Great. 'Let's just hope they do then.'

Monroe checks his watch. 'I need to get going, get things set up.'

'Can you get the playing cash?' I ask.

Monroe nods. 'I hope so. What did Critten tell you to bring for the buy-in?'

'Fifty thousand dollars.'

Monroe's mouth falls open. 'Jesus. That's a lot of federal money. Just how good a poker player are you?'

I glance at JT. Grimace. 'Let's say yesterday was my first time.'

Monroe mutters something under his breath. 'Then you'll probably need to buy yourself back into the game a few times to have a hope of hanging on in there until you're at heads-up.'

'Yeah,' I say. 'So can you get the money, because without that we may as well—'

'Quit nagging, I'll get us the goddamn money.' He shakes his head. 'You'd better damn well win.'

I cross my arms. Think, *Like I don't already know that*. Say, 'Good. You'd best get on it then.'

As he walks towards the door, Monroe gestures towards the poker set over by the coffee maker. 'And you'd better get practising. We can't afford to blow this.'

Asshole. I'm risking everything for this, and he's treating me like I'm some rookie.

I clench my fists. Look over at JT and see his jaw is set rigid and there's anger in his eyes. This will be our last time working with Monroe, on that I'm real sure.

After this we're done.

11

Monroe plays like he lives – hard and dirty. It's a little after two in the afternoon, and we're an hour into our first practice game as a trio. Monroe's up, JT's about even, and I'm struggling to stay in the game.

'So what've you got?' Monroe looks at me over his cards. His eyes have a manic glint – like he's jacked up on the adrenaline of the game. 'You think you're going to beat me? I doubt it. You're not playing well. You best quit, because you're not going to beat me. I'm going to win. I'll take all those chips.'

I look from Monroe to my own cards. Try not to let him rile me. I know the taunting is part of his game play; he's trying to distract me. In my hand I've gotten a pair of jacks. Not a bad hand, but the odds say it can be beaten. Biting my lip, I take my decision. Count four chips from my diminished stack and slide them across to the middle of the table. 'Call.'

Monroe lets out a little squeal and rubs his hands together. 'Yes siree, the lady wants to play.'

JT adds four chips to the pot, matching the bet. Then he deals the next three cards, placing them face up, one by one onto the table: queen of hearts, ten of diamonds, jack of hearts.

I feel a fizz of excitement as I realise I've got three of a kind, jacks.

'Now that makes things interesting,' Monroe says, taking another four chips from his stack and pushing them to the centre of the table. 'Raise.'

He's looking at me. Watching for my move. I take another four chips and add them to the pot.

Shaking his head, JT throws his cards into the middle of the table. 'Game's too rich for my blood. I'm out.'

'Just me and you, Lori,' Monroe says, grinning. 'Bring it on.'

My heart hammers in my chest as JT deals the next card. It's the jack of spades. I've got four cards of the same kind – jacks. It's a good hand. It can be beaten, but it's pretty up there.

'Raise.' Still grinning, Monroe puts another four chips in the middle of the table. He holds my gaze. Winks. 'What you going to do now, Lori?'

I hate how he keeps on using my name and the way he's trying to goad me. I hate it, but I react to it, because I'm human and I sure as hell don't want him to win this; to buy into the game in Skyland Tower I need $50,000 of the FBI's money, and Monroe's the only person who can vouch for me to get it.

I look at my chips – only nine left. My hand is good, but there's a possibility Monroe could have a straight of cards in numerical order that will beat it, or if his cards are hearts he could be on his way to a flush of five cards from the same suit. The safe thing here would be to fold. I glance again at my cards. I don't want to play things safe, I want to wipe the smile off Monroe's smug face.

I push the whole stack into the centre of the table and bet everything I've got. 'All in.'

He whoops. 'Things just got interesting.' Counting out nine chips he adds them to the pot. 'Come on then, I'll see you.'

I turn over my cards. 'Four of a kind, jacks.'

Monroe is smiling. 'Nice hand.'

JT looks worried.

Monroe turns over his cards. They're the two of hearts and the nine of hearts. He looks at JT. 'Why don't you deal us the last card?'

Taking the final card from the top of the pack, JT deals it face up on the table. It's the three of hearts. Monroe whoops and claps his hands. Disappointment punches me in the belly.

JT nods to Monroe. 'Flush beats four of a kind.'

With that last card Monroe got five cards in the same suit – hearts – a more valuable hand than mine. I cuss under my breath. Annoyed that I let myself get carried away with the game.

JT leans over towards me. 'I told you not to just play the cards. You've got to play the players as well.'

I glare at Monroe who's still gloating. 'I was doing that, but he was—'

'Listen to him, he's giving you good advice,' says Monroe. 'People try to hide their tells, but it's rare they truly can. You need to watch for their reactions and play the person, but you need to think about what you're giving away yourself too. You were easy to read, Lori. You bite your lip when you've got a good hand, and when you try to hide it your cheeks flush.'

I look from JT to Monroe. Feel angry, ganged up on. 'Why don't you play in the goddamn game?'

Monroe looks at me seriously. 'You know it has to be you. The men at the game tonight are regular high-stakes players. You play like you just did, they'll sniff you out as a rookie like a shark smells out blood, and then they'll hunt you until you're bled dry.'

Thrusting my chair back, I stand up from the table. 'I may as well not go then, because I doubt I'm going to be getting any better before the game tonight.'

Monroe holds his hands up. 'Don't be so hasty.' He gestures towards my cards. 'This thing you've got going on, the impulsiveness, it's a big part of the problem. Your game play is good, it's being such a damn hot head that you need to get under control.'

Frowning, I turn and walk over to the coffee maker and pour myself a mug. 'My head's just fine thanks.'

JT shakes his head. 'Don't let him get under your skin. You let him get to you in the game, that's why you lost. Your ego overruled your logic. If you'd have studied the board better you'd have seen the potential for that flush.'

I turn back and look at JT. 'I did see it.'

JT holds my gaze. Looks disappointed. 'You can't afford to get

overexcited. Tonight isn't going to be some beer-keg poker party.'
He looks real serious. His tone is calm, steady. 'In that last hand
you were reckless. Monroe's right when he says that you need to
curb that. Impulsive play is a sure-fire route to losing.'

Anger flares inside me. My tone is sharp, irritated. 'But he was
goading me the whole time, and I couldn't concentrate. I wanted
him to quit it.'

'I get that, Lori,' JT says. 'But it was intentional distraction. Not
every player is going to sit quiet and play like a gentleman; some
are going to try and rile you anyway they can, especially if you do
well in the opening hands.'

'I'm not going to go big in the opening hands, we talked about
that.'

Monroe nods. 'Good strategy.'

'Yeah,' JT says, fixing Monroe with his gaze. 'I've warned Lori
about how some players get. Advised her it's best to sit back and
let them get the dick-waving out their system before she gets full
into the game.'

Monroe ignores the jibe. 'Agreed. You need to stay in the game
long enough to go heads-up with Cabressa.'

'Sure. I'm real clear on what I need to do. I was the one with
Critten when he issued the instructions.' I don't keep the sarcasm
from my tone, and I don't say staying in the game past the first
round seems like one hell of a tall order. Instead I change the
subject. 'Did you bring the micro camera with you?'

Monroe shakes his head. 'No, I've got to pick it up this afternoon, along with the money and the rest of the chess pieces. I'm
briefing the SWAT team at nine, then I'll come back here and get
you set up.'

Nerves fizz in the bottom of my belly. 'Okay.'

Monroe holds my gaze. He looks real sincere, disconcertingly
so. 'I appreciate this, Lori. I know what you're putting on the line
here.' He looks from me to JT. 'The both of you are doing a good
thing.'

'You didn't give us much of a choice,' I say. Monroe forced us into this job – he got me out of a tight fix in my last job on the condition I did this one for him. I had to give him my word; and if I go back on it, he's threatened to arrest me and JT on the same trumped-up bullshit charges he'd made go away – so his faked sincerity doesn't mean a thing.

Monroe shrugs. 'One way or another, debts have to get paid.'

I watch him as he gets up and heads towards the door, the implicit threat hanging in the air between us. I owe him, and JT owes him. Without Monroe's assistance we'd both be back trying to prove our innocence – of crimes we didn't commit, but with no evidence to corroborate our stories. We needed Monroe and he helped us, but it was like making a deal with the devil. And now the devil's called in the favour.

'Keep practising,' says Monroe as he opens the door. 'See you tonight.'

As the door closes behind him I glance at JT. We don't speak, but I can tell from his expression that we're thinking the same.

What happens if we can't pull off this job?

12

'I'm not going to tell Monroe.'

JT's just gotten out of the shower. The white towel wrapped around his hips makes the tan of his chest look even deeper. Now I've told him my plan he's frowning, looking unsure.

'You think that's wise?' he says.

Sitting on our bed, I cradle the knight in the palm of my hand. It's heavier than it looks and it sure is real pretty – solid gold, with a line of emeralds around the base. I stroke the smooth sides. Thinking. 'Thing is, I'm not sure he's telling us *his* whole plan.'

JT's frown deepens. 'How so?'

'I can't see how this exchange at the poker game will get him what he wants. The point of this operation is to catch Cabressa in the act of *buying* knowingly stolen goods. If he wins them, or is gifted them as I'm instructed to, we're not fulfilling that brief.'

JT sits down on the bed next to me. Looks real thoughtful. 'I can see that's an issue, but surely Monroe would say something if he thought it was a problem. Could be he thinks the video from the micro camera is enough.'

I watch a trickle of water glide from JT's shoulder, down his chest to the fluffy towel at his waist. Nod. 'Could be.'

We sit side-by-side, not speaking for a moment. The only sounds are the slow drip of the shower in the bathroom and the hiss of the coffee maker.

I exhale hard. 'I just don't think he's telling me everything, and that worries me. Most non-Bureau people Monroe works with have a tendency to wind up dead or in jail. I don't want that happening to us is all.'

'For sure,' says JT.

I turn a little ways further towards him. 'That's why I think we need my back-up plan.'

JT runs his hand over the two-day-old stubble on his jaw. 'So you hold the knight back from the deal at the poker game. Then what?'

'When Cabressa realises it's missing, I offer it to him for an extra fee.'

JT cusses under his breath. 'That's a real dangerous game, Lori.'

'For sure, but if Cabressa is as obsessive about completing this set to keep alive the memory of the last time he saw his son, then he'll pay. I'll meet him somewhere public, do the exchange – dollars for the knight – and get it on film. That way Monroe will have evidence that'll stick without doubt.'

'Cabressa could get real pissed, Lori. He'll think you lied to him.'

'I'm pretty sure I can talk him around.'

JT holds my gaze a long moment, then nods. 'Monroe will be pissed too, and that footage you'll have of Cabressa will also show *you* selling stolen goods. Monroe could use that against—'

'Monroe only wants the evidence on Cabressa, and we'll have gotten it for him. He's got enough bullshit claims against us already; he's FBI for God's sake – if he decides he wants us in jail he can make that happen. This way he gets what he wants and we'll be free. We can be out of this city and back with our little girl.' I clench my fists. 'And we won't ever have to work with Monroe again.'

'I get that's why you want to do this, for sure I do.' JT looks at me all serious. 'But I just don't—'

'You got a better idea?'

He shakes his head. 'Can't say that I have.'

I turn the knight over in my hand, thinking. He's right about Monroe – there's no guarantee he'll keep to his word, and he could throw me in jail. My best chance to prevent that is to give him what he wants – a watertight case against Cabressa. I stand up, turning towards JT. 'Well then, my way is the way it's going to go down. Doubling down on getting Cabressa – it's our best shot.'

JT nods. 'I don't like it, but you know I'll support you.'

I smile. Feel relieved that he's not going to fight me on this. Need to get this job done and get out of this city. I step closer and put my arms around him. Lean down and kiss the top of his head. His dirty-blond hair is damp against my lips. 'I'm counting on it.'

*

I hide the knight in our hotel room. Standing on a chair, I use the screwdriver from the tool set in my go-bag to undo the screws holding the grill over the central air vent in the corner of the room, and remove it. With JT standing beside me, watching, I place the knight inside. I glance at JT. 'Okay?'

He nods. 'Yup.'

Taking the grill from him, I fix it back into place with the screws and step down from the chair. From the ground I can't see that there's a knight hiding behind the grill, but from certain angles I can see the light glinting off its golden body. Figuring that's good enough, I put the chair back behind the desk and check my watch – it's almost a quarter after five.

'You want to have another practice game?' JT asks.

'Sure,' I say.

Anything to help me kick ass tonight.

13

Use whatever you've got to get the job done – that's a rule I made for myself when I started bounty hunting and one that I'm using tonight.

JT whistles as I come out of the bathroom. 'Well damn.'

I smile, pleased with his response. 'You think it'll work as a distraction?'

'I'm real sure.'

I exhale, relieved. The low-cut black dress is tighter and shows a whole lot more of me than anything I'd usually wear. In truth I'm a jeans-and-tee kind of girl, but I need to get into character. The dress is my disguise for this evening, the costume of a bold and experienced poker player – a female poker player joining a table of male players. I'm guessing those boys will have all kinds of tricks up their sleeves for trying to distract and outsmart a new player in the group, and I figure the dress will help me cause a little distraction of my own. Like I said, you gotta use what you got to get the job done.

There's a rap on the door. Nerves start to fizz in my stomach.

JT answers and stands aside to let Monroe and one of his team enter the room. They're both wearing dark suits – the FBI uniform – but that's where the similarities end.

'This is Dirk, the tech guy,' says Monroe pointing to the younger, skinny guy with acne scars and black-framed glasses. 'He's going to get you set up.'

The young guy raises his hand in hello. He's as smart as Monroe is crumpled-looking.

Monroe looks at me expectantly. 'You ready?'

I nod. 'Yes.'

'Good.' Monroe looks at the tech, and gestures towards me. 'Go ahead.'

The young guy puts his bag down on the desk, and points towards the chair. 'Would you mind taking a seat for me, Miss Anderson.'

His voice is deeper than I'd have imagined. I nod and do as he asks, watching as he pulls a small metal box from the bag and opens it carefully.

Taking a piece of shiny card from the tin, he carefully removes something from it with his index finger and then turns towards me. 'I'm going to position this in your hairline so it captures whatever you're looking at.'

'Is that the micro camera?'

'It is.' He moves it closer so I can take a look. It's tiny. A flesh-coloured dot that looks nothing like a camera.

'That's going to film stuff, for real?'

'Totally,' he says, nodding enthusiastically. 'It's been tested in the field with great results. It's sweat resistant and should blend with your natural skin tone. Just tilt your head back a little for me, and I'll get it fitted.'

I do as he says. He pulls back the hair to the right of where my hair parts and presses the dot firmly against my scalp. Holds it for a few seconds, then releases the pressure. I can't really feel anything now he's removed his fingers.

As the tech guy arranges my hair back into place I glance at JT. 'What do you reckon?'

He squints at my hairline. Shakes his head. 'I can't see it from here.'

I take that as a good thing.

The tech guy rummages in his bag and hands me a compact mirror. 'Take a look for yourself.'

Holding the mirror close, I look. At first I don't see it, but on my second scan I notice the slight change in skin tone an inch behind my hairline. The micro camera is so small that it blends in, unnoticeable. 'Okay,' I say.

Reaching into his bag again, the tech guy pulls out a device the size and shape of a cellphone. He switches it on, and as the screen comes to life I feel the micro camera high in my hairline buzz.

'What the—?'

'I'm just activating it, sorry, should have warned you it'd vibrate as the pairing was made.' He taps a few things on the screen of the device he's holding, then turns the screen to face me.

'Wow.' My word repeats from the device's speaker a fraction of a second after I've said it. The image on screen is clear and almost the same as what I see in front of me. The only difference is that the micro camera's vantage point is a few inches higher. 'That's so clever.'

The tech guy grins. 'Told you it was neat.' He takes a set of ear pods from the bag, and hands them and the device to Monroe. 'You're all set. It's transmitting live via the paired satellite link and recording simultaneously.'

'Good work.' Monroe gives the tech guy a pat on the back. 'You can go back and join the others.'

'Yes, sir.' The tech guy packs up his equipment and moves to the door. Pulling it open, he turns before he exits and catches my eye. 'Good luck, Miss Anderson.'

'Thanks.'

The door clicks shut behind him.

Monroe puts in the ear pods and pockets the device. 'How did your practice go this afternoon?'

'Fine.' I don't go into detail; I had quite enough of his help earlier.

He gives me a smile. 'You're going to be fine. I'll be watching the whole time; if something goes wrong I'll send in the cavalry.'

'The last time I did a job for you, you told me that if things got messed up I'd be on my own.'

Monroe glances from me to JT. JT crosses his arms. I keep my stare fixed on Monroe.

He sighs. 'Look, sure, I did say that, but that job was off-the-books, whereas you're part of an official operation this time. You're my asset, and I'll protect you.' He clears his throat. 'And speaking of which, I'm going to need you both to sign this.'

I take the sheet of paper from him. Take in the FBI logo, the official wording. 'What is this?'

Monroe waves his hand dismissively at the letter. 'Standard procedure; you and JT need to say you're entering into this willingly, you know the risks associated, yadda, yadda, yadda.'

'So you can absolve yourself of any responsibility if things turn bad?'

Monroe looks shifty. 'So the Bureau can, or something like that.'

JT looks real pissed, and I get where he's coming from, but the paper looks legit, and we already know we can't trust Monroe. If this piece of paper proves we're working with the FBI that could benefit us later down the line if Monroe decides to try and double-cross us. Grabbing a pen I sign on the dotted line and hand it to JT who, after a moment's hesitation, does the same.

'There you go,' he says, handing the paper to Monroe.

Monroe adds his signature then takes a photo on his smart-phone and hands the letter back to JT. 'For you to keep.'

'Great,' JT says, in a tone that implies anything but.

Turning away from Monroe I walk over to the mirror on the wall by the closet and look at my reflection. Even when I lift up my hair I can't really see the micro camera attached to my skin. I turn back to face Monroe. 'I still don't get how this camera is undetectable when they sweep me for bugs.' I narrow my eyes, trying to gauge Monroe's reaction. I'm unsure whether he's really in my corner or if he's hedging his bets and has got some other plan running alongside the one I'm about to put into action for him. 'I've never heard about anything like this.'

'The US Government doesn't like to share its technology innovations with the public,' Monroe says. 'I'm not trying to stitch you up here. I've got your back, Lori.'

'Then tell me exactly how it is that they won't be able to detect it.'

He shakes his head. 'No can do, that's classified.'

I shrug. Look at JT then back to Monroe. 'Yeah. Thought so.'

Monroe sighs and runs his hand through his hair. 'I need you on this, Lori. For God's sake just believe me when I say I'm not messing with you.'

I hold his gaze. He looks sincere, but I've met one of his assets before, and after the operation they were doing went bad, the asset got arrested and thrown into jail for multiple homicides they didn't commit. Monroe left them in jail for two years before agreeing to help. A few months later, Monroe's help cost that man everything he loved. Monroe didn't show any remorse, only anger that the job didn't get finished. That's how I know he only cares about himself and his career. And he needs this operation to go right if he's going to get his career back on track. If he can't then he's screwed. So I know that whatever he tells me, he'll always do what's best for him and to hell with everyone else. He'll make JT and me collateral damage if it means saving his own skin. And if there was nothing personally at stake here, I'd have walked away a real long time ago. But there is – I need the deal Monroe's promised me: one last job, then I'm free of him for good. So I stay, and I play my part. 'Okay.'

'Good.' Monroe nods. He hands me bricks of fifty-dollar bills bound in elastics. 'This is your buy-in money, plus enough to let you buy yourself back in twice.'

'Thanks.' I take the cash and pack it into the leather carryall beside the box containing the chess pieces and my Taser.

Monroe raises an eyebrow at the Taser. 'You know they're going to take any weapons off you before you play?'

'Sure, but it'll make me feel more secure if I know it's close by.'

Monroe shrugs. 'Well okay then, it's your call.'

I nod. Say nothing. There's less than an hour before I'm due at the Skyland Tower. In the short amount of time we've had, I'm as prepared as I'm going to be. Now all I want is to get this the hell over with.

Monroe seems to sense the vibe and turns to leave. 'I'll be in room 5209 if you need me.'

I nod. 'Sure.'

JT and me are silent as Monroe leaves. Once the door closes behind him I pull out my cell and find Dakota's number. I'm wrestling with the urge to FaceTime her, but it'll be just gone 11.00 p.m. in Florida. It's real late to call her, and I don't think it's smart to speak to her face to face right now anyways; she's real perceptive and chances are she'll see that I'm feeling stressed. I don't want her to worry about JT and me doing this job, there's no kind of sense in that. So I put my own needs aside and tap out a message instead.

Night night honey. Love you xxx

I stare at the words. They just don't seem enough.

JT moves closer to me. He sees the message on the screen of my cell and slides his arm around me. 'It'll be okay,' he says. 'We'll be back with her soon.'

'Yeah,' I say. I know that he's trying to make me feel better, but I also know that words don't mean a damn. We both know there are no guarantees in the life we've chosen and the job we do.

We take a moment. Stand with our arms around each other, sharing the hope that things will go our way.

Eventually I break the silence. 'I should tell Red we're doing the job tonight.'

JT nods. 'Good call.'

As I tap out a second message, JT splashes two fingers of bourbon into two glasses. He holds out one to me. 'Some liquid courage for the road?'

I press send on the message to Red then take the glass. I clink it against JT's. 'To staying safe and going home.'

'Amen to that.' He gulps down the whisky as I take a sip of mine. Looks at me all serious. 'Lori, you know you don't have to wear that goddamn camera. Hell, like I keep saying, you don't even have to do this job.'

I give JT a sad smile. Monroe will be watching, listening, to this conversation. There's no way we can back out now, it's just not going to happen. I put my hands on JT's chest and smooth down a wrinkle in the black shirt he's wearing. 'It's okay. We've got this.'

On tiptoes I reach up and kiss him, long and slow, savouring the feeling, before slowly pulling away. JT smiles at me, and for a moment I feel like the luckiest woman alive. Then I switch my mind to the job at hand. Know I need to focus hard, we both do, and that from here on in the job is the only thing we can think about.

I take a breath and think about what comes next, then I pick up the carryall with the chess pieces and buy-in money and I turn to JT. 'Let's get this done.'

14

The Skyland Tower is the tallest building I have ever seen and all kinds of fancy – marble floors, marble-clad walls, oak concierge counter and uniformed staff. The doorman opens the door for us, and we stride boldly into the foyer. Our footsteps seem overly loud against the pale marble floor.

Fake it. Play the part. That's what tonight is all about.

I stand a little taller. Tilt my chin up. Pretend like my ass isn't so clenched that you couldn't drive a straight pin up it with a ten-pound sledgehammer. Instead I act like I own the whole damn place. Beside me JT walks quiet and confident. He looks around us, constantly assessing for threats, just as good close protection does, especially given that the carryall in my hand contains assets worth over one and a half million bucks.

The uniformed man behind the concierge desk clears his throat. He's groomed real nice with a symmetrical goatee and the wrinkle-less forehead of a Botox user. 'Welcome to Skyland Tower,' he says. 'Who are you visiting with tonight?'

I stride up to the counter, tall on my heels. My heart's pounding in my chest, but my voice is calm and authoritative. 'We're visiting suite 6311 as guests of Carmella Davies.'

'Can I take your names, please?' The concierge's tone is real polite, but there's a hint of caution to his smile now, a kind of fixed-ness.

'Lori Anderson, and my associate, James Tate.'

The concierge checks our names on his computer, then gives us a broad smile and gestures towards the line of elevators on the far wall. 'Take elevator one to the sixty-third floor, and have a great night.'

I thank him, then JT and me stride across to the elevators. I press the call button for elevator one. Take a breath and try to ease the pounding of my heartbeat.

We wait. I face the elevator, staring at my reflection in the mirrored doors. In my high heels, tight black dress and with my hair pinned up into a chignon I look a whole lot different to usual. And although I'd rather be in my Levi's, I'm hopeful this look will prove a useful distraction to my fellow players and help me get the job done.

JT faces the foyer, still alert to threats. Taking my cell from my pocket, I dial Monroe.

He answers after two rings. 'You okay?'

'I am,' I say. 'Things alright with you?'

'Audio and video good.'

'Great.' I end the call.

The elevator announces its arrival with a ping. We step inside. On the control panel, the buttons for the sixty-third floor are specific to each of the four penthouses. I press the button for 6311. As we start to ascend my stomach flips.

JT leans towards me. His lips caress my cheek, and he whispers, 'You've got this. Just stay focused. I'll be right by your side the whole time.'

I nod. Try not to think about my last job, and how it turned into a massive shootout between two warring factions of the Miami Mob and the FBI. The walk out of the farmhouse I'd been holed up in, past all the bloodied, broken bodies, will forever be etched on my mind. I never want to be in a situation like that again. Never want to see so many wasted lives. I look at JT. 'We play poker, get the transfer done and get out. No shooting.'

JT smiles. He takes my free hand and squeezes it. 'Deal.'

I squeeze his fingers. Try not to think about what's at stake; about Dakota sleeping on Red's houseboat, and the hold Monroe has on me, and what a dodgy son-of-a-bitch he can be. Instead I think about poker, the chess pieces and staying in the game long enough to go heads-up, one-on-one, with Cabressa.

I take a breath. Smile at JT. The odds might be against us, but together, I know we can get this done.

The elevator opens straight into the lobby of the penthouse. If I thought downstairs was fancy, this place is on a whole other level. Black-and-white marble floors, high ceilings with crown mouldings and wood-panelled walls. There's a hat stand, a coat closet and two heavy-set security guards. They look like a pair of massive bookends. Both are dressed in black with their dark hair closely cropped. Their weapons belts are fully loaded. I eye their guns and feel glad I brought my Taser.

The guy closest beckons me forward. 'Good evening, Miss Anderson. Please step this way.' His voice is soft and friendly, but that doesn't mean his words are any less of an order. He looks at JT. 'Sir, if you could unholster your weapon and hand it to my colleague, I'd sure appreciate it.'

JT glances at me with an 'I told you so' expression, and starts to undo the buckle.

I move over to where the security guy's standing.

He's holding a scanner wand and uses it to gesture towards my carryall. 'What's in the bag?'

I put the carryall on the ground. 'My buy-in and collateral for the game. There's a Taser as well.' I glance over to JT, who's handing his gun over to the second security guy. 'I'm guessing you'll be wanting to remove that.'

The guard unzips my carryall and lifts out the Taser. He carries it across to his colleague and puts it into the metal box on the table beside him. I notice that the box has the name *Anderson* written on the front label.

He returns to where I'm standing. Meets my gaze. 'Please adopt the stance, Miss Anderson. I'm going to do a sweep.' His voice remains soft, kind. 'It's just a formality, you understand. For your safety and ours.'

Nodding, I spread my arms wide. Hold my breath. And hope to hell the micro camera is as undetectable as Monroe claimed.

15

The wand beeps and the security guard waves it back over the area again. There's a second beep, followed by a third. Outwardly I stay still and try to act calm. Inwardly, though, it's a whole different story. If these guards find the micro camera it's real likely Cabressa will find out. That happens and he'll be having his people skin my hide and nail it to the barn door.

The security guy looks across at his pal. 'Got a problem here.'

The other security guard steps over to join us. I feel like a minnow beside two sharks. I'm wishing I were a minnow with a Taser.

I clench my fists. Get ready to defend myself. We can't fail yet. We've not even made it into the poker room.

'Hold still, Miss Anderson,' says the first security guy. He moves the wand inch-by-inch over me working from the bottom up. The closer the wand gets to my head, the sicker I feel. It beeps as it passes my chest.

The guy scratches his head. 'I'm sorry, I'm going to look under your dress.'

I stare at him a moment. There's no way of doing this and keeping my dignity. JT looks unhappy, but I can't exactly refuse. Luckily the material is stretchy enough I can peel it down over my shoulder.

The guard's cheeks flush as he slowly passes the wand over my chest again. It beeps as it gets to the bottom of my lace bra. He glances at his buddy and for a minute I think they're going to tell me to take off my bra. Then he gestures towards my bra and says, 'You got metal in there?'

'Just the underwire.'

'That'd be it,' he says. 'Let me just go over you with the bug de-
tector to be sure.' He produces a small, silver device from his belt.
Switches it on, and passes it over me. He gives me a smile. 'You're
all set. Sorry about that. But I'm sure you appreciate we have to
ensure the safety of all our guests.'

'Of course,' I say. My body is still on high alert – adrenaline
pulsing through me, ready for flight or fight. I clasp my hands together to stop him seeing they're shaking.

Having put JT's gun into the metal box with my Taser, they
seal the top and put it on a small trolley alongside six other ident-
ical boxes. The security guard hands my carryall back to me. 'Your
weapons will be held downstairs in the security room until you
leave. They will be returned to you at that time.'

I nod and move towards the door that leads through into the
rest of the suite. Before I get to it, the door swings open and a tall,
beautiful woman wearing a fitted black dress and jacket and sky-
scraper heels, a leopard-print scarf tied around her neck, steps into
the foyer. She smiles at me and then at JT, and beckons us through
the door. 'Welcome, Miss Anderson. Please come this way.'

I step through the doorway and into the lion's den.

*

The penthouse is more luxurious than anything I've seen.
Carmella leads us through into the main open-plan living space.
The walls are painted pure white. The floors are stripped oak –
solid wood not laminate. It feels more like an art gallery than a
home, with huge Modernist paintings filling the wall space. I
glance at JT and I can tell he's thinking the same. This place is a
whole other world.

We stop in the living space. The kitchen is at one end, all sleek
white units, marble countertops and stainless-steel appliances,
with the huge island separating it from the rest of the area. From

there it flows through the sitting area, filled with colour-popping modern couches, a white baby-grand piano, and through to the table at the far right of the space. It's a full-sized poker table, laid out ready for play. I notice the packs of cards, still in their shrink wrap, sitting on the green felt beside a Shuffle Master machine. All along the far wall are bifold glass doors. Half have been opened, and through the sheer white drapes, which are billowing gently in the breeze, I can see a paved terrace area and the twinkling lights of the city beyond.

Carmella turns to me and smiles. She gestures towards the kitchen, where a young woman in a black skirt and white blouse is pouring champagne for a group of men. 'Come this way, please,' she says. 'Let me introduce you.'

As I follow her, I see one of the security guys wave JT over to an open door leading away from the living space. I halt, unsure of what's happening. The security man steps over to us. Looks towards my carryall and then at JT. 'Please bring the bag this way.'

JT meets my gaze. I know the etiquette of this game is to be respected. It seems while the players gather in the main open-plan area, have a glass of champagne and get introduced, their close protection take the buy-in money into a side room – a bedroom, I remember from the floorplan – and wait while the cash is counted. I don't want to be separated from JT, but it seems I have little choice. I pass the carryall to him. Force a smile.

'I'll be right outside that door,' he says.

As he walks away with the security guy, I turn and follow Carmella. Over by the island unit I'm handed a glass of champagne. It's then, as I feel all eyes turn to appraise me, that I'm hit with it. Aside from Carmella and the server, I'm the only other woman here in the suite.

'Good evening, gentlemen.' Carmella looks at me. 'And lady. And a warm welcome to this month's game. As you know the buy-in for tonight stands at fifty thousand dollars. For those who have brought additional funds or have a line of credit with the house, you're permitted two subsequent buy-ins. While the buy-ins are being counted, please enjoy your champagne. We'll be starting in a few minutes.'

The men start talking among themselves. I take a sip of the champagne. It's smooth and dry, but I'm careful not to drink too much. I'm going to need all my smarts if I'm going to make it through to heads-up.

Carmella steps towards me. 'Miss Anderson—'

'Call me Lori, please,' I say.

She smiles graciously. 'Okay, Lori. Can I introduce you to the rest of the players?'

'Thank you, yes.'

Carmella puts her hand on the arm of a tall black guy whose arm muscles rival those of the security. 'Otis Valha, can I introduce you to Lori Anderson. She's a new player joining us tonight.'

Otis smiles and shakes my hand with his gold-ring-clad fingers. 'Pleasure to meet you, Lori.' He gestures to the older, balding, thick-set guy in a blue suit and brown brogues he's talking to. 'You come to take Carl's money off him?'

I smile. 'Let's hope so.'

Otis clinks his champagne glass against mine. 'We'll have some fun.'

'Who's having fun?' A red-faced, tubby guy in a red polo shirt and chinos is staring at me. He holds out his hand. 'I'm Anton Peck.'

'Lori,' I say as I shake his hand. His palm's sweaty, and his grip is too firm. He pumps my hand up and down longer and harder than is necessary. I figure that when we first sit down to play, this guy will be one of those who try to dominate the play.

Releasing my hand, he tugs on the sleeve of one of the men whose back is to me, talking to two others. The man turns. He's about six feet tall, I'd say in his fifties and looking good on it. Cropped dark hair with a few greys around the temples, black suit, beautifully tailored, and shiny black loafers. When he smiles it's the mega-watt smile of a movie star. 'I'm Mikey Fitzgerald,' he says, taking my hand and holding it in both of his. 'From the mayor's office.'

'Lori,' I say. Damn, this man knows how to hold some intense eye contact. I pull my hand away first.

'And I'm Johnny, Johnny Keto,' says the athletic-looking guy with a shaved head and a big, bushy beard who's standing beside Mikey.

I frown. Tilt my head to one side. 'How do I know that name?'

Johnny grins. 'You a fan of baseball, Lori?'

'I am.'

'Maybe you've seen me in action then.'

I nod. 'Could be that I have.'

'Miss Anderson?' The group goes quiet as the man at the back starts to speak. His Chicago accent is stronger than any of the others. And as he approaches, Mikey and Johnny move aside to let him through. 'So nice to finally meet you.'

He looks younger than the late-fifties I know him to be, with gelled black hair and a deep tan. I recognise this man from the pictures Monroe has shown me. He's got the athletic bulk of a man who boxed in his younger days and carries himself in a way that suggests he still does and rarely loses. My heart rate accelerates but I stand my ground. Hold out my hand and smile, conscious that all eyes are on me. 'Pleased to meet you, Mr Cabressa.'

He grins, laughter lines deepening around his eyes as he does so. 'Likewise, Miss Anderson. I'm told you play a good game.'

I fight to keep my smile in place. Despite his obvious strength, his handshake is damp and flaccid. 'I like to think so.'

He lets go of my hand, but the smile is still on his lips as he says, 'Let's hope that's true.'

16

I'm still staring at Cabressa when the door of the bedroom opens and one of the bookend security guys appears. Seven guys – JT plus six others I've not seen before – file out of the bedroom and back towards the foyer. I catch JT's eye. He looks worried, but I can't do anything to find out why without attracting attention.

JT and the rest of the guys exit into the foyer behind the security guard. As the door closes behind them the second bookend security guy appears from the bedroom. He makes his way to the door, then stops and turns towards us.

Carmella looks at him and raises her eyebrow.

The atmosphere suddenly feels all kinds of tense. Something's up. Every player is watching Carmella. I turn towards her as well and wonder what the hell's going on.

The security guy gives Carmella a nod.

There's an audible exhalation from the players around me. Otis Valha's shoulders drop as he relaxes. Johnny Keto slaps Mikey Fitzgerald on the back.

Carmella smiles and raises her glass. 'Our administration is complete and everything is in order, so let's play.'

It's like a stampede at a rodeo as the men rush to find their seats, racing each other to their favourite spots. I hang back, watching. It's my first time at this kind of rodeo and I need to learn the way things work.

I take a seat at the table opposite Carmella and between Carl Reynolds, the banker, and Otis Valha, the boxer. Cabressa has taken the seat at the head of the table – to my left, along past Carl. I notice how Carl and the man sitting on the other side of

Cabressa – Johnny Keto, the ball player – slide their chairs a little further from him. Their expressions don't give anything away, so I can't tell whether the movement is motivated out of respect, and they're giving the city's premier mobster more space, or whether it's part of the game. At the opposite end of the table from Cabressa is the guy from the mayor's office, Mikey Fitzgerald. I watch as he takes a pair of shades from the inside pocket of his suit and puts them on. Carmella catches my eye and raises an eyebrow, then looks away and removes the packaging from a fresh deck of cards before loading them into the Shuffle Master. On her right, Johnny Keto, the ball player, is watching her movements like a hawk. To her left, sitting between her and Mikey, Anton Peck, who I learn from the chit-chat around the table is a realtor, switches his cell onto silent before putting it back into the pocket of his pants.

I glance towards the door to the lobby. The heavy-set security guy is standing with his back to it. There's no sign of JT returning.

The server leans between me and Otis, and tops up our champagne glasses. Once she's finished, she positions six full champagne bottles in freestanding ice buckets around the table, and then she leaves through the door back towards the elevator. As the door opens I try to see whether JT is still in the foyer.

When I realise he isn't I start to get concerned. I turn back towards Carmella. 'When do our security people come back in here?'

'They don't. During the game only the players and myself remain in the suite.' She gestures to the security guy over by the door. 'The exception being Thomas who stays at the room for *all* our security.'

I frown. Wonder where the hell they've taken JT if he's not in the suite. 'Did you ask them to leave?'

She gives a little laugh and shakes her head. 'Of course not, they're waiting down on the sixty-second floor, where we have a special room laid out for their comfort. If you need to leave the table for any reason when cards are in play, you can request your security personnel returns to take your seat while you're absent. Otherwise, it's just us until the game is won.'

I'm irritated that I've been separated from JT, but I don't let on. None of the other players seem fussed so I'm guessing this is the usual way the game is run. 'No problem.'

Carmella gives me a tight smile. 'Alright then.'

Next she deals the first hand.

*

The first few hands are fast and bold. Remembering JT's warning, I take them easy, folding early with cards that might have been useful, because I don't want to get caught up in the early-game dick-waving. Cabressa pulls into an early lead, beating Johnny, who was chancing his arm on a bluff, and taking half the ball player's chips in the process.

I try to focus on the players, on the way they act before they bet, and how they react when things don't go their way. It seems to me that there's a distinct hierarchy with the players. It's real obvious Cabressa is top dog here, with Mikey from the mayor's office coming in a close second. They talk as equals – Mikey jokes with Cabressa and sometimes Cabressa even cracks a smile – while the rest treat Cabressa with reverence or apprehension. Anton and Carl are next in the pecking order. Johnny and Otis come after that, with Otis having the slight edge on Johnny. They're friendly to each other but I wouldn't say they seem like friends. There's tension in every interaction between the two of them, in their words and their body language. It's clear these men do not trust each other, but they're trying real well to hide it. I don't like secrets. And, the way they're acting makes me not trust either of them.

Correction, I don't trust anyone around this table, even

Carmella, as it could be that she's on Cabressa's payroll. The longer I sit at the table and the longer the game plays on, the more it feels like I'm a shrimp invited to a shark's dinner party.

Carmella deals the next hand. Johnny and Anton pay the blinds.

Reaching onto the green felt of the table, I slide my cards towards me and take a peep.

A pair of aces, known as pocket aces in the game. I try not to let my excitement show. Put the cards back flat on the table. Look up.

Cabressa is staring at me, a slight smile turning one corner of his lips up. I look away. The others are doing their best to hide their thoughts, but I can tell from how Otis is jigging his leg up and down and Anton is, seemingly absentmindedly, scratching his left wrist, that they have cards worth keeping in play.

'Mikey, what are you going to do?' Carmella prompts.

His face shows no emotion, no tell – good or bad – but Mikey takes two five-hundred-dollar chips from his stack and pushes them towards Carmella. 'I'm in.'

Otis matches his bet, and then it's my turn. We've been playing round about forty-five minutes, so I figure they should've gotten the first flush of recklessness out of their systems. I take a thousand-dollar chip from my stack and put it on the table.

'Well lookee here,' Anton says, rubbing his pudgy hands together. 'Seems you're not just a pretty face.'

I keep a neutral expression, pretending that his sexist remark hasn't bothered me none, even though what I'd really like to do is dry-fire my confiscated Taser into his balls.

Next to me, Carl, the banker, folds. Straight after, Cabressa does the same.

Johnny necks another glass of champagne – I've lost count of how many he's had already – and throws two five-hundred-dollar chips towards Carmella. 'Why not, I'll come along for the ride too.'

Carmella looks to Anton. 'Your move.'

Smiling like a goddamn sexist Cheshire cat, Anton chucks two thousand-dollar chips onto the green felt. 'Let's make this a bit more interesting, shall we?'

'Oh man,' Johnny says, groaning.

Mikey adds another thousand to the pot. Otis dithers, looking at his cards, putting them down, then picking them up again for another look. A tut and head-shake from Cabressa has Otis make up his mind and add his own thousand-dollar chip to the pile. I do the same.

'Fine, fine,' says Johnny, throwing two five-hundred chips to join the rest.

Carmella deals the next three cards: ace of hearts, king of diamonds, ten of clubs.

Otis's leg is jigging faster. Anton stops scratching his wrist.

I stare at the cards on the table. I've got three of a kind, aces, now – my two plus the one from the table. It's a good hand, but there's danger too. If someone has a queen and a jack they're on for a royal straight, and that'd have me beaten.

Carmella looks to Mikey.

He shakes his head and pushes his cards across the table to her. 'I'm out.'

Otis puts in a three-thousand-dollar bet. His leg doesn't stop jigging.

I match him. Don't hesitate this time.

Johnny throws three thousand worth of chips onto the board. 'May as well see where this river runs.'

Anton smiles, and puts a five-thousand-dollar chip on the table. 'I see y'all.'

I bite my lip.

He adds a second chip. Winks at me. 'And I raise you.'

Otis's leg stops jigging. He looks back and forth from his cards to the river, as if he's trying to calculate if his odds are good. Shakes his head and pushes his cards towards the middle of the table. 'Nah, I'm done.'

Damn. I feel the fizz of adrenaline – the thrill of competition

– but I'm cautious. I chased down Monroe in our practice game and wound up losing. I need to be logical, steady. I glance at my cards again. It's a good hand. I need to stay in.

'I'm in,' I say, faking more confidence than I'm feeling. And push another two thousand in chips onto the board to match Anton's bet.

Anton whoops. 'Nice, really nice.' He looks at Johnny. 'You coming too?'

Johnny cusses under his breath. Throws his cards onto the table. 'You're killing me, man.'

Anton laughs. Licks his lips and says to me, 'Now we get to find out which of us is riding the other.'

I force a smile and think about firing my Taser into him again.

Carmella deals the turn. It's the queen of hearts.

Hot damn. If Anton has a jack in his hand then with what's already on the table he's gotten all he needs to make himself a royal straight. I rap my knuckles on the table. 'Check.'

Anton gives a loud bark of laughter and pushes his stacks of chips onto the board. 'That's me all in.' He grins. 'What you going to do about that, princess? Ready for me to ride you?'

I try not to let my disgust show. Need to figure out my move. JT warned me not to be impulsive, and that I need to play the long game. I lost the game with Monroe because I ignored what was on the board and let my competitiveness get the better of me. I can see what's on the board here and I know there's a straight to be had. I think of Monroe watching and listening via the micro camera, and suddenly wish it had two-way comms. I'm gambling with the FBI's dollars. Things go wrong, Monroe will find a way to punish me.

Anton is leering across from the other side of the table and there's nothing more I'd like to do right now than to beat him at this hand. But there's a whole night ahead of us, and I have to stay in the game to get heads-up with Cabressa. I only have enough money for two additional buy-ins, and the way things are going so far I'm not sure it's enough.

I shake my head. Fold my cards and push them into the centre of the table. 'Too rich for my blood.'

Anton punches the air. 'Show us your cards.'

I hesitate. I know I don't have to, but all eyes are on me.

'I'll show you mine if you show yours,' says Anton, and flips over his cards.

I cuss under my breath. He has a six and a queen. All he's got is a pair of queens. I reach onto the board and turn over my cards.

Anton claps his hands. 'Well damn, would you take a look at that.'

Otis shakes his head. 'It's not cool to gloat.'

'He got us all,' Johnny says. He meets my eye. 'Got you the worst though, man.'

I glance at Cabressa. For the first time since I met him he's showing some emotion – he looks real disappointed. I guess he's thinking on whether I've got what it takes to make it to heads-up, and if I don't, how he's going to get his hands on the chess pieces.

'Hey Lori,' says Anton, laughing as he gathers the pot off the board. 'You got spooked by the queen of hearts but who says romance has to be dead. You want to give me a kiss with these chips? Go some place we could have ourselves a real ride?'

I imagine slamming my fist into his smug asshole face. Shake my head. 'You've more chance of seeing God twice in the next five minutes than me and you ever doing anything.'

'Ouch, that's quite a burn,' says Johnny with a laugh.

Anton looks pissed. 'Don't be a little—'

'Back in your pants, Anton,' Cabressa says.

Anton scowls but stays silent as he finishes raking up the chips and starts stacking them up alongside the rest of his stash.

Carmella deals the next hand. The drinks keep flowing. Mikey lights a cigar.

I take a deep breath and wonder how long I'll be able to stay in the game.

17

They took his weapon. JT can understand that, the game involves a lot of money so you need tight security in case anyone gets out of hand. What he doesn't get is why they've taken him and the other player's security people one storey down in the elevator – to the sixty-second floor – and have them holed up in another room. This room. It's a hell of a lot smaller and far less luxurious than the penthouse above.

He hates that he's been taken from Lori's side. Wonders how the hell he can protect her from here. She might try to tough it out, pretend she's okay, but he knows her too well, can see through her act. Truth is, she's real anxious about this job. The massacre at the Bonchese compound last month – all those people dying around her – messed with her confidence. She's been fearful since. Doubting herself, even though she shouldn't. She's the strongest woman he's ever known. Hell, she's stronger than any man he's known too.

JT looks at the other men. Seven other close-protection guys for the players, plus one of the identikit security guards who work for Carmella, the organiser of the game. All of the guys are huge. None of them seem bothered about getting cooped up downstairs while their bosses play poker in a penthouse on the floor above. Most are on their cells, and one is reading a Jack Reacher novel. The identikit security guard is pondering over a puzzle book.

Still, it doesn't feel right to JT.

He leans over towards the man sitting to his left – a man mountain with a thin goatee and an open-mouthed style of chewing his gum. 'This normally happen?'

The man looks at him, confused. 'What?'

'This.' JT gestures at the room, the other guys. 'Not staying in the penthouse during the game.'

'Yeah.' The bearded guy keeps chewing. Stares blankly ahead. 'Standard procedure for Carmella's games.'

JT sees the white ear buds in the guy's ears. Recognises the sightless stare of a person zoned out listening to music.

'You're new to this scene, eh?' says a man with a deep voice, like treacle over gravel.

The voice comes from a guy over to his right. JT turns towards him. The guy's huge – like a shaggy-haired WWF wrestler in a suit. JT nods. 'Yup. First time.'

'You with the woman?'

'I am.'

The wrestler guy licks his lips. 'Looks like one hot piece of ass.'

JT fights the urge to punch the guy in the face. Needs to stay in character, play his role of employee; not arouse suspicion. 'She's a good boss.'

'I bet she is.' From the man's tone it's obvious what he means. 'Good fringe benefits.'

JT ignores the implication. 'So what's the deal here? How does it work?'

The suited wrestler-looking guy smiles and pulls his chair closer to JT. 'So the game runs every month. Carmella, she runs a bunch of smaller games each week, but this right here is the big one. Big players, top money, if you know what I mean.'

The guy is looking at JT expectantly. JT doesn't know what he means, but he can guess so he nods. 'Yup.'

'So my guy, Johnny Keto, he's here every month,' the wrestler guy continues. 'Not all of them are. Some come every few months. Some we only see once, and they're gone. A few, like Johnny, are regulars.'

'Which ones?'

The guy scratches his jaw. 'Well, Johnny, like I said, plus Carl and Anton. Of course, Mr Cabressa is at every game. Always has been from what I understand.' He leans closer to JT. 'The way I heard it, this might be known as Carmella's game on the outside, but everyone who's anyone knows that Mr Cabressa is the money behind her outfit.'

Interesting, thinks JT; a bad kind of interesting. If Carmella is bankrolled by the Cabressa family, that makes this a mob game, not a neutral location.

'So your boss, what is she?' asks the suited wrestler-type guy. 'She some kind of ringer?'

JT shakes his head. 'She's in the city for business. Likes to play a few hands to let off steam.'

The wrestler guy raises an eyebrow. 'What kind of business?'

JT shrugs. 'Like she'd tell me.'

'Tell me about it.'

They sit in an easy silence for a long moment. JT scans the other close-protection guys. None seem to be paying him, or the conversation, any mind, although he suspects that could just be what they'd like him to believe. He's seen the side-eyes and the furtive glances. They're curious about him, but they're keeping their distance. So far this wrestler-looking guy is his only chance at learning more.

He leans closer. Keeps his voice low. 'So tell me, what are the players upstairs like, and who'd you put your money on to win?'

The guy glances around, and then lowers his voice conspiratorially. 'Well, it's interesting you ask that because I've got this theory that...'

JT nods along as the guy speaks. He knows this man's type – a grandstander who likes the sound of his own voice and to show off his knowledge. In usual circumstances he gives folks like that a wide berth, but right here and now he's thankful for the man's indiscretion. Any knowledge about how this game works could be helpful. JT needs to know what to expect so he can anticipate any issues. He nods encouragingly as the wrestler guy jaws on.

When he finally draws breath, JT asks, 'And so this game is on the level?'

The wrestler type frowns. 'How'd you mean?'

'They're all just here to play poker?'

The guy leans closer. 'Well, see the thing of it—'

The identikit security guard over by the door clears his throat. JT glances over at him. He's not working on his puzzle book any longer – he's staring real hard at the wrestler-looking guy.

The wrestler guy notices it too. He stops talking. Looks away.

'You were saying?' JT prompts.

The guy gives a little shake of his head. 'Nah, it's nothing. Look, this is a good game. That's all you need to know.'

JT knows he's just seen a warning being given. There's something going on here; far more than just a poker game. JT wants to know what that is.

He glances at his watch and realises the game's been going near on two hours already. In the scenarios he'd worked through with Lori they figured she'd be done in a little more than two hours, depending on how fast the blinds went up.

The identikit security guard is staring at him, unblinking. Whatever else is going on in this game, JT knows they think he's on to it. He tries to stay relaxed, feign boredom, not look suspicious, but in truth his mind is working through a bunch of possibilities and scenarios. None of it makes him feel any better. He's got no weapon, no Lori and no idea what the hell is going on here. Not yet anyways.

But one thing he's damn sure of is that he's going to find out.

18

Carl Reynolds, the banker, is the first out of the game. After losing everything to Otis, he got reckless in his first hand of his second buy-in and took Anton on in one of his all-in bluffs, only it turned out not to be a bluff, and Carl lost his chips. He bought his way back in for a third time, but three hands later lost everything for a second time to Anton. After that, he stayed out.

I'm hanging on in the game, but it hasn't been easy. Johnny, Otis, Mikey and me are all on our third buy-ins. Anton is on his second. Only Cabressa is still on his first.

As Carl gets up from the table, Carmella opens a fresh deck of cards and loads it into the Shuffle Master. Carl pours himself a glass of champagne and stands behind the chairs, ready to watch the next hand. He looks at Cabressa. 'You know who this Herron guy is?'

All the players stop fussing with their stacks and whatnot, and look at Carl. There's surprise on their faces, and I wonder if he's broken some kind of a rule.

Cabressa shakes his head. 'I do not.'

'Yeah, right, Herron, I've heard that name,' Anton says, running his hand over his chin. 'There's this guy in construction I work with a lot, he said a bunch of their equipment has gone missing – big stuff, backhoes and shit. Word is, this Herron guy was behind it.'

'Who's Herron?' Otis asks, taking a sip of his drink.

'Fucked if I know,' says Johnny with a shrug.

'We've heard the name,' Mikey says, looking at Carl over the top of his shades. 'Police have connected him to a couple dozen incidents in the past few weeks.'

Cabressa nods. 'I've had word of some problems on the streets – product getting stolen from our stores, overseas shipments going missing – those involved have named this Herron as the perpetrator.'

Carl puts his hands together and cracks his knuckles. 'It's not good for business.'

Mikey nods. 'It isn't good for the city. A man like that causing trouble, it creates unease.' He looks at Cabressa. 'Someone needs to fix it.'

Cabressa holds Mikey's gaze. 'I'm sure they will.'

There's a moment of silence. Then Carmella deals the next hand.

Thoughts of Herron are forgotten as we look at the hands we've been dealt. Johnny stares at his cards. Otis jigs his leg up and down. Both of their stacks of chips are critically low.

'We should talk about that place you've got over on the west side,' Anton says, glancing at Cabressa. 'The area's coming up good, I could make you a lot of—'

'We're here to play, not do business,' growls Cabressa.

Anton either doesn't get the hint or ignores it. He gestures towards Carl. 'But haven't we already been talking business? You know, all that stuff about Herron and—'

'I said not here,' Cabressa says, his tone full of steel.

Anton puts his hands up. 'Steady there. I'm just talking, putting some ideas out there.' He leans across the table towards Cabressa. 'We're talking really profitable ideas for—'

'Not. Now.' Cabressa waves Anton away like he's an annoying bug.

Anton shifts back in his seat, looking confused. 'But usually—'

'I said enough,' Cabressa says, glaring at Anton. 'Keep quiet, we're trying to play here.'

Cabressa's voice has only raised a couple of notches, but the effect is dramatic. Anton's piggy eyes widen, and his red cheeks drain of colour. It's the first time he's been quiet since the game began.

Carmella raises an eyebrow. Looks at Otis. 'Are you in?'

'Okay, sure,' he says, pushing a five-thousand-dollar chip onto the table.

I fold – my hand is nothing special – as does Mikey. Cabressa, Johnny and Anton call.

Carmella deals the flop.

Otis shakes his head and throws his cards onto the table. 'I'm out.'

Cabressa takes a ten-thousand-dollar chip and places it on the table. He looks around the table and smiles.

Johnny's looking agitated. He's got less than ten thousand in his stack so if he's going to bet, it's all in or nothing. He glances from Cabressa to Anton, as if trying to work out if they really have good hands. Then he cusses, and tosses his cards onto the board. 'No, I'm out.'

Cabressa smiles a little wider. Looks at Anton.

Anton fiddles with the chips on his stack. He looks nervous, like he doesn't want to bet but thinks he has to. Slowly, he pushes his stack towards the middle. 'All in.'

'Good,' says Cabressa. He adds some chips to the ones in the pot to match Anton's bet, then sits back and nods to Carmella.

Anton turns over his cards. All he has is a pair of eights.

Cabressa reveals his hand. When combined with the cards on the table he's got a full house, jacks and threes.

'The pot goes to Mr Cabressa,' says Carmella.

Anton cusses. Pushing his chair back from the table, he gets up and stalks over to the window. I hear him muttering something about how I shouldn't have been allowed to play, that because of me being here he'd been put off his game. I frown. If Anton saw women as real people, not just sex objects, maybe he wouldn't have let himself get distracted.

Otis leans closer to me and whispers, 'Don't go taking what he said personal. Anton always takes losing bad and he always has to blame someone else. He's got money problems, you know.'

I wonder why the hell he's still playing if he has money problems. It makes me think of all the times my ex-husband, Tommy Ford, stumbled home blind drunk as dawn was beginning to break. Depending on his mood, he'd take out his frustration on me with his fists, or crawl into bed apologising for losing that month's rent money at the poker table. It might have been over ten years ago now, but sure as dammit I still remember every punch and every empty apology. I shudder. And push the memories away. Anton's out the game now, I need to forget about him. I turn my attention back to the table and the game.

Carmella deals and we play on.

A few hands later things get interesting again. Cabressa and Johnny have folded. Mikey, Otis and me are still in the game. My bet is on the table – a cool five-thousand-dollar chip. Mikey's up next and is looking all kinds of uncomfortable.

'In or out, Mikey?' Carmella asks.

He dithers. Fiddles with the cufflinks in his shirt and makes a real performance of huffing and sighing, but eventually he matches my bet.

'Otis?' says Carmella.

Mikey and me look at Otis.

'Give me a minute here.' There's sweat on Otis's upper lip and his leg has stopped jigging. He fiddles with his stack, lifting the chips off the table and then putting them down again.

As we wait, I feel eyes on me and glance back along the table. At the far end Cabressa is watching me, unblinking. His expression is impossible to read, but his eyes, cold and hard, make me suddenly shiver.

'I'm going to have to hurry you,' Carmella says.

Otis's leg starts jigging again. He wipes his lip and his brow. Shakes his head. 'Okay, fine. I'm going all in.'

He pushes his stack onto the board. Jeez, there must be ten thousand in chips. I hadn't figured on the betting going so high. But my hand is good – a low straight – and I can't see much potential for a better hand on the board with just the final card to be dealt. JT and Monroe said I needed to play the players, not just the cards. I study Mikey and Otis. They were both chilled earlier in the game, but their luck hasn't been great, and as the hours have passed they've looked increasingly tense. Now Otis is sweating again, and Mikey is ramrod straight, a sure sign that he's trying to hide the urge to fidget. I think they're bluffing. I take another chip from my stack and add it to the pot. 'I'll go with you.'

Mikey huffs, then pushes the few chips he has into the middle of the table. 'Me too.'

We've all bet slightly different amounts, as Mikey and Otis are all in, so as Carmella counts the chips, calculating who will get what, dependent on who wins, I count what's left of my own stack. It's not much, only three thousand in chips. If I don't win this hand, I'll be dead in the water.

I glance at Cabressa. His hands are steepled on the table, with his chin resting on the top of his fingers. He's staring at the cards.

'Here's your last card,' says Carmella.

I hold my breath. Watch her as her red-nailed fingers deal the next card face up onto the table. It's the ace of diamonds.

My pulse pounds at my temples. This is the moment of truth.

I turn my cards over, showing my straight.

Shaking his head, Otis flips over his cards, revealing a pair of jacks, ace high. 'Nice hand,' he says to me. 'Played good too.'

'Thanks.'

Mikey stares at the cards over the top of his shades for a few seconds longer, then shakes his head and pushes his cards onto the table, face up. He has three of a kind, eights, but it's not enough and he knows it. He takes off his shades and holds up his hands. 'You got me.'

I exhale, and take the pot with trembling hands. I was bold and it worked. And thankfully my stack is a whole lot healthier than before, which is a real good thing. It's down to just three of us now – me, Cabressa and Johnny.

I glance at Carmella, and there's a flicker of a smile as her eyes meet mine. Then her poker face returns, she readies the cards and deals again.

Cabressa wins the next hand by default, vacuuming up the blinds when Johnny and me fold. I can't see them, but I can hear Carl, Anton and Otis whispering to each other over by the piano. Anton doesn't sound happy, and every now and then I hear my name mentioned. There's the clinking of glasses as more champagne is poured, and I guess that the losers are trying hard to drown their sorrows.

Carmella loosens the leopard print scarf around her neck a fraction and then deals the next hand. Johnny hunches over his cards, munching through a bowl of roasted peanuts as he studies them. Cabressa watches him closely – he's not drinking and he's not eating – his expression giving nothing of his own hand away. The air conditioning is cranked up to the max, and I shiver as I look at my cards – six of clubs and queen of clubs. They're not great, but I'm in for the big blind anyway, so I figure I may as well see what the next cards bring if no one raises the bet.

They don't. Cabressa makes up the small blind to match the big. Johnny puts in his chips too. We're all in the game. As Carmella deals I catch a waft of scent from the huge display of lilies in the vase on the baby-grand piano. I grimace. I hate lilies; the scent of them makes me feel sick. Try to focus on the cards.

Seven of diamonds. Nine of clubs. Three of clubs.

I bite my lip, then immediately stop. I've been warned that it's my tell, I mustn't let the others see. When I look at Cabressa he's looking at his cards and smiling. He never gives anything away about his cards, so I doubt they're the cause of his smile. I think he's figured out my tell.

I glance at Johnny. He's murmuring to himself and swigging back champagne. Hot damn, he's drunk at least a bottle, most likely more like two, and his words are starting to sound a little slurred. As I watch him I notice he's leaning over to one side in his chair, resting his elbow on the table, and cradling his beard-covered chin on his hand.

Carmella looks at me. Raises an eyebrow. 'Your move.'

I take eight thousand-dollar chips from my stack and push them onto the green. 'I'm in.'

Cabressa matches me. Johnny takes another gulp of champagne and then does the same.

Carmella deals the next card. It's a six of hearts.

I've got a possible flush, or a guaranteed pair. The flush could win the hand. The pair is real unlikely to do anything good. If I stay in, it's a real gamble. But if I make a medium bet, let Johnny think I'm being cautious, and reel him in alongside me, I could win his stack and get him out of the game.

Johnny's trying to look confident, but his eyes are drooping and there's champagne splattered down his beard. Cabressa sits straight-backed, with his expression impassive. He doesn't look at the rest of us, just continues staring down at the table.

I push a ten-thousand-dollar chip onto the board. Cabressa folds. I need Johnny to come with me. I alter my posture, hunch over a little, put an anxious frown on my face. Fake that I'm nervous.

Johnny watches me a moment, eyes narrowed. Then he pushes the last of his chips onto the table. 'Go on then, I'm all in.'

Carmella counts Johnny's chips, then looks at me and says, 'You need to add a couple thousand more.'

As I push the chips onto the green felt my heart quickens. I have to win this.

'Ready?' Carmella asks.

We nod and she deals the last card. It's the king of clubs.

Johnny's shaking his head, guessing he's already beat.

I turn my cards over. 'I've got a flush.'

'You sure got me good,' slurs Johnny, pushing his chair back from the table. 'I don't got nothing that'll beat that.'

Carmella collects up the cards and pushes the pot towards me.

I take the chips, arranging them into neat stacks. I've made it to heads-up. I played the gamble, took the risk, and it worked. I give myself a virtual high five.

Cabressa nods, a thin smile on his lips. 'Nicely done, Miss Anderson.'

'Yeah, good work,' Johnny says, raising his empty champagne flute towards me. Then he stands and staggers over to the piano to join the others.

'We're now heads-up,' says Carmella. Putting the deck we've been playing with aside, she unwraps a fresh deck and puts them through the Shuffle Master.

I take a sip of my champagne and glance at my watch. It's almost two in the morning. We've been playing for hours. I hope JT is okay. I hope Monroe is getting the video and audio from the micro camera, and I hope to hell that this is almost over.

Carmella looks from Cabressa to me and says, 'Let's play.'

That's when the shouting starts.

19

'You been coming to these games a while then?' JT says, adjusting his weight in the chair.

The wrestler-type guy shrugs. 'I guess.'

'Since the big game started?' JT asks.

Again the guy shrugs and looks noncommittal. He glances over at the identikit security guard. Seems he's not so talkative now.

JT follows his gaze. Sees the guard's staring over at them again. He can tell what's going on – the guard's trying to figure out if he's a threat. He needs to convince him that he's not. He turns more towards the wrestler guy. Frowns. Acts agitated. Raises the volume of his voice enough for the guard to hear real easy. 'Have you worked for your boss long?'

'Couple of years, I guess.' The wrestler's tone implies he doesn't want to talk anymore.

JT needs to persuade him otherwise. 'Look, maybe you could give me some pointers? This is my first time running point on a close-protection gig, and to be honest this set-up is freaking me out. I had orders not to let her get out of my sight.' He shakes his head. 'Feels like I've fucked up already.'

'You just followed orders, dude. That's all you could've done.'

'I don't have eyes on her though, do I?' JT scrubs his palm over his hair.

'You didn't have a choice,' the security guard says. He's looking at JT with something bordering pity now rather than suspicion. 'She can't fire you for that.'

JT acts like he's not convinced. 'Hope not.'

'It'll be alright, dude,' says the wrestler guy.

The conversation ends. The security guard goes back to his puzzle. The wrestler guy starts playing with his cell. JT checks his watch again. The game's been on for three hours; longer than they'd anticipated. He scans the rest of the close-protection guys. No one looks bothered.

JT's worried though. He hates not knowing what's going on. He debates messaging Monroe. The man's a worm, but he's watching the live feed from Lori's micro camera. He'll be able to tell JT how she's doing. He glances at the others again. Every now and then one of them side-eyes him.

It makes him feel uneasy. Outwardly they're trying to give the impression of being relaxed, okay with the situation, but there's something more going on. The wrestler guy stopped telling JT the way things worked after the warning look from the guard, the gum-chewing man mountain didn't want to get involved from the get-go. The rest of the guys have tried to avoid eye contact. The guy with the Reacher book is tapping his forefingers against the cover as he reads. The pony-tailed guy sitting next to the wrestler is playing Candy Crush, but he's tense – so tense that his neck muscles are popping out his neck.

A heavily tattooed guy with shaggy brown hair gets up and steps over to the refreshment table. It's a fine spread – bagels, muffins, chips and a selection of sodas – but this guy's the first JT's seen use it. As tattoo guy starts loading up a plate, another of the guys gets up and moves over to join him. This guy's the smallest of the bunch, but he's still real big – like a rhino rather than a bull elephant. He's got shoulder-length dreads and carries himself with the grace of an athlete despite his bulk. When he reaches the table, the tattooed guy leans over, says something to him. JT can't hear what, but from the grim expression on the guy's face, he's guessing it's not good.

He wants to know more.

Getting up, JT saunters over to the refreshment station. He nods a casual hello to the two guys. The tattooed guy flicks his gaze to the dreadlocked man, then looks back at JT and gives a small nod back. The guy with the dreads keeps loading his plate.

'This free?' JT asks. He knows that it is, but it's as good a conversation starter as any.

The dreadlocked guy ignores the question. The tattooed man nods again.

JT grins. 'Good spread.' He gestures to the food. 'Any recommendations?'

Both guys ignore him. The identikit security guard is looking over at them, frowning.

JT raises his voice a fraction. 'You hear me? I asked a question.'

'I heard you,' says the tattooed guy, glancing towards the security guard, then moves away from the table. 'And I ain't got nothing to say to you.'

JT turns after the tattooed guy. Holds his hands out, making like he's all confused. 'But I—'

'Stay in your lane.' The dreadlocked guy elbows JT hard and hisses, 'Quit asking questions. That's not how things works here.'

JT holds his hands up again. He's seen all he needs to. 'Okay, I hear you.'

The guy with the dreads picks up his plate and heads towards his chair. The security guard focuses back on his puzzle book.

Their act is good for sure, thinks JT. They're so good it's almost believable, but he can tell that they're faking. These men aren't ruling this roost – they're not warning him off because they're guarding their territory, as they'd like him to believe. This is real different.

He can see it in their eyes, behind the faked posturing and macho bullshit.

These men are afraid.

20

Anton storms towards us.

'You two are heads-up?' Anton yells, his flushed complexion getting redder by the second. He stabs his finger towards Cabressa. 'You did this – fixed the game – didn't you? Tonight's been a goddamn set-up right from the get-go.'

Carmella freezes. For a moment her eyes widen and I see fear on her face, then a moment later it's gone, replaced with the neutral mask she's had the whole game. The rest of the players inch closer to us. Johnny's swaying, clinging on to Otis for support.

Cabressa calmly finishes counting his stacks, and then looks up at Anton. 'And why would you think that?'

'Because *you* brought *her* here.' Anton points at me as he spits out his words. '*You* vouched for her. But she's not a whale, is she? She's a goddamn ringer.'

I know what Anton means, but I stay silent. A whale is a rich person who's a weak poker player – someone the other players can easily beat.

'You're talking horseshit,' says Cabressa. 'She's a distinctly average player who you've allowed to get the better of you, most likely because she's showing a bit of cleavage.'

Anton cusses under his breath. Balls his fists.

Carmella stands up and moves over to Anton. She puts her hand on his arm. Her voice is a purr as she says, 'Anton, honey, you need to stop making a scene, okay?'

'No. No, it's not okay.' Anton shakes her off. Takes another step towards Cabressa. 'You said you were bringing a whale.'

Over by the door I see the security guy, Thomas, put his hand on his gun.

I stay in my seat. I wish I had my Taser, but figure that if Anton gets all up in my face, I should be able to take him down with a hard one-two and a roundhouse to finish.

Carmella steps between Anton and Cabressa. 'I don't allow that kind of game play at my tables, you know that.' The purr is gone, now Carmella's voice is firm, and real business-like. 'Everything in this game is fair and squared away. What you're saying right now puts my reputation at risk; is that what you want, Anton? You want to ruin me and stop the games?'

Anton opens and closes his mouth a couple of times. Takes a step back. 'No, I didn't mean that. This isn't about you, Carmella, it's about—'

'You need to think very carefully about what you're saying.' Carmella holds his gaze. Her voice is tough as steel. 'If you're at my table and you're badmouthing my game, then believe me when I say that what you're saying is absolutely about me, and that makes it personal. Trust me, you do not want to do that.'

Anton hangs his head like a naughty school kid. 'I just ... I didn't mean it that way. I don't want the game to stop.'

Carmella eyes him for a moment. 'If that's the case, are we good here?'

Anton glances towards Cabressa, then back to Carmella. Nods. 'Sure.'

'Well, that's okay then,' Carmella says. Picking up one of the remaining bottles of champagne in the ice buckets, she refreshes his glass. 'I'd hate to lose you – you're one of my most valued players.'

'Of course not, I would hate that too.' Anton drifts away towards the others. He looks bewildered, like he can't quite grasp what just happened.

Respect to Carmella; she's a real smooth operator.

Along the table, Cabressa looks untroubled by what's just gone down, and I'm left wondering how, as such a distinctly average player, I'm going to manage to pull off a convincing win. Anton and the other guys are going to be watching us real close. Cabressa won't be able to just throw me the game. It's a problem, but that's not the only thing I have to worry about.

As Carmella reshuffles the cards, Cabressa leans towards me. 'I don't know if you were told this before the game, but when we get to heads-up I like to make things more interesting. So, enough of these chips, let's bet something more valuable than cash.' Cabressa pats his jacket pockets until he feels something, then pulls out a set of keys. 'I'll bet you my new Rolls Royce. Custom made, two weeks old. Cost eight hundred thousand dollars.'

'Jeez!' says Johnny, swaying towards the table. 'That's one hell of a sweet ride.'

My mouth goes dry. I hadn't expected Cabressa to put something big on the table, but now I see I should have anticipated this, it's the only way for me to put the chess set in play without it seeming odd or like I've gotten special privileges.

'You got anything like that you can bet, girly?' says Anton.

The men gather closer around the table. All eyes are on me.

I look towards Carmella. 'There's something in my bag for this purpose; can Thomas go grab it?'

Carmella nods at Thomas and he disappears into the bedroom, returning a few minutes later with the wooden box that contains the chess pieces. He sets it down on the table in front of me and then returns to his post by the door.

'This is a unique set of chess pieces,' I say as I unfasten the lid of the box. 'It was made for a famous match in Las Vegas back in the eighties, and is valued at one point three five million dollars. But, as one of the pawns is missing, I think it should be a close enough match for the Rolls Royce.'

Cabressa watches my fingers undoing the clasps. His focus is as intense as a turkey buzzard on a blue jay.

I fold back the lid, and remove one of the pieces – a queen – to show the players. 'They really are one of a kind.'

Carmella looks at Cabressa. 'Are they acceptable?'

He takes the queen from me. Holding her up to the light, he runs his index finger over her in a way that looks kind of sexual. He closes his eyes a moment and sighs deeply, then looks at Carmella. Nods. 'They're satisfactory.'

I say nothing even though it seems this is one mobster whose chess fascination takes things to a whole new level of fetish. I take the queen back from Cabressa, place her in the box and fold down the lid entirely so all the pieces can be seen. Cabressa stares into the box, seemingly fixated by the pieces. I'm glad. I figure maybe they'll distract him enough to let me win the next hand.

The other players gather round. Carmella deals.

Then Cabressa slams his palms down onto the table, cussing loudly.

The chip stacks tumble. I flinch and look at Cabressa.

'It's not complete,' Cabressa shouts, his voice shaking with fury. 'One of the knights is missing.'

21

Cabressa glares at me, his eyes blazing. His whole body is trembling with anger.

He points at me, his finger stabbing towards my face. 'What the hell have you done with it? Where is the knight?'

I consider lying, but when you're in an unfamiliar city and the king mobster of that city has you as their guest in a high-stakes poker game, I think it's better to tell the truth. 'It must still be where I was storing the set.'

Cabressa puts his hands together in his lap. His voice is unnervingly calm. 'How?'

This is the moment when I lie. It's a matter of self-preservation and keeping my cover story intact. 'I was keeping the pieces in a safe place – away from prying eyes. I must have missed the knight when I was packing them into the box to bring them here. It's not a problem, I can—'

'Get the knight here, now.'

I frown. 'You want me to go and—'

'You aren't going anywhere, Miss Anderson. I trust you have an associate who can fetch you the piece? I'm told you're not without friends in this city. Get one of them to bring the piece here. Your security man can meet them in the lobby downstairs and bring the knight here to the penthouse.'

My associate? Friends in the city? I'm struggling to think on who Cabressa means. Has he figured out I'm working with the FBI? Does he mean Monroe?

Cabressa taps his gold watch. Glowers at me. 'Miss Anderson, the clock is ticking.'

I look from Cabressa to Carmella. Carmella's expression is blank, as if she hasn't heard a word that's been said. Mikey, Anton and Carl are watching us with the rapt attention of the blood-thirsty crowd at a gladiator match. Johnny's barely conscious, slumped in the seat at the other end of the table. Otis looks concerned, but as I catch his eye, he looks away fast.

There's no help for me inside this room, but that's okay, I know how to handle myself. I meet Cabressa's gaze. Keep my voice strong and calm, and say, 'I need to step outside and make a call.'

22

The call comes at a quarter after two.

JT's sitting in his chair, sandwiched between the man-mountain gum-chewer and the wrestler type in a suit. No one has spoken for the last half hour and an uneasy silence has settled over the group.

The call changes all that.

The identikit security guard nods as the person at the other end of the call speaks. He frowns. Looks over at JT. Then says, 'Yeah, I'll do it now.'

The guard puts down his puzzle book and heaves himself up from his seat. JT feels the men on either side of him tense and shift in their seats so there's more distance between them and him. Across the room the guy with the dreads glances at the tattooed man. The fear is stronger in his eyes. Makes JT think this can't be part of the usual routine.

As the security guard moves across the room JT watches him in his peripheral vision. He wishes he'd gotten his weapon. Figures from the way the other men are acting things could be about to go bad. Real slow he slides a little further forward on the chair, putting more weight onto the soles of his feet. Ready to move fast – defend or attack – if the situation demands it.

The security guy stops a yard or so from him. 'You're JT right? The one with the woman?'

'Yup.'

'You're needed upstairs.'

JT sees the shock on the faces of tattoo and dreads opposite. The wrestler guy turns towards him and the guard, looking confused. JT looks up at the guard. 'Why?'

The guard shrugs. 'Don't know. My instructions are to escort you to the elevator. Thomas will meet you in the penthouse.'

JT gestures towards the metal footlockers with each player's name on – his and Lori's weapons are inside. 'Do I get my stuff back?'

'Not until the game's over.'

Given what's happening isn't the norm, he'd prefer his gun to hand, but knows he doesn't have the collateral to push it. He stands. 'Lead the way.'

As the security guard walks him out of the holding room and towards the elevator, JT wonders what the hell has happened with Lori and the game. And what it is that he's going to be walking into.

*

The elevator doors slide open on the sixty-third floor, and JT's met by the other identikit security guard – Thomas. He grimaces at JT. 'Your player's causing us some issues and delaying the game. You need to sit in her place as a substitute.'

JT frowns. Doesn't like the sound of that. 'What kind of issues?'

'She's made an incomplete bet, and she needs to sort it.' Thomas glances towards the door at the end of the foyer that'll take them to the living space and the game. He looks real anxious. Takes a few steps towards the door, gesturing for JT to follow.

JT doesn't move. 'An incomplete bet? I don't understand.'

Thomas lowers his voice. 'Look, just between us, this is pretty unorthodox. She's head-to-head with Mr Cabressa and put a special bet on the table – a set of gold chess pieces – she said a pawn was missing but there's a knight missing too. Mr Cabressa is insisting that the knight is brought here to the penthouse before the game plays on.'

JT grits his teeth. That goddamn knight. 'Don't you want me to go get the piece?'

'No, she's calling someone else to do that. She wants you to sit in her chair – watch her cards – while she's out of the room.'

Seems they want him to literally take Lori's seat. He nods. 'Okay. I can do that.'

Thomas looks relieved. 'This way,' he says, ushering JT across the foyer and into the living space.

As soon as they're inside, JT takes a quick appraisal of the situation. The lighting is softer here in the penthouse, mostly coming from a few lamps dotted around the space. The brightest area is the poker table, lit by a suspended rig of spotlights all focused on the felt green of the table. But despite the low lighting and soft music playing in the background, he can tell the atmosphere is anything but relaxed.

Over at the poker table, Lori's back is rigid, her body tense. She's doing a good job of trying to hide it, but JT can see her fingers are clenched into fists in her lap, and the two worry lines she gets between her brows when she's concerned have appeared.

Lori and Cabressa sit at right angles to each other across the poker table. Carmella, who looks to be dealing, is opposite Lori. Cabressa's body language is closed – arms crossed, chin tucked down – and he's glaring at the organiser, Carmella. JT follows the mobster's gaze. Carmella's expression – neutral, verging on vacant – makes her look outwardly calm, but JT can see that's not the true story. She's fiddling with a poker chip from the house's stacks – flipping the blue chip over the knuckles of her right hand and under her palm, over and over. It's a neat trick, but a nervous tic when done on autopilot and on repeat.

The other players are gathered around the table. They're standing, leaning over the chairs – ready for a show. JT guesses they're waiting for Cabressa to bawl Lori out, or maybe that's already happened. One thing's real clear – her plan's backfired.

JT recognises Johnny Keto, the wrestler's charge, from his time playing ball. Back then he'd looked in peak fitness, real alert, but now the ballplayer looks drunk – his eyes are glassy and the movements he makes as he leans across towards the man JT recognises as Otis Valha, the boxer, are overly large and uncoordinated.

JT takes a look at the rest of the players. Aside from Otis Valha they're all looking well on their way to being drunk. That's not good. Alcohol has a habit of making situations more volatile. Last thing they need is for this to escalate. The plan now is clear; they need to get the knight, get this handoff done, and then get the hell out.

JT follows Thomas across the room to the poker table.

Lori smiles when she sees him – a fleeting gesture, automatic, before she recomposes her features into a more neutral expression. Her voice is tougher than usual when she speaks – playing her role as boss. 'Good, you're finally here. Take my seat while I make a call.'

As she stands and steps away from the table, JT moves towards her chair.

'Watch my cards,' she says to him. She looks at Cabressa. 'This won't take long.'

Cabressa stares at Lori, his voice heavy with threat. 'It had better not.'

As he watches Lori walk out of the living space and onto the terrace, JT fights the urge to slam the heel of his hand into Cabressa's throat. He mustn't, he knows that. It's not just that Lori is more than capable of fighting her own battles and she wouldn't appreciate him stepping in, it's also because they have to work with this mobster asshole until the exchange is sorted. Soon as it's done they're going to get gone. They'll be rid of Cabressa and the Chicago mob, and free of Special Agent Alex Monroe. That's the goal – the only reason he and Lori agreed to do this. So they could get rid of two assholes with one set of chess pieces.

JT takes Lori's seat. He believes violence is only ever a last resort, never the first answer in a situation, and he's always operated on that basis. But still. Right now he stares into Cabressa's eyes, and he smiles as he imagines punching the man's smug face into a pulp.

23

I make the only play I have open to me. I call Monroe.

He answers after a single ring. 'What the fuck, Lori! Where's the knight? You were tipped for the exchange and you blew it – you fucking blew it.'

'I need you to go get the piece for me.'

'You're killing me here.'

I glance back through the drapes into the penthouse. The guys are talking around the table. I can't hear what they're saying, but I don't want to be away from them too long. The situation is heated. It won't take much to turn things hostile. 'Look, it won't take long. Once I've got it I can make the exchange.'

Monroe cusses. 'I thought we had him. I thought we damn well had him.'

'We have,' I hiss. 'I just need you to do this one thing for me.'

'I'll get it, obviously.' Monroe sounds anxious, pissed. 'I just don't get why you didn't take the whole set. Why leave the knight behind for God's sakes? Why, Lori?'

I don't have time for this. But I need Monroe to focus fast. 'I was worried the poker exchange wouldn't be enough to charge and hold him. And if you did charge him he'd be able to use lack of knowledge as a defence and claim he never knew the pieces were stolen, that he accepted them in good faith. Basically, with the legal help a man like him will have on retainer, if the chess pieces are a gift or a win he'll be able to wriggle out of the charges real quick. By removing one I was going to instigate a second hand-off. One that he'd ask for, and would happen after the game. When we're away from the game I'd let slip that the set is stolen

– that way Cabressa would be knowingly handling stolen goods, and you'd have the evidence on camera.'

Monroe's silent.

'You still there?' I ask.

Monroe exhales hard. 'Your plan was good. Makes sense. Just wish you'd told me earlier.'

'Yeah.' I don't say I'm sorry. I'm not sure that I am.

'I'll go get the knight for you. Where is it?'

'It's in the central air vent in my hotel room. Unscrew the grill and you'll see it lying on its side.'

'Okay, it'll take me thirty minutes, maybe a touch more.' Monroe sounds anxious again. 'It looked tense at the table. You think you can keep things calm until I'm back?'

I glance back inside. The guys are still talking, and there's no yelling, so I'm hoping that's a good sign. 'I hope so.'

'Just hang in there,' Monroe says.

His voice is so sincere that if I didn't know better I'd think he was a good person. But whatever he's done before, I trust that he'll do this: he'll fetch the knight – and do it because it's in his best interest. 'It's all I can do.'

'I'll be as fast as I can,' says Monroe.

'Good.' With the cellphone still to my ear, I turn away from the penthouse and step over to the edge of the terrace. It feels strange to be this high; the view is like something from an airplane window. Sixty-three floors below the city streets stretch out under me, lit up by thousands of buildings and streetlights. It looks kind of beautiful. But I don't have time for beauty. 'Because it's getting kind of hostile.'

'It's nearly done.'

I tell myself he's right – I only have to stay with these people a little while longer. Soon this will be done, finished. JT and me can go home and be back with Dakota. And no matter how gorgeous the Chicago cityscape looks all twinkling below me, I sure can't wait for that moment.

I take a breath. Get ready to hang up with Monroe and head back inside.

'Lori?' Monroe's voice sounds stranglehold tight.

'Jeez,' I say, clutching my free hand to my chest. 'Oh shit. Monroe, are you seeing this?'

I watch in horror as one by one, building by building and street by street, the lights on every block in the city go out.

Within seconds the whole of Chicago is engulfed in darkness.

24

'Monroe, can you hear me?'

His words are distorted, metallic sounding. 'Lori, what's...?'

There are three beeps and the call disconnects. The backlit screen of my cell seems overly bright in the eerie gloom of the blacked-out city. Nothing's twinkling anymore. I press Monroe's number and wait for the call to connect, but it doesn't. Nothing happens.

I check the screen. Hot damn. There's no cell service, no 4G, and no wi-fi, zip – just like the city's power, they've all been switched off. I wonder what the hell this means and how the hell a thing like this happens. Wonder if it's some kind of terrorist attack.

There's a loud click behind me, and I whip round. The penthouse is in darkness aside from several cellphone screens illuminating small patches of the poker table. I take a step towards the building. There's another click, as loud as before, followed by another. Then a whirring sound starts up, like a small motor. I realise the noise is coming from above the balcony windows.

At first I feel relief – if something's working surely that means the penthouse still has some power. Then I realise the terrace doors are moving, closing. I think back to the blueprints of the building – the whole suite of the penthouse is designed as a panic room. The blackout must have caused it to automatically activate.

The penthouse is going into lockdown. The doors are sliding closer. JT's inside, I'm out. And if I don't move my ass I'm going to get stuck out here on the terrace.

Sprinting across the tiled floor, I squeeze between the final door and the wall – just making it inside before the door closes and the lock clicks shut. The motor pauses a moment, then metal shutters lower over the windows.

'What the hell's going on?' Johnny slurs from over by the poker table, his face made ghostly in the light of his cell. 'What's happening to the windows?'

'They're armoured shutters.' Carmella's voice is clear and calm. 'It's part of the panic-room protocol. If there's a power problem in the building, or any other perceived threat to the inhabitants of this suite, the protocol is activated. The blackout will have triggered it.'

'Can't we un-trigger it?' Otis sounds out-of-breath, all sorts of anxious. 'I hate the dark, and I don't like enclosed spaces.'

'The penthouses all have back-up generators,' says Carmella. 'We should have power again really soon, you don't need to worry.'

'My cell's got no service,' says Carl, stabbing at the screen. '911 isn't connecting.'

'Why are you calling 911?' says Carmella.

'Because this is an emergency,' Carl says, his tone patronising. 'There are no lights.'

Mikey looks at his cell. Shakes his head. 'I've got nothing.'

'There's no service, or 4G or wi-fi,' I say. 'I checked already.'

'That's not normal, is it?' Otis is speaking fast, his words coming out in a tumble. 'I get that wi-fi would be affected, but the 4G, the cell service? How's—?'

'It could have taken out the cell towers,' says JT. His voice is gravel deep and steady. Hearing him makes me feel calmer.

'I just don't like it that we're locked in here. What if there's a fire? What if we want to—?'

'It's okay,' says Carmella. In the glow of the screens I see her move over to Otis and put her hand on his arm. 'There's a landline in the study, I'll call the concierge and ask them to override the panic-room protocol.'

'Thanks,' Otis says, still sounding breathless. 'Really appreciate it.'

She rubs his arm. 'It's no problem.'

Thomas goes with Carmella as she leaves the living space to go make the call. The rest of us stay where we are. I switch on the torch app on my cell. Otis looks tense over at one end of the table. By the piano, Mikey, Anton and Carl are discussing the power grid and what could have caused such a huge outage.

Sighing, Johnny sways over to the huge L-shaped couch and sprawls at one end of his, slurping his champagne.

Only Cabressa, who's still seated at the head of the table, seems unbothered. He turns to look at me. 'Did you reach someone who can bring the chess piece?'

'Yes.' I think fast. Want to buy myself more time to figure out a way I can still get watertight evidence on Cabressa. I meet his cold, hard gaze. 'But the cell service cut out before I could tell them where to find it.'

Cabressa grips the edge of the table in both hands. The light's too dim to see if his knuckles are going white, but I can tell for sure that he's angry from the way he's clenching his jaw. He glares at me. 'We'll just have to hope the blackout, and lack of cell service, doesn't last for too long, won't we.' It was not a question.

I nod. Act meek. Know that I won't be done with this job until Cabressa is behind bars. There's a calm kind of menace, a cold evil, about this rather nondescript man that gives me the heebie-jeebies. I've heard the stories of what he's done, how he's ruled the streets of Chicago for over twenty years, and anyone who's gotten in his way – criminal or honest citizen – has been threatened, exploited or killed. I also know, just from looking into his eyes, that once this deal is done and he has the full set of chess pieces, this mobster intends to kill me. I glance at JT, see the concern on his face, and I know he's guessed Cabressa's intentions too.

If Cabressa gets his way, neither me or JT will ever leave this city. We'll be set into the concrete foundations of one of his mob-money-financed skyscrapers, or weighted down and cast into Lake Michigan from an isolated spot out near the purification plant.

Our baby girl, Dakota, will become an orphan at just ten years old.

I clench my fists. Give JT a meaningful look.

Because there is no goddamn way I'm going to let that happen.

25

'How long does the generator take?' Carl's sounding more anxious than a few minutes ago. The silence and the darkness are getting to all of us. And it's getting hotter and more humid inside this sealed penthouse with the central air shut off.

'Give it a minute,' Mikey says. 'It's probably never been used before, the building's so new.'

'Never been used?' There's a tremble to Otis's voice. 'You mean it's not tested, it might fail?'

'No,' says Mikey. 'I meant it might take a few minutes to get started.'

Anton picks up one of the bottles of champagne. Looks at Mikey and Carl. 'We may as well have another drink while we wait.'

'True,' says Mikey, holding out his glass.

Otis shakes his head and starts to pace up and down in the gloom. His path is illuminated by the torch app on his cell, and in its glow I can see that his lips are moving as he mutters to himself.

Johnny watches him a moment, then sticks his leg out as Otis gets close to where he's sprawled on the couch, blocking the boxer's path. 'Chill. We're in a penthouse with champagne. It's all good.'

'It is not all good,' Otis says between gritted teeth. 'It's far from all good.'

I look at JT. 'You okay?'

'Yup.' But I can tell from the way he says it that he isn't. He's under par, still supposed to be convalescing from the stab wounds and heart attack he had a couple of months back. The wounds are healed, but the muscle damage remains. The physical therapy's been helping, but I know he'll be worrying about his ability to keep us safe, keep me safe. He worries like that, even though I looked after myself and Dakota just fine on my own for the best part of ten years before JT and me got back together.

I give a small nod, conscious that Cabressa is studying me. 'It'll be fine. We just need to wait for the back-up generator.'

He opens his mouth to reply, then stops as Carmella re-enters the open-plan area. From the look on her face, I can tell that the news isn't good.

Otis hurries towards her. 'Did you tell them to unlock all these things?' he says, waving towards the shutters. 'How long will it be until the generator's working?'

Carmella shakes her head. 'I couldn't call anyone. The phone system is Internet-based; even the internal calls aren't connecting.'

'It's not surprising,' Carl says, running a hand over his smooth pate. 'Everything needs power. We've just got to wait it out.'

'That's my plan,' says Anton, filling up Carl and Mikey's glasses again. He looks at Carmella. 'I just hope we've got enough fizz to keep us going?'

'There's plenty,' says Carmella. 'And the fridges are stocked. We can survive here for days, not that that'll be necessary, of course,' she adds, glancing at Otis.

Otis is shaking. He stops by the table. Grips the back of one of the chairs. 'We. Need. To. Get. Out.'

'It'll be okay,' Carmella says. 'I'm sure it'll be fast.'

'But it's not, is it?' Otis snaps back. His voice is getting faster, louder. 'It's been forever, and there's still nothing. We're locked in here. The phones are out. And we're trapped. Prisoners. I can't...' Turning, Otis sprints towards the door. He's real fast for a man of his size and muscle mass.

Leaving JT at the table, I chase after Otis.

Carmella follows close on my heels. 'Otis, wait,' she shouts. 'This isn't helping.'

He doesn't listen. Keeps sprinting.

Thomas looks ready to step into Otis's way and stop him, but Carmella waves him away. Thomas steps aside as Otis reaches the door.

Otis yanks it open, and hurtles into the lobby towards the elevator. Sliding to a halt beside it, he stabs at the call button. Switches his weight foot to foot. Mutters, 'Come on, come on.'

Carmella and me stop next to him. We glance at each other.

'Please, come on,' Otis pleads. He's near to tears. His whole body is shaking.

'It's not working,' I say, as gently as I can. 'It needs electricity to function.'

'But it has to.' Turning to face me, Otis's face crumples and he seems to deflate in front of me. This tall, muscular boxer is defeated by fear. Shaking his head, he sinks slowly to the floor, his back against the wall, and pulls his knees into his chest, hugging his arms around them. 'I can't stay locked in here. I can't.'

'You can and you will,' I say, my voice calm but firm, as if to a child. I put my hand on his shoulder. 'You're with friends. However long it takes, you will be fine.'

He looks back towards the door into the living space. 'They're not *my* friends.'

I try not to act surprised. He'd seemed buddy enough with them earlier, but then there was the hierarchy I'd noticed. For the first time, I wonder if I'm not the only one who was invited to the game for a reason. Otis had been playing well and then he virtually threw the game. I'd put it down to bad luck, or tiredness setting in, but maybe it was intentional. It could be he was given a seat at the game in order to repay a debt to Cabressa or one of these other men. For all I know the whole thing's been rigged from the get-go. I squeeze his shoulder. 'Well, you're with us, anyways.'

He frowns at me, and then looks at Carmella.

She nods. 'You can't stay here, Otis. We need to get back to the others.'

He does nothing for a moment. Then takes a ragged breath. 'Okay.'

I put out my hand. 'Come on.'

He takes my hand and I help him up. Carmella and me guide him as he takes wobbly steps out of the lobby. I can feel him shaking, but at least he's not in flight mode anymore.

'The wanderer returns,' laughs Anton, raising his glass in Otis's direction as we move into the open-plan living space. 'Come get some fizz, might help your nerves.'

'Don't,' Carmella says, shooting him an angry look. 'Give him a break.'

Johnny waves. 'Glad you're back with us, dude.'

Carmella and me help Otis over to the poker table and into one of the chairs. He sits, slumped, head resting in his hands. Looking like a broken man.

JT meets my gaze. 'It's getting all kinds of hot in here.'

He's right, with the central air off the heat's rising, and the humidity too. I can feel sweat running down my back between my shoulder blades. But I don't think JT's just talking about the room temperature.

JT keeps his voice low. Nods across the room. 'Some people are making matters worse.'

In the light from my cell I follow his gaze. Across the room, Johnny is lying back on the couch with his eyes closed. Over by the piano Mikey looks flushed, and Anton's face is almost puce.

Carl's removed his jacket, revealing huge sweat marks under the arms of his pink shirt. He's talking fast, voice rising in volume and pitch. 'We need to stop him. It can't carry on, you know. This Herron is going to sink our—'

'We will. But not right now,' Anton says, cutting him off. He points at Carl's chest. 'Right now, you need to cool it.'

I wipe the sweat from my forehead. This heat isn't helping the situation. Everyone's getting restless, and that's when things get more unpredictable. In hot, humid, stressful situations like this irritations can have a real nasty habit of turning violent.

Carl's shaking his head. Squaring up to Anton.

I glance at JT.

He raises his eyebrows.

Next moment Anton grabs Carl by his shirt and shoves him hard against the piano. Carl bellows, striking out at Anton, and they both crash to the floor, fighting.

That's when the back-up generator kicks in.

26

First there's a loud buzz, then the lights switch on. A few seconds later, the central air kicks in and chilled jets blast through the vents. Anton and Carl stop fighting. Everyone cheers. I feel all kinds of relieved and grin at JT. He gives me a half-smile, but I can see he's still worried.

'The back-ups kicked in, that's a good sign,' I say.

'It's not finished yet.' JT glances towards the terrace. 'We're still in lockdown.'

He's right. The metal shutters are shrouding the consortia doors and the windows. We're still locked inside. I think back to the blueprints and the building notes we'd studied for Skyland Tower. In a power outage, once the back-up generators kick in, if no threat is perceived, the panic room protocol reverses itself.

I bite my lip. Cabressa and Carmella are sitting real close, so I can't talk about this to JT because I'd have to reveal that I've looked at the design of the building and its security systems, and as far as they'd know I'd have no cause to do that. As I look across the table at JT, I see the concern in his eyes and the tension in his body – like he's ready as a momma bobcat to jump into action – and know he's thinking it too. If the security system is still active, what threat has it detected?

The others, unaware of how the system works, are high-fiving and cheering. Anton puts his hand out and helps Carl up. Carl slaps him on the back. They're laughing. Mikey's pouring more champagne. Otis goes over and sits with Johnny. Johnny hugs him. Even Cabressa cracks a smile.

We all flinch as two loud beeps come over the room's integral speaker system.

Otis looks around. His eyes widen, panicked. 'What the hell is—?'

'Main power to the Skyland Tower has been disrupted,' says an electronic-sounding voice. *'Secondary power has been activated. Do not be alarmed. For your safety, panic-room protocols are in operation until main power is re-established.'*

That isn't right; that isn't what the building's systems manual said it was programmed to do. I frown at JT. He's looking concerned too, but flicks his gaze towards Cabressa and gives a little shake of his head. *Don't say anything, not right now.*

I stay silent.

Carmella loads the deck into the Shuffle Master and looks to me and Cabressa. 'Now we've got the power back, are you ready to continue the game?'

Cabressa narrows his eyes. 'I'd rather wait until the knight is reunited with the set, but given this situation I suppose we can play forward.' He fixes me with a hard stare. 'Just know that I won't consider the bet paid in full until the chess set is complete.'

I stare at him. Don't like what's happening, or the attitude he's giving me, but seeing as we're locked in this penthouse suite for God knows how much longer, I figure I need to keep him sweet and play along. So I nod. Force a compliant smile. 'Understood.'

JT gets up from my player's chair, and I settle back into the seat. JT stays close behind me, and I'm thankful for it. Feels like I'm in a snake pit going head-to-head with a cobra. I'm real glad JT has got my back. The rest of the guys gather closer around us, watching. As Carmella's about to deal I hear Anton cuss.

She stops, the first card poised over the green, and looks over at him. 'Problem?'

Anton turns his champagne flute upside down and says in a childlike voice, 'There's no more fizz.'

A flash of irritation passes across Carmella's face before she supresses it with her mask of professionalism. 'There's plenty more.' She looks over to Thomas, the security guy, who's still standing by the door. 'Could you bring more champagne for our guests?'

'Sure.' He leaves his post and strides through to the kitchen area.

There's a clink of bottles, then he reappears carrying four more bottles over to the poker table. Thomas gives the first bottle to Anton, who fills his glass, and then those of Carl and Mikey. The second bottle goes to Johnny, who abandons his glass in favour of drinking straight from the bottle. Thomas sets the other two bottles in the ice buckets.

'Thanks,' says Carmella.

As Thomas moves towards the door, two loud beeps sound over the penthouse's speaker system again. He stops, and turns back towards us looking confused. 'What's that about?'

Then the electronic voice begins to speak again, and everything changes.

27

'*It's time to play a different game. Not everyone in the suite tonight is who they say they are. All ten of you are hiding secrets.*'

My stomach flips. What the hell is this?

Everyone falls silent, listening. Otis's leg starts to jig.

The electronic voice continues, booming out from the penthouse's speakers:

'*Here are some facts you might not know about each other:*
One of you is a police informer.
One of you is a thief.
One of you is a killer.
One of you is an addict.
One of you is a cheater.
One of you is bankrupt.
One of you is a wife-beater.
One of you is a fraud.
One of you has an illegitimate child.
One of you is HERRON.'

'Is this some kind of joke?' Anton says, wiping his brow.

'Don't sound like no joke,' says Otis. His leg jigs faster. 'Sounds like some freak's trapped us in here on purpose.'

'You can't be taking this seriously?' Carl says. He laughs, but it sounds forced and hollow. 'It's just some sick fuck—'

The electronic voice interrupts him. '*Herron is taking over the city. He's disrupting business deals and politics, interfering with shipments, and co-opting gangs into his empire. His identity has been carefully guarded as he hides behind his lieutenants, staying anonymous and untouchable, expanding his reach in the business and*' *criminal worlds. He's a threat to all of you and your businesses, but one. So this is your challenge – work out which of you is Herron. The panic-room lockdown protocol will deactivate once you've made the correct choice. How you decide to use that information will be up to you. Good luck.'*

Everyone stays quiet a moment, waiting to see if the electronic voice is going to continue. When it doesn't, all the men start talking at once.

'Where are they?' says Otis. Wild-eyed, he scans the room. 'Where's the voice coming from?' He hugs his massive arms around his torso, but it doesn't disguise the fact that he's trembling. 'They're watching us. They've trapped us in here, and now they're watching us.'

Carl's shaking his head. 'It's pre-recorded, you fool, no one's watching. You need to chill the fuck out.'

Otis is shaking. 'We're screwed. We're totally screwed, man. We're like rats in a sack.'

'How do they know we're here?' says Mikey. His voice is loud, strident. His fists are clenched. 'How can they possibly know that?'

'They can't, can they?' says Anton. 'No one knows we're up here. We didn't sign in when we entered the building, it's—'

'But there are cameras,' Otis says, looking wildly around the living area. 'The cameras are everywhere, man. They're watching us. Oh jeez, they're watching us.'

'I said chill. The fuck. Out,' says Carl, glaring at Otis, and sounding anything but chilled himself. 'They didn't mention our names. It's a bluff, some asshole making a joke. So just chill.'

JT moves closer to me and slips into the empty seat to my right, away from Cabressa. He leans towards me. Whispers into my ear. 'This is bad, we need a plan to—'

'I need to confess something,' says Carmella.

The talking stops. All eyes are on Carmella.

JT sits up.

Carmella clears her throat. 'Look, I know I should have told you this before. Hell, I should have cancelled the game, or moved locations or something but, well, my cell was stolen yesterday.'

Everyone stares at her. No one speaks.

'I'd already sent the messages about the game,' Carmella continues. 'And all the details, and your names and numbers were in the cell.' She looks around the group. Her professional mask is slipping, and the fear beneath is starting to show in her eyes. 'I thought it'd be okay, because I had it wiped remotely. But it wasn't wiped immediately. Whoever took it had it almost an hour before that, so if they'd figured out the code then...'

'That's how they know,' Otis says. 'It's all true. It's all—'

'You did this.' Anton points at her. 'You stupid bitch, you fucked us; you're responsible.'

Carmella's cheeks flush. 'I didn't think—'

'Yeah, that's more than obvious.' Anton steps towards her. 'You didn't think at all.'

'Calm down,' Mikey says, stepping between Carmella and Anton. 'We can't turn on each other. We need to work out who's doing this and how to stop them.'

'This is crazy,' says Johnny, staggering a few steps closer to the table.

'It is,' agrees Mikey. 'And that's why we've got to think logically about this.'

'It all started with the blackout,' says Carl, running a hand over his bald head. 'They used the penthouse security protocol to lock us in.'

'Yeah, but how could they have known about the blackout?' says Mikey, looking thoughtful. 'It would have been impossible to predict.'

'Unless they caused it?' Johnny slurs.

'Really, have you any idea how difficult it would be for someone to do that?' says Mikey. 'Anyways, if they just wanted to trap us, all they needed to do was cut power to the building, not the whole city.'

'Yet here we are,' says Anton.

'I don't care how they did it,' says Johnny, crossing his arms. 'I'm not playing this fucker's game. Count me out.'

'You can't elect to be out,' says Anton. 'You're here, that automatically makes you part of this.'

Johnny shakes his head. 'I won't—'

'It can't be pre-recorded,' says Otis, his voice trembling. 'They know exactly who's in the room. They have to be watching us.'

Carl frowns. 'Not necessarily, they could have used the information in Carmella's cell and—'

'No, they couldn't.' JT's voice is real serious. 'If it was pre-recorded they'd have said nine not ten. I'm only in here because of Miss Anderson having to leave the table to make a call. Technically, I shouldn't have been in here; I should have been with the rest of your security people downstairs. But the voice mentioned ten people, so they know exactly how many people are inside this suite. That means it can't have been recorded before the power outage.'

'I was right, they *are* watching us,' Otis says, the tremble in his voice becoming more pronounced. 'Oh my God, they're watching us right now.'

Johnny turns and sways across the room towards the far corner. Climbing onto the couch, he walks along it, barely keeping upright. 'There's got to be some hidden cameras here somewhere.'

'Wouldn't the power outage have taken the cameras out of action?' asks Carmella.

Mikey shakes his head. 'Maybe before the back-up generator kicked in, yes. But now we've got power again, I'd say any cameras will be back running too.'

I swallow hard. Sure, there might be other cameras built into the penthouse; after all, fancy places like this have all kinds of security measures put into them as standard. But aside from anyone who could be observing the penthouse through the building's cameras, there's one other person who I know has been watching the whole night for sure. Monroe. He's dodgy as hell, I know that, but setting up this situation – the power outage, the panic-room protocol and the electronic voice's accusations – it all seems far too elaborate for Monroe to have planned. The prize he wants is Cabressa – he's had a hair up his ass for him for years – and this is the closest he's ever gotten to getting an arrest that'll stick. I'm pretty certain he wouldn't do anything to jeopardise that, especially for some new player on the block, like Herron. I'm pretty damn sure, but I'm not a hundred percent.

I sit for a moment, as the others argue around me, and think on it. Feel sick as another realisation hits me. Monroe's been watching this whole time. There's no reason why someone else couldn't have tapped into the feed.

I glance at JT and then at Cabressa. Unlike all the others, Cabressa hasn't spoken a word. But now I realise he's thinking about something. It's real easy to see: his lips are pursed into a thin line and a deep frown is etched into his brow.

When he notices me watching him, he narrows his eyes. Clears his throat. And bangs his fist hard against the table. When all the others have stopped talking and are looking at him he says, in a hard-as-steel voice, 'So which of you assholes is Herron?'

28

Everyone looks at Cabressa.

'Whoever's got us locked in here knows one of us is Herron.' The mobster looks from person to person. 'It's not me, so it has to be one of you, and I want to know who.'

The tension feels heavy in the air. No one speaks.

I hold my breath, waiting to see what happens next. Beside me, JT moves forward in his seat – a tiny adjustment, but I know he's getting into a position ready to go on the defence if things escalate.

Johnny, seemingly a brave drunk, gestures towards Cabressa. 'What's to say *you* aren't Herron?'

Otis inhales sharply. Carl shoots a worried look at Mikey.

Cabressa uses his index fingers to smooth his thick, dark eyebrows into place. 'A fair question. The voice said each of us had a secret, and listed out those secrets for us. Among us are a police informer, a thief, a killer, an addict, a bankrupt, a wife-beater, a cheater, a fraud, the father of an illegitimate child, and Herron.'

'This is one sick game,' says Anton, grimacing.

Otis's shaking his head and looking like he might throw up.

'Seems like a cheap riddle to me,' says Mikey, lighting a cigar.

'Not so cheap when Herron has cost some of us big money these past few months,' says Carl. 'If we could get rid of him tonight, that'd be a win in my book.'

Thomas, the security guard, puts his hand on his gun. 'There'll be no getting rid of anyone. I'm here for all your safety. Nothing can happen inside this building.'

Johnny stares at Cabressa. 'You've not answered my question yet. How can we be sure *you* aren't Herron?'

Cabressa nods. 'I'll make my confession first, shall I? I don't have anything to hide. I'm the father of an illegitimate child. Two children in fact – Kirsten and Toby; they're five and nine. Their mother has been my personal assistant for the past twelve years. Sadly my wife has been unable to have children, therefore we have an "arrangement".' He looks from person to person. Holds my gaze the longest as he says, 'I am not Herron.'

'So who is?' says Anton, eyes narrowed, looking from person to person.

No one speaks. Everyone avoids eye contact.

Otis's leg is jigging at double speed. 'Look, if we're going to get out of here, we have to work it out. It's the only way, man.'

Thomas shakes his head. Keeps his hand on his holster.

Cabressa looks at Anton. 'I know you're the bankrupt, so given the parameters of this game you can't be Herron. But if you find me Herron, all the cash brought here for this poker game is yours.'

On the opposite side of the table, from behind Carmella, Thomas steps towards Cabressa. 'That's not how things get done here.'

Anton frowns.

Thomas keeps approaching. When he gets level with Anton things seem to shift into fast forward. Anton shoves Thomas towards the table. Thomas, big and lumbering, falls sideways, his balance lost, vulnerable. Anton ploughs after him. Pinning Thomas against the table, he brings his knee up hard into the big guy's stomach. As Thomas doubles over, arms flailing, Anton punches him in the side of the head. The security guy drops to the ground, out cold.

Hot damn. Anton sure moves fast for a man of his bulk.

Otis is staring at Thomas's collapsed body. Carl and Mikey seem in a state of shock. Cabressa looks unbothered as he flicks a speck of fluff from his jacket.

I look across the table at the spot on the floor where Thomas is lying. No matter how I think on it there's no fast or stealthily way for JT or me to get to Thomas. As I glance at JT I can tell from the intense expression on his face that he's trying to figure it out too. We need to, and we need to do it real fast. Because sitting in Thomas's holster is a Glock 27.

JT starts to stand.

Johnny, wide-eyed with shock, turns to Anton, who stands statue-still beside Thomas, his fists still clenched. 'What the fuck did you just—?'

'I want *all* the money,' Anton says to Cabressa. 'Everything that was put on the table and held in reserve in the back room.'

The mobster nods. 'That's what I said was yours: all the money. Only the chess pieces and the car are off limits.'

'Okay,' says Anton. He bends down toward Thomas's body. 'I'm happy with the cash.'

I can't see what he's doing, but I've got a damn good idea. There's no time to stop him. All we can do right now is try not to draw attention. Think on our best move. I turn to JT.

He grimaces and slides back into his seat. He leans towards me, but his eyes are on Carmella, as he whispers, 'Brace yourself.'

Carmella is vigorously shaking her head. 'Anton, you can't have the money. That's just not going to happen.' She turns to Cabressa. 'It's in my care. It's not yours to give—'

'The rules have been changed, Carmella,' says Cabressa. 'This is out of your hands now. Tonight we're playing a new game.' He nods at Anton.

Anton straightens up. The Glock 27 is in his hand. He points it at Carmella. Adjusts his posture – his legs are splayed, and both hands grip the gun. The exaggerated stance makes him look like a cartoon figure, a make-believe cowboy. But the Glock is very real. So is the danger.

'You caused this, bitch,' says Anton. He puffs out his chest. His tone is fuelled with macho bullshit. 'You let your cell get stolen. You deserve to die for your damn stupidity.'

There's a pause. A brief moment of silence. Then JT speaks.

'Put the gun down,' JT growls. 'No one needs to die here.'

29

Anton looks at him real surprised. Anton's inexperienced with a gun, JT can tell that from the way he's holding it, and the exaggerated stance he's adopted, but that doesn't make the man any less dangerous. He might be a fool, but a fool with a gun is a dangerous fool.

'This isn't a good play,' says JT, real firm. 'You need to lower the Glock. Get it out of the lady's face.'

Anton keeps the gun pointed at Carmella. 'Looks a good-enough play from where I'm standing.'

Carmella starts to cry. JT starts to stand.

Anton swings the gun towards JT. 'Stay sitting where you are, cowboy.' He points the gun back at Carmella. 'You shut it.'

Carmella is shaking her head. Her eyes are pleading with Anton. 'Please, I didn't...'

'I told you to shut your mouth,' Anton yells.

This is bad. JT can see the sweat on Anton's flushed face. The man's hands are shaking around the gun. JT knows if he can't defuse this situation it'll go bad real fast. But it's a tricky balance. Anton's got the gun and is acting all powerful, but he's stressed too; power and stress – the worst kind of cocktail.

JT puts his hands up, palms out. Tries to look non-threatening. 'Why don't you lower the gun and we talk about this?'

'No. She's not going to let me have the money, and I need it, I need it all. I deserve it. All the people I've brought to her games, all the money they've put on her tables, and she wants to screw me, fuck me over.' Anton's voice is rising. Beads of sweat are dripping down the side of his face. 'I can't let her stop me.'

Goddamn. The man's a mess. JT decides to take a different tack. 'You need her.'

Anton frowns. 'Why?'

'She puts the poker games together, right?'

Anton keeps his eyes on Carmella. 'Yeah, I guess.'

'And before you get to join the game you go through a vetting process, am I right?'

Anton gestures at Carmella with the gun.

'Yes,' she says, 'I do background checks on all new players.'

'That's why you need her,' says JT.

Anton still looks confused.

'Because she knows the most about all of us. Think about it: you know some of the players because you've played with them a long time or whatever, but none of you know everyone equally well.' JT gestures to Carmella. 'None of you except her.'

Cabressa nods thoughtfully. Mikey leans over and whispers something to Carl. Otis and Johnny stare at what's happening like they've been hypnotised.

Beside him JT can feel that Lori's tense as a bucking horse in a rodeo trap. He doesn't want her exploding out the gate. Doesn't want her drawing Anton's attention to her and putting herself in more danger. She needs to focus on getting the job done with Cabressa. JT needs to take this load. He meets her gaze. Give a slight shake of his head. Hopes she interprets it as intended: *Let me handle this.*

He looks back at Anton. 'There's no sense you getting the money if you can't get out of here, right?'

Anton stares at him a long moment, looking like he thinks JT's trying to trick him with the question. Eventually he answers. 'True.'

'So put the gun down and let's talk. Figure this out.' JT forces a smile and tries to appeal to Anton's better nature. 'You're not a killer. You're a businessman.'

Anton looks thoughtful. He moves his gaze from Carmella to

JT. Shakes his head. 'Right now I'm the man who's got the gun. I'm going to work out who Herron is and I'm going to have that money.'

JT senses the situation is about to escalate. 'Why don't you lower the gun and we talk about this like gentlemen.'

'No, that's not going to happen.' Anton turns his gaze back to Carmella. He's taking deep breaths, getting himself set to do something. He raises the gun so it's pointing at Carmella's head and runs his finger along the trigger. 'The bitch brought us all here, got us into this situation, didn't warn us that she'd lost her phone and the game had been compromised. None of that makes me feel like acting gentlemanly towards her. No, it makes me mad. She let this happen, us getting locked in here.' He takes a step closer to Carmella.

Carmella shrinks away from him. The rest of the players are silent, watching. Everyone tense, aside from Cabressa. Lori shifts in her seat next to JT. JT hopes she's not going to try something.

Anton takes another step closer to Carmella. Gives her a sickly smile. 'You know you deserve this.'

That's the moment JT realises for sure that he's wrong.

Anton *is* ready to kill.

30

Keeping the gun pointed at Carmella, Anton takes a few steps closer to her and presses the gun against the side of her head. 'Keep still, bitch.' He looks at the rest of us. 'We're locked in this place because of her. She brought us here and she compromised our security. This is all her fault.'

Carmella is trying to stay still but she's crying and her whole body's shaking.

JT gets up from his seat. 'Put the gun down. This isn't the answer.'

Anton swings the gun from Carmella to JT. 'Stay the fuck where you are.'

My stomach flips. Memories of the horrific bloodbath I witnessed at the Miami Mob compound flash across my mind's eye. I feel lightheaded, like I might throw up. Can't let that happen here. 'Anton, please. Let's talk about this.'

Anton ignores me. Keeps staring down the barrel of the gun at JT.

'This isn't the way, dude,' Johnny slurs. He wobbles towards Anton. 'You need to just—'

Anton swings the gun towards Johnny. 'Stay back. Don't make me shoot you.'

Johnny puts his hands up. 'I'm not making you do a thing. I'm just saying—'

'Well, don't. Stop talking.' Anton waves the gun around. His eyes are wild. It looks like he's losing his shit. 'All of you stay still.'

'Like Anton says, it's best if everyone stays where they are until we've got this situation resolved,' says Cabressa. He sounds calm, looks unbothered. He glances around the group, scrutinising each of us, then repeats his original question. 'So which of you is Herron?'

No one speaks.

Our silence hangs awkwardly in the air. The only noise is the whir of the central air. No one moves. No one makes eye contact.

Seconds tick by. Still nothing happens, no one speaks. I glance at JT, and he gives a small shake of his head – *Say nothing*. I sit, and I wait, and I hope to hell I can think of a way to get us out of this. I think of our baby girl, Dakota, waiting back in Florida for us, and I know I can't sit passively any longer. I grip the base of my chair, and get ready to spring across the table at Anton.

I'm beaten to it.

There's a roar, and Thomas, the security guy, leaps up from the floor and launches himself at Anton. I don't know how long it's been since he came round from getting knocked out, but he's wide awake now and punching Anton with all he's got. Anton tries to fight back, but he's tubby rather than muscular, and without the element of surprise on his side, as it was before, he's struggling to defend himself.

Thomas rains blows down on Anton. Anton tries a grab and misses, but manages to hook his leg around Thomas's and destabilises him. As he falls, Thomas pulls Anton with him. They land hard. Anton drops the gun and it goes skittering across the floor. I drop to my knees, looking for it. When I see it, my breath catches in my throat. It's smack up against Cabressa's foot.

Cabressa's long, thin fingers close around the grip of the gun. 'Enough!' he yells, straightening up and firing the gun once into the floor. The force of the shot in this contained space vibrates in my chest. The noise makes my ears ring. The noise around me is muffled, like I'm underwater.

Anton and Thomas spring apart.

'Asshole,' says Anton, glaring at Thomas. 'Know your fucking place.'

Thomas lunges for Anton again.

I jump as Cabressa fires the gun a second time.

Carmella screams.

The bullet hits Thomas between the eyes. Red mist plumes like a stained halo from his head, and he staggers backwards, his body propelled by the force of the shot, but already dead.

'What the...?' Anton looks on in horror as Thomas's body slumps to the floor at his feet.

'Oh my God.' Carmella's crying again. Thrusting her chair away from the table she rushes to Thomas's body and kneels beside him. Puts her hand on his arm then glares up at Cabressa, anger chasing away her tears. 'You killed him. Why the hell would you do that? He was a good man. He had a family.'

Cabressa stares back at her, unmoved. 'A security guard needs to be able to follow directions. I told him to stop. He disobeyed.'

She shakes her head. Tears run down her face, and she wipes them angrily away. 'You're an animal. You disgust me.'

Cabressa shrugs. He gestures to Carmella's empty chair. 'Sit back down, so we can get this done.'

I watch as Carmella presses Thomas's eyes closed and then removes her fitted jacket and places it over Thomas's face and chest. Getting to her feet, she steps around the puddle of blood that's spreading out from his head and across the hardwood floor, and returns to her chair. She looks pale, deeply shaken, but there's rigidness to her movements, and her jaw is clenched. I recognise her expression and what it means. I've felt that way too. Carmella is a woman whose anger is turning into a need for revenge.

Cabressa, gun in hand, seems unaware. He looks around the group. Nine of us remaining of the ten that we were. 'Let's try that again, shall we? Who is Herron?'

'Don't you realise that none of us are Herron?' Carmella says, her tone frosty, her anger seeping into every word.

'Aren't you?' Cabressa says.

'It's just some twisted game,' says Carmella. 'Someone is messing with us. Probably someone who wanted to join the poker game and didn't make the cut.'

'You sure about that?' Cabressa says. 'All this seems overly dramatic for a disgruntled poker player to instigate.'

'I am sure,' she says. But even though she's nodding, she doesn't look completely certain.

'Look,' says Mikey, 'like you said earlier, Mr Cabressa: if each of us owns up to our secret shit then we'll be able to see who's Herron by a process of elimination.' He lights another cigar and takes a long drag, trying to seem unconcerned. It almost works, but as he takes a second drag I see that his fingers are trembling.

I'm feeling real concerned myself. I can't admit that I'm a police, or at least an FBI, informant – if I do Cabressa will kill me for sure. But if I don't own up to something then he'll think I'm Herron, and then he'll kill me anyways. I glance at JT. His expression is grim. Of the secrets on the list there's one both of us could admit to being. It's not something either of us are proud about.

'Okay,' says Cabressa, a sneering smile on his lips. 'Let's try this again, people. It's time to share your secrets.'

JT, Carmella and me stay silent. Mikey and Carl glance at each other, then Johnny. Anton stands like a sentry beside Cabressa, rubbing his jaw. He doesn't look worried, I guess because he's already shared his secret and made his alliance with Cabressa.

Otis clears his throat. Looks at Anton and then Cabressa. 'I'm not who you want, man. I'm not Herron, I swear.' He takes a breath. Puts his hand on his chest. 'On that list they read out, I'm the addict.'

Cabressa's smile widens. He cocks his head to one side. 'Tell me about your addiction.'

Otis swallows hard and glances at Carmella, and then me.

'Don't look at anyone else,' Cabressa says, his finger tracing the trigger of the Glock. 'It's me who needs to believe you.'

Otis's hands start to shake. He clasps them together. Nods. 'It started when I was—'

Two loud beeps sound over the penthouse's speaker system. Otis falls silent. No one else speaks. We're all waiting for the electronic-voiced message we expect will follow. But the message doesn't come immediately. Instead there's a pause, then another set of two beeps.

I look at JT. And mouth, 'What's happening?'

He frowns. Shakes his head: *I don't know*.

That's the moment the central air cuts out and a strange whistling sound starts up from behind the vents.

31

'Why's the air conditioning switched off?' Johnny slurs.

'You think the generator's failing?' says Anton, looking towards Cabressa.

Otis – wide-eyed and afraid – rocks back and forth on his chair. 'No, no, this is just ... I can't do the dark again.'

Two beeps sound again. Everyone goes quiet. Otis stops rocking.

The electronic voice booms over the speakers. *'While the panic-room protocol is activated, this penthouse is a sealed unit. It is airtight. Until you have completed your challenge the penthouse support systems will shut down, one by one, every thirty minutes. The first system to shut down is central air and ventilation. The decontamination programme has been activated and is now removing the oxygen from the suite. You have approximately one and a half hours before the oxygen level reaches critical and the air becomes unbreathable.'*

Otis stops rocking. 'Oh man, this isn't—'

'In thirty minutes time the lights will turn off,' continues the electronic voice. *'Thirty minutes after that all power will be lost. Thirty minutes later you will be dead by suffocation. The only way out is to solve the challenge: who is Herron?'*

'This is some weird goddamn shit.' The seriousness of the message seems to have sobered Johnny up. He's still trying to act unbothered, but the performance is falling flat. I can hear the fear underneath the light-hearted tone.

Mikey looks serious. He stubs out his cigar. 'It's like Mr Cabressa here was saying – we need to find out which of us is

Herron. And as it seems no one is willing to put their hand up to it, a process of elimination is our best option.'

Carl's been silent a long while, but now he speaks. 'I agree. The only way out of here is to find out who's Herron.'

'But is it?' I say. 'If whoever set the challenge already knows Herron's identity, why is it so important for us to discover it too? It makes no sense.'

JT nods. 'True. This isn't about finding Herron's identity, the person who's trapped us in this suite has already done that. It's something to do with us personally. Question is, what?'

'That's of no matter,' Cabressa says, waving away our concerns with the barrel of his gun. 'If we want to get out we have to complete the challenge they've set, and for that we have to learn which of us is Herron. That is our focus.'

'I'm with you on that, Mr Cabressa,' says Mikey. 'I sure as hell don't want to be in here when the oxygen runs out.'

'Me neither,' Carl agrees. 'Let's get it done.'

Otis and Johnny nod. Carmella's looking at Thomas's body, seemingly not listening.

'So we're agreed,' says Cabressa. 'We have ourselves just under thirty minutes of light left. Let's use that time to work out which secret belongs to each of us.'

'Elimination time,' says Anton.

*

Cabressa herds us to the far end of the room, gesturing with the Glock for us to take a seat on the L-shaped couches. Mikey and Carl sit beside each other, then Otis, Carmella, Johnny, me and JT. Cabressa sits on a dining chair, facing us across the wooden coffee table. Anton stands a few paces to his left, armed with two carving knives taken from the kitchen and a slightly manic expression.

The set-up feels like some mock court or tribunal, only, unlike a legal trial where justice is sought, here Cabressa has appointed himself judge and executioner. It's bizarre, I think. And it makes me wonder if he's behind all this. But still, he has the gun, and we know from what he did to Thomas that he's willing to use it.

'Each person will take their turn under the spotlight,' Cabressa says, looking slowly around the group. He strokes his finger against the Glock's trigger guard. 'All of you will reveal your secret, or face the consequences.'

No one speaks.

'Otis, let's start with you.'

'Okay,' says Otis, his leg jigging up and down double quick. 'But, man, I already told you, I'm an addict.'

Cabressa fixes him with a hard stare. 'Tell me more.'

'It started in my teens. I was too skinny, not enough bulk behind my punches to be a serious contender. Old Mo who ran the gym suggested I take something to help. He was my coach; he taught me everything and I owed him some good wins.' Otis hangs his head. Fiddles with the gold skull ring on his index finger. 'I thought I could control it, that I'd know when to stop. So I took the pills.'

'And now?' prompts Cabressa.

He exhales hard. 'It's not just those pills. I've got arthritis in my hands, man. The pain gets real bad. I need something to take the edge off. But those kind of drugs, they're bad; you get used to them, need bigger doses.' He shakes his head. 'When I have to go cold turkey before a big fight I feel like I'm crawling out my own skin. It's like—'

'Isn't that enough?' I say.

Cabressa frowns. He glances pointedly at the gun, then at me. 'I'm the one in charge here.'

'Sure,' I say, keeping my tone conversational, non-aggressive. I don't want to rile him. 'But Otis has confessed to his secret so shouldn't we move on? The clock's ticking after all.'

The mobster considers it for a moment before nodding. 'True.

Time is of the essence.' He looks at me, a shark-like smile on his lips. 'Time for you to take the hot seat, Miss Anderson.'

'No problem,' I say, holding his gaze, and trying to bluff my way through the feeling of dread gnawing away at my guts. My heart is punching against my ribs, but I can't afford to show weakness. I can't tell Cabressa the truth, either. I think of the options left open to me; informer, thief, killer, wife-beater, cheat, fraud, Herron.

This is just like poker; I have to hide my tells.

I make my decision.

'Which one are you then?' he says.

I take a breath, and keep my voice clear and steady as I answer, 'I would have thought it was obvious, given what you already know about me. I'm the thief.'

Carmella raises her eyebrows.

Johnny's mouth hangs open. 'You are?'

I nod. 'See those chess pieces over there on the poker table. They're worth one point three five million dollars.' I look back at Cabressa. Stay real cool. 'I stole them from a dead man on a yacht.'

Cabressa watches me for a long moment, then nods and looks towards JT. 'What about your man, there?'

'I would have thought that was obvious too, he—'

'He can answer for himself,' says Cabressa.

'Sure.' I let JT take over.

JT fixes Cabressa with a steely gaze. His voice is steady. 'I'm the killer.'

Cabressa raises his eyebrows. 'Is that right?'

'You find the police informant and you can get them to have their cop pals run my rap sheet.' JT smiles, but there's no warmth in the gesture – he's playing the role of cold-blooded killer in an Oscar-worthy performance. 'It sure ain't pretty.'

'Tell me.'

'State trooper out in Polk County, three of the Miami Mob in West Virginia, bounty-hunter in Savannah,' he says, his tone gruff. 'I could go on.'

Cabressa doesn't speak. He's watching JT real close. Cocks his head to one side. 'How'd you get security work with that history?'

JT nods towards me. 'Miss Anderson isn't too choosy about that sort of thing, as long as you can do the job she wants.'

I stay looking straight ahead. Don't look at JT. He's spinning the lie, embellishing it, making it sound real. I don't want to risk giving away the truth.

Cabressa nods. 'Okay. You're the killer.' He looks at Carl. 'Let's hear from you next.'

Over on the far side of the couch, Carl looks nervous. He loosens his tie. Runs his hand over his smooth pate.

'Carl?' Cabressa's voice is firm. He gestures towards Carl with the Glock. 'We don't have time to wait around. Tell us.'

His mouth opens and closes a few times before any words come out. Then he inhales hard, and starts to speak. 'It just sort of happened, the first time. Things were bad at work. I'd gambled on a few investments that were, you know, shaky at best, and it looked like they were all going to go bad the same month. And she'd been spending, I mean, *really* spending, so much money, I just...' He hunches his shoulders, hangs his head. 'When she burned the dinner I saw red. It was done before I really knew what happened. I felt ... hell, I felt awful, like a shit. I said I was sorry. I *was* sorry. And I promised I'd never do it again.'

I'm surprised. Of all the men here, I'd have had Anton pegged as the one who took his inadequacies and frustrations out on a woman. But now I know Carl's done it once, I doubt that was the only time. It never is. I learned that from experience. My ex-husband Tommy was that way too. I stare at Carl. 'But you did do it again, didn't you?'

'I...' Carl shakes his head. The sweat patches beneath the armpits of his pink shirt are getting bigger, and beads of sweat are forming above his upper lip. 'Yeah. I did.'

'Tell us what you are,' says Cabressa. There's a slight smile tweaking up the corners of his lips. He's enjoying this. 'Be clear about which of the secrets is yours.'

Carl swallows hard. Avoids eye contact with everyone. 'I'm a wife-beater.'

'That's low, man.' Otis is frowning. 'Real men don't beat on women.'

'You're a fucking addict, don't judge me,' snaps Carl.

'We can judge you,' says JT, looking at Carl with disgust. 'And we are.'

Cabressa is nodding. 'Very interesting, let's—'

Two loud beeps over the speakers interrupt him. We all go quiet, listening. My heart's pounding. Beside me, JT leans a little closer. The warmth of him against me gives me a little comfort.

Then the electronic voice begins to speak.

32

'*You have fifteen minutes until the lights go out. Use this time wisely. Find Herron*,' says the electronic voice.

'We need to do this faster, man,' says Otis, his leg jigging frantically. 'I can't go back in the dark. I just can't.'

'That's why we're doing this,' says Cabressa. The note of irritation is clear in his voice. 'To solve the challenge and get out of here.'

Everyone is tense. Otis looks sceptical. I am too.

I still think there's more to this than we're being told. If the person setting this challenge already knows Herron's identity, why do they need us to uncover it too? It makes no sense. And what the hell is their motive for doing this? In an hour and fifteen minutes the air in the penthouse will run out.

Right from the get-go Cabressa – a stoic mob boss – has thrown himself into completing the challenge. This is a man who takes orders from no one, yet he's willing, even happy, to do this challenge without question. Again, it makes me wonder if he's got something to do with it. Has he manufactured the blackout and the challenge in order to confront Herron in a sealed environment of his own making? Cabressa owns this city; he'd have the power to organise a blackout and the challenge. Is he behind this? Has he created a messed-up game of human poker with the stakes raised to life or death? I think there's a strong chance he has. But I can't share any of this with JT, not with Cabressa and Anton tooled up and watching us. We can't afford to let them know me and JT are a couple; if they learn that, it's real likely they'll find a way to use it against us.

'I need a goddamn drink,' says Johnny, getting up. He takes a few steps from the couch, then Anton steps into his path.

'Sit back down,' says Anton, brandishing the knives towards Johnny.

'What?' Johnny looks from Anton to Cabressa. 'A man can't get a drink? It's getting awful hot in here.'

He's right. With the central air switched off, the heat and humidity are building by the minute.

'I said sit, the fuck, down,' Anton says, his voice booming. He runs the two blades of the kitchen knives together. Holds them as if they're swords.

Johnny steps back. Puts his hands up in surrender. 'Woah, dude, really?'

'Sit down,' says Cabressa. 'Let's look at your dirty secret next.'

While attention is on Johnny, I lean closer to JT and whisper, 'We need to figure a way out of here before anyone else dies.'

JT nods. Keeps his voice soft, quiet. 'For sure.'

Johnny plonks himself back down onto the couch. 'This is all wrong.' He looks at Cabressa. 'You sure this is what you want?'

Cabressa nods. Anton takes a step closer to Johnny, and clenches his fists tighter around the knives.

Worry flashes across Johnny's face. 'Fine. You really want me to say, then I'll say.' He looks at Cabressa. 'But don't say I didn't warn you.'

Cabressa gestures with the Glock for him to continue. 'Go right ahead.

Johnny shrugs. 'Suit yourself.' He looks at the rest of us. 'I'm a cheat. *The* cheat. A ringer, if you like. Sometimes I'm paid to win a game, sometimes to lose.' He looks at Cabressa. 'Tonight, I was told to strike out when it got to the last three. Like always, I did as I was told.'

I raise my eyebrows. Cabressa rigged the game. It doesn't surprise me. I was right about not being the only one put in the game for a reason; Johnny was too.

'Why?' asks Mikey, rubbing his forehead.

Johnny nods towards Cabressa. 'Ask him.'

'We don't need to get into that now,' says Cabressa.

'I think we do,' says Mikey. 'I've put a lot of money through this game over the months. I win and I lose, and that's all good unless it's fixed. If that's the case I'm mad as hell, and I want a damn answer.'

'Tonight was special,' Cabressa says. 'I needed to guarantee an outcome.'

Carl looks towards the speakers. Gestures towards the metal shutters over the concertina doors onto the terrace. 'Yeah, special – we got that.'

'Nothing to do with all this,' says Cabressa. He points at me. 'To do with her.'

'Why?' Mikey asks. 'Why'd she need to go heads up with you?'

Cabressa doesn't answer.

'It's those chess pieces, am I right?' Mikey says. 'It struck me as odd before, you know. The way you got all riled up when one of the pieces was missing – that just isn't normal. This is a poker game; you accept the bet collateral, or you don't. But you had her make a call.'

Johnny's looking thoughtful. He puts his hand up. 'You know, she went outside to the terrace and made that call, then a couple of minutes later the blackout started.'

'You caused this?' Carl glares at me, his mouth contorts into a snarl. 'Who the fuck are you really?'

I hold my ground. Don't let the asshole shake me. 'I'm just a thief, like I said. The blackout was nothing to do with—'

'They're working together,' says Carl. 'That has to be it. She caused the blackout, and this challenge bullshit is some sick game of yours, Cabressa.'

Otis looks at me, eyes pleading. 'Make it stop, please make it stop.'

Mikey ignores Otis. He looks across at Carmella. 'Did you know about this?'

She opens her mouth to speak.

'Enough,' shouts Cabressa. He doesn't look so cool anymore. His face is flushed, and there's sweat beading on his forehead – a combination of the rising heat in the suite and the increasing pressure from the group. He's trying to sound in control, though. 'So I rigged a couple of games, it's no big deal.'

'There's a lot of people in this room who'd say different,' says Mikey.

'It's no worse than what you've been doing,' Cabressa spits, pointing at Mikey. 'All your side deals, and creaming thousands off the top of the city's budgets. You're as crooked as I am, so don't get all holier than thou.'

Mikey leaps to his feet. Fists clenched. 'Take that back. I'm an official of this city. I've never done—'

'I'm speaking the truth and you know it,' says Cabressa, leaning back in his chair, seemingly relieved to have moved the spotlight from himself to Mikey. 'You're just as much of a criminal as me, you just lie about it.'

'You bastard,' yells Mikey, lunging towards Cabressa.

Anton steps into his path. Both knives are raised.

Cabressa swings the gun up.

Two electronic beeps blast out of the speakers.

The lights go out. We're plunged into darkness.

The gunshot sounds louder in the dark.

33

'Get down,' whispers JT, pulling me off the couch and onto the ground.

Carmella screams. Otis whimpers. Someone, a man, bellows in pain.

Two beeps sound again. Then the electronic voice says, *'Thirty minutes has been reached. The lights are now off. In thirty minutes all power will cease. You must identify Herron before that time.'* There's a pause, then the voice continues. *'In sixty minutes the de-contamination process will reach eighty percent. At that time the oxygen level will be critical and you will be unable to breathe. Your only option is to find Herron.'*

The bellow has turned to groaning. It's coming from some-where to my left. I resist the urge to ask if the person's okay. Any more sounds they make will alert Cabressa and Anton to where they are, and that could result in more violence. And whatever happens next, one thing is clear – we must be out of this pent-house before the next hour is up.

'We need to turn our flashlights on.' JT's voice is clear, strong, from the darkness beside me.

'Go right ahead,' says Cabressa. 'No law against it.'

JT doesn't switch on the flashlight app on his cell straight off the bat. I can guess what he's thinking – the darkness gives a level of protection from Cabressa taking any more shots, but once we turn on the flashlights we'll be illuminated, and become easy targets.

Cabressa seems to sense it too. 'You more comfortable if I do it first?'

'Yup,' says JT.

The back-lit screen of Cabressa's phone appears from a way over to my left. From the height of it, he's standing now. There's the shadow of another figure beside him, Anton I assume. Moments later the backlight changes into the bright-white light beam of the flashlight app.

JT switches on his cell's flashlight. Carl is next, followed by Carmella. Otis switches his cell on but keeps on the back-lit screen, not the flashlight app. Johnny doesn't switch his on, but I can see him beside Otis. Mikey isn't standing where he was before the lights went out.

I peer into the gloom. 'Mikey?'

'He fucking shot me.' Mikey's words are laboured.

Switching on my cell's flashlight, I scan the area Mikey's voice came from.

'Get the light out my eyes,' he says, shielding his face with his arm. 'Don't blind me too.'

He's lying on the floor near the piano. From the blood trail on the wooden floor it looks like he dragged himself there in the dark after Cabressa shot at him.

'Quit moaning, Mikey,' says Cabressa. There's a smirk in his voice. 'Whining isn't becoming of an official from the mayor's office.'

I'm not going to stand by and do nothing. He's hurt, and from the blood trail it looks bad. I scoot over to Mikey. 'Where'd you get hit?'

He nods towards his right arm. I follow his gaze and see that his hand is a real mess. It's hard to see the damage with all the blood, but if I had to bet on it I'd say it's a through-and-through in the palm.

'Bad, isn't it?' says Mikey through gritted teeth.

'We need to stop the bleeding.' I turn back to the group and make eye contact with Carmella. 'Is there a towel we can use to stem this bleeding?'

She starts to get up. 'Yes, sure I can—'

'Don't move.' Cabressa points the gun at her. 'Everyone stay exactly where you are. No leaving this room.'

'He's bleeding bad,' I say to Cabressa. 'I need something to—'

'I said no.'

'Here, use this.' Carmella unthreads the leopard print scarf from her neck and throws it across to me.

'Get back over here,' says Cabressa, gesturing to my spot on the couch with the gun.

I ignore him and take the scarf from Carmella. I can tell from the feel that it's pure silk, real expensive, but something this light-weight isn't going to be able to absorb much of the blood. Still, given Cabressa is being an asshole, it's the best we can do. I look at Mikey. 'Take a breath, this is going to hurt.'

I don't wait for him to respond before I start. I bind his injured hand tightly with the scarf using a figure-eight pattern to keep it secure and put maximum pressure on the palm to try and stop the bleeding. Ripping the end of the scarf, I tie it in a hard knot over the wound. Hope to hell it works.

'Try to keep it raised a little,' I say to Mikey. 'That'll slow the blood to it. Help it stop bleeding.'

He nods. In the beam of the flashlight I see there's a sheen of sweat across his face, but his body is shaking as if he's cold. Shit. He's going into shock. This is bad. I turn to JT. 'He needs medical attention.'

'We need a way out of here,' says JT. 'There has to be a—'

'No. We need to uncover Herron,' Cabressa growls, brandishing the gun. 'We've less than thirty minutes.'

No one speaks for a moment. All we can hear is the sound of Mikey's laboured breathing and the whispered mutterings of Otis praying for help.

'Like Mr Cabressa says, we need to get this done,' says Anton.

'There are two secrets left and two people.' Cabressa flicks the beam of his flashlight towards Thomas's body. 'Although only one of them is alive.' He switches the beam to focus on Carmella's face. 'So which secret is yours; are you a police informer or Herron?'

'Obviously, I'm not Herron,' says Carmella, blinking in the light.

Cabressa narrows his gaze. 'You sure about that? I mean, you seemed awfully certain none of us were Herron, but the person about to cut our air off seems sure it's true.'

'I am certain.' Her tone is hard. 'But I'm not a police informer either.'

Cabressa rubs his jaw. 'Well now that gives us a problem. If you're not the informer *or* Herron, who are you?'

'I'm the fraud.'

Johnny glances towards Mikey – the guy who's already owned up as being the fraud. Mikey stays hunched over by the piano. His good hand keeps pressing his injured one. He grimaces from the pain.

I glance at JT. This is going to be a problem.

Cabressa gestures at Carmella with the barrel of the gun. 'I'm listening.'

Carmella clears her throat. 'I'm not from New Jersey originally, like I've always told you. I grew up poor in a very different city. When I was fourteen I ran away. I lived on the street and dabbled in a bunch of things, few of them legal, before I got into poker. Then, a good few years ago, I ended up in New York and started working the tables, learned a lot, began to run my own games. But I got too good and it attracted the wrong kind of attention.' She takes a breath. Keeps her eyes locked on Cabressa. 'When the mob in New York moved me on, I came here. You know the rest.'

Cabressa makes a steeple with his hands and rests his chin on them. He looks thoughtful, and glances from Carmella to Mikey. 'You can't both be the fraud.'

Mikey clutches his injured hand to his body. Looks real anxious.

'Someone's Herron, and someone's the police informer,' says

Anton, looking at each of us in turn. 'You need to own up, or we're all going to die.'

'What about him?' says Mikey, his breath coming in gasps as he raises his good arm and points at Thomas's body. 'He's included in our number, so one of the secrets must have been his.'

'Yeah, for sure, but I'm more interested in who these two are,' says Cabressa, looking from Carmella to Mikey. 'Could be that they're both frauds, but as far as our captor is concerned, there are ten secrets, and there was ten of us – so Carmella and Mikey aren't both *the* fraud.'

'No, we're not,' says Carmella. Meeting his stare with her own. 'Question is, who do you believe?'

Cabressa rubs his finger along the trigger of the gun. 'Who indeed.'

Carl looks twitchy. Otis's leg is jigging faster. Even Johnny's stopped drinking the champagne and is looking worried.

I check my watch. Another five minutes gone.

Anton turns to face Cabressa. 'So which of them is Herron?'

Cabressa gives a small shake of his head. 'Neither.' He points at Carl. 'He is.'

'What the...?' Carl's face flushes red. 'That's a goddamn lie. I'm not him. It's bullshit, you've got to believe me.'

'I don't believe I do. See, I've always known Carmella isn't the Jersey girl she's always made herself out to be; she is a fraud. And although Mikey's a fraud too, he's something else as well, something that our captor knows about.' Cabressa looks at Mikey, shakes his head with disgust. 'He's a dirty rat.'

Anton's mouth drops open. He points one of the knives at Mikey. 'Wait, what, you inform for the police?'

Mikey avoids Anton's gaze. Grimaces. And gives a single nod.

Johnny's shaking his head. 'I don't believe it, dude. You tell stuff to the cops? I thought you were one of us. I thought you—'

'Shut the hell up.' Carl's voice cuts over Johnny. He turns towards Cabressa. 'So how does this make me Herron?'

Everyone looks at Cabressa. We all want to know.

He smiles. In the beam of the flashlight it makes him look ghoulish. 'Because I know all about your side hustle – the drugs and the girls. We've been watching you for a while, my family and I. You thought you could take a part of this city for yourself, didn't you? A part of *my* city. But you didn't stay in your plush offices and take the cream off the top like Mikey here. No, you decided to get some skin in the game.' He points the gun at Carl. 'What you need to understand, Carl, is that the game isn't for people like you. You should stick to massaging figures and doing backhanded deals. You don't have the stomach for my world. You should have stayed in yours.'

Carl looks nervous. His eyes dart left to right. 'Sure, I did that – I set up some stuff – but I've never used the name Herron. It was Mikey there that told me about him, before that I hadn't—'

'Enough,' says Cabressa. 'I've made the decision.'

I glance at JT. He meets my gaze. Gives a slight nod. From the tightness in his jaw and the tension in his body I can tell that he's thinking real similar to me – that whether Carl is Herron or not this isn't going to end well. Cabressa's calm has disappeared. Anger is virtually vibrating out from him. If he's right about Carl then our best move is to get out of here as soon as the panic-room protocol is deactivated. If we don't, we'll end up in the middle of a mobster taking his revenge on a friend who has disrespected him, and I really don't want to get taken out in the crossfire.

'So Herron is Carl,' says Anton. He walks over to the nearest speaker. Looks up at it as if it's a camera. 'Carl Reynolds is Herron. That's our answer.'

We wait.

Two electronic beeps pierce the silence.

34

'*You have fifteen minutes until full power shutdown.*'

'Oh Jeez,' says Otis, wide-eyed in the glow of his cell-phone screen.

'Don't worry, dude,' Johnny says, his words are less slurred now. 'We've got the answer. We'll be out of here in no time.'

In the beam of the flashlight, I see Cabressa frown.

No one speaks for a long minute. Instead we wait, thinking there'll be something more – a verdict on Cabressa's decision that Herron is Carl. But there's nothing – no beeps, no electronic voice. The whistling from behind the air vents seems to grow louder.

I wipe the sweat from my upper lip. Lift my hair off the nape of my neck to let it cool. Breathing feels harder now. I look across at Mikey – his breaths are rapid, shallow. Carmella has moved alongside him. It looks as if she's struggling to breathe deeply too – her mouth is open, her eyes fearful, as she helps put pressure on the makeshift bandage wrapped around Mikey's hand.

If we've only got fifteen minutes more power, we've got forty-five minutes before the decontamination process takes the oxygen in the suite down to a level that will kill us all. We have to get out of here.

Anton glances round at Cabressa, then turns back to the speaker. 'We answered you. Herron is Carl. Let us go.'

Again we wait.

Again nothing happens.

'Maybe they unlocked the elevator,' says Johnny. 'I'll go check.'

'But the shutters, man,' Otis says, the tremor still in his voice. 'They're still down. And the lights are off. We're still prisoners.'

'I'm checking anyways,' says Johnny, getting up. 'We'll feel really stupid if the elevator door's been unlocked the whole time.'

'It didn't work when I tried it.' Otis sounds doubtful, but there's a hint of hope in his voice. 'Suppose looking won't cause any harm.'

'Do it,' says Cabressa. 'Leave the door to the hallway open.'

Johnny heads out to the hallway. None of us speak. Then we hear him cuss.

When he returns he's shaking his head. 'Thing's still locked. Buttons don't respond.'

'So what does that mean?' asks Carmella.

'It means we're screwed,' Anton says, spittle flying from his lips. Cussing, he stabs one of the kitchen knives into the far end of the coffee table. The table shudders from the impact. The knife remains standing upright, part embedded in the wood.

I stare at it. Trying to work out, if I launched myself towards it, whether I could grab the knife before Anton. I glance at JT. He grimaces. Doesn't think it's worth the risk. And it could be that he's right.

'It means that I'm not Herron,' says Carl.

'But if that's true, who is?' Carmella says, panic in her voice. 'The air feels weird, kind of thin. We've got to get out of here.'

'Agreed,' says Cabressa. 'So that leaves us with the question, again. Who is Herron?'

'Maybe it's just a sick joke,' says Carl. 'And none of us are, just like Carmella said before.'

Cabressa shakes his head. 'No, we've been over this, our captor believes Herron is in this room. We have to find the answer they want in order for them to free us, and once the power goes they won't have ears or eyes on this place – they won't be able to hear our answer or set us free.'

Otis starts to rock again.

Johnny wipes the sweat from his face. 'But who the hell can—'

Two electronic beeps sound. Then the voice says, *'Five minutes until total power down.'*

DEEP DARK NIGHT **151**

'Just say ... our names one-by-one ... to them,' says Mikey. His eyes are closed. His body is shaking. His shirt's drenched in sweat. 'One's got to stick.'

'That's not the way it works,' says Anton.

'Isn't it?' Cabressa turns to him. 'How would you know? You got some rule book the rest of us haven't seen?'

Anton puts his hands up. The second knife glints in the beam of the flashlights. His red polo shirt has dark patches under the armpits. 'I don't, I just...' He points his knife towards me. 'I reckon it's her. She's the new bitch in town.'

'We talked about that already.' Cabressa's tone is hard. 'Seems like you're trying to deflect attention.'

'Deflect from what?' Anton says, his voice rising in volume.

Cabressa cocks his head to one side. 'From the fact that you're Herron.'

I feel my breath catch in my throat. This is bad. Real bad. Anton is a loose cannon and he's holding a knife. I push my palms against the couch. Tense my body, getting ready to move, react, to whatever happens next. Beside me, I can feel JT doing the same.

'I'm not Herron.' Anton takes a step towards Cabressa. Points the knife at the mobster. 'Take. That. Back.'

Cabressa shakes his head. 'I don't think so.'

'Tell them it's him,' says Otis. 'Please. Just get us out of here.'

'You fucker, you should have had my back, all of you should.' Anton throws himself towards Otis.

Cabressa raises the gun. He doesn't hesitate in pulling the trigger. The shot is thunder loud. The air smells like it's burning.

Mikey shouts, 'Don't!'

Carmella screams.

Anton drops to the ground. One side of his head is missing. Chunks of bone and blood are splattered across the oak boards. The knife he was holding skitters across the floor and under one of the couches.

Carmella is sobbing. Otis is whispering a prayer.

Getting up, Cabressa steps over Anton's body, taking care not to tread in any of the blood, and walks over to the corner speaker.

In my head, I try to figure out how many bullets Cabressa has left in the gun. A Glock 27 holds nine. If it was fully loaded when he took it from Thomas, by my reckoning he's gotten five left. That's five more than I'd like. I look at JT. Mouth the words, 'We need to get the gun.'

JT nods. His face is flushed; the intensity of the heat and humidity in our locked and sealed prison must be getting to him. And, like me, I can see his breathing is shallower now.

I lean closer to him, and whisper in his ear, 'If we don't act soon, we'll be too weak.'

He nods again and puts his hand over mine, for just a brief moment, and squeezes. 'Agreed.'

Cabressa's voice is clear and calm as he says towards the speaker. 'Anton Peck is Herron.' He turns back, and pokes Anton's body with the toe of his shoe. Shrugs. 'Correction, he was Herron.'

We wait. I look around the group: they're all listening, watching, for a sign that Cabressa is right, all apart from Carmella. She's got her head bowed, and is sobbing as she continues to keep the pressure on Mikey's hand wound.

'You're wrong,' says Mikey. There's a breathless gasp to his words. 'Anton was an asshole, but he wasn't Herron.'

Cabressa gazes across to where Mikey's lying beside the piano. He points the gun at Mikey's head. 'Are you giving us a confession?'

'No, I'm saying that it doesn't add up right that Anton would be Herron.' He looks at Cabressa. 'For one thing, Anton wasn't smart enough.'

Cabressa gives a single laugh, a loud 'ha'. 'Very true, Mikey. So very true.' He frowns. 'But if Anton wasn't, then who is?'

'You ever think they're not going to let us out?' JT's voice is calm, just a touch of breathlessness to his usual gravelly rasp.

Cabressa swings round to face him. The gun is still raised. 'You calling me stupid?'

'No, I'm calling whoever's doing this to us a liar.' JT meets Cabressa's stare with one of his own. 'Seems to me they just wanted to occupy us until the oxygen runs out. They never had any intention of letting us go, even if we figured out who Herron is. They were always going to leave us here to die.'

'Man's got a point,' says Johnny.

Carl and Mikey are nodding. Otis prays louder.

Carmella is staring at JT with an intense expression on her face. When she sees me watching her, she says, 'But why would they target my game? I don't get it.'

'We can work that out later,' I say. 'Right now we need to figure a way to get free of here before the oxygen runs out.'

As if on cue two electronic beeps blast through the speakers. The electronic voice says, *'One minute until full power shutdown. Thirty-one minutes until oxygen levels reach critical.'*

'We could do that,' says Cabressa, walking around Anton's body and back to the space between the two L-shaped couches. He stands a couple of yards in front of us. The gun is in his hand, and his finger is against the trigger. 'Or I could keep shooting until I get the right person. That way I'm free, and Herron is dead.'

'Jesus, no,' Otis says. 'Have some humanity.'

Carmella shakes her head. Tears are streaming down her cheeks.

Johnny's eyes widen. Carl looks frozen in fear. Mikey closes his eyes as he struggles to breathe.

'That's not the answer,' JT says. His eyes fixed on Cabressa. 'Let's find a way out of this place, together.'

Cabressa cocks his head to one side, as if considering it. Then he smiles like a messed-up Cheshire cat as he raises the gun and aims.

My breath catches in my throat. My stomach flips.

The gun is pointing at JT's head.

'Right now,' says Cabressa, still smiling as he looks down the barrel of the Glock at JT. 'I'm thinking I'll start with you.'

35

What happens next goes down real fast.

Leaping from the couch, I lunge for Cabressa. I don't think, don't hesitate; just move. Slam my shoulder into his chest and my elbow into his gut as he fires.

We fall – he goes down backwards, I'm on top. We hit something on our way down – a chair, the coffee table, I'm not sure which, but it's hard and resists our weight for a fraction of a second before breaking under the impact. Then we hit the floor.

Cabressa takes the worst of it. I use him as a shield. Jab my elbow into his face as we roll. Tighten my knees around his legs to keep him still. It's not easy – this dress seemed stretchy before, but under this amount of strain it's limiting my movements. I can't get my legs wrapped around Cabressa far enough. I'm losing my grip.

He's a fighter, that's for damn sure. He bucks beneath me, twisting out of my grasp and catching me with a left hook to the side of my head that almost has me seeing stars. Now he's trying to grab my arms; wants to take away my power. I can't have that.

I fight back harder. Fight dirty. Bite down on the soft flesh of his inner arm. Straddle him and slam the heel of my hand down into his face. Feel his nose crack, and a warm dampness on my hand as I pull it away. A split second later he sucker-punches me in the chest. I kick at him, thrust him away, but I can't breathe.

I'm wheezing. Tears stream down my face as I struggle to breathe. I don't know where Cabressa is now. In the darkness I hear footsteps thundering away across the wooden floor and panicked voices. See dark shadows moving in the gloom. Everyone's fleeing. They're leaving me.

Oh Jeez. I can't breathe and they're leaving me. Panic crashes through me.

I try to move, but I'm too weak. Need to breathe.

A shadow crouches beside me. It's JT's. He grips my shoulders, and looks into my eyes in that intense way he does. 'Slow. Steady. You're okay. I've got you.'

I believe him.

I try to breathe.

Slow. Steady.

It works, and I feel the panic leaving me. I look into his eyes. 'I had to do something.'

'I know,' he says. A smile flashes across his lips before he frowns. 'We need to get out of here. I told the others to go to the roof garden stairwell. I think I've figured out a way to make it through the security door back there.'

'How can you do—?'

Cabressa groans.

JT grabs my hand. 'We need to move.'

He helps me up. I feel unsteady, on jello legs. There's an ache deep in my chest. I wheeze as I breathe.

In the gloom I see Cabressa push himself up to sitting. He hunches over, clutching his busted nose.

'Come on.' JT yanks me along faster. 'We've got to get out of here.'

My lungs feel on fire. My head is spinning.

Cabressa bellows at me to stop.

We round the door to the hallway. I know from the blueprints there's a door that leads to the security door for the roof at the end of the hallway, after the elevator.

Just inside the hallway we almost fall over Mikey. There are bloody handprints on the walls and floor. Otis is trying to help him, but Mikey looks real bad. From the way he's floundering he can't seem to support his own weight. That's when I realise the shot I diverted from JT must have hit Mikey in the leg.

I try to slow down to help, but JT pulls me past them, towards the first of the double doors to the roof. He yanks the door open. Crammed inside the small space between the first door and the metal security door are Carmella, Johnny and Carl.

Spooked, I skid to a halt. 'We'll be trapped in there. Like fish in a smaller barrel than the whole suite. Why do you—'

'I've got my lock picks, and some of my tools,' JT whispers urgently. 'I remember the blueprints – the type of lock the security doors have. I can get through this.'

'In a few minutes?' I say. 'Because that's all we've got left.'

'Yes. Come on. We've got to go now.' JT's words are fast, urgent. Then his focus shifts to something behind me. He cusses.

I hear it before I feel the impact. Jump from the crack of the shot. Flinch as the bullet embeds itself in the oak board a half-yard from my feet.

'Stop where you are,' Cabressa yells.

Slowing, I turn. My stomach lurches.

Cabressa has the Glock to Otis's head.

Otis is crying, spluttering out prayers. 'Oh Lord, please be merciful on—'

'It isn't God who can save you now,' says Cabressa, with an evil smile on his face. 'Only person who can do that is Miss Anderson.' He pushes the gun barrel harder against Otis's head. Otis whimpers. 'Go through that door, Miss Anderson, and Otis here dies.'

'Come on,' JT says. 'We have to go. If we don't get out of here now, everyone dies.'

I stare at Cabressa. I have no doubt he means to do as he says, that he'll kill Otis if I don't stay with him.

I gaze into JT's eyes. Know what my decision has to be. I can't have another person's death on my conscious. I cannot be responsible.

'I love you. I'll find another way out.'

'No, Lori, don't you do this,' says JT. He clutches my hand tighter. Tries to pull me through the door.

Shaking my head, I slip my fingers from his and take a step back from the doorway. 'I have to. I'll see you on the other side.'

36

'Lori don't,' JT shouts. He pushes against the door, grabs for her hand again, but it's pointless. 'Don't do—'

There are tears in her eyes as she slams the door shut. Locking him inside the double door airlock space and her still in the foyer of the penthouse. He slams his fists against the door. 'Goddammit, Lori.'

There's no answer from the other side. He doubts he'd be able to hear her even if she tried to speak. He pounds on the door again. Beating his frustration onto it, every blow echoing in the confided space. The lack of oxygen makes him weaken fast. The airlock is part of the same lockdown and decontamination system; unless he can get them through the exterior door they'll run out of oxygen. The helpless feeling makes him even angrier.

He hates this. Hates that he's separated from her. Especially now. There are just minutes left before the oxygen runs out. He hates what she's done but he understands her reason. The deaths at the Bonchese compound at the end of her last job hit her hard – she wouldn't be able to bear the weight of Cabressa killing Otis because of her actions. He gets it, but now he's feeling the fear. Lori could die on the other side of that door, and there's not a goddamn thing he can do to stop it happening.

'What now?' Carmella's voice is laboured, breathless.

JT resents her because she's here and Lori isn't. He knows that isn't fair. But this whole situation isn't fair. This isn't how the job was supposed to go. He whacks his right fist against the door again, then his left. His hands are aching now. He knows he has to stop.

He presses his palm against the door. Imagines Lori on the other side. He has to believe in her. Have faith she'll get out of the penthouse before the air's gone. She's stubborn once she's made up her mind on something, and she's real resourceful too. JT knows she'll do whatever it takes to get free and clear. Neither of them is ready to say goodbye anytime soon.

'Cowboy, you going to do something here?' Johnny calls, breathlessly. 'We're running out of air, you know?'

JT turns. Carl, Johnny and Carmella are looking at him. Waiting for him to get them free. Red-faced and wild-eyed, Carl looks ready for a meltdown. Johnny's watching JT real closely. Carmella's eyelids are half closed, there's a layer of sweat over her skin; she's wilting and fit to drop. It's hellishly hot in here, squeezed into this tiny space. And it's getting hotter.

JT nods. Can't keep fretting. Needs to act.

Stepping around Johnny, Carl and Carmella, he strides towards the second door and studies the lock. He pulls the thin tool belt from under his shirt, glad that the security guards missed it when they patted him down and that he hadn't been body-scanned the same way Lori had. Unzipping it, he removes his lock picks and gets to work.

Everyone's relying on him to get them out of here alive.

37

The elevator is our only chance. We've got nine minutes left before the oxygen level hits critical. Then it'll be all over. I can't let that happen. I have to get back to JT. And we have to go home to our baby, Dakota.

'Can you get it open then?' Cabressa says. He's still waving the gun around.

'Having that gun in my face isn't helping none,' I snap as I run my fingers around the outside of the elevator doors. 'This isn't my usual thing.'

'You're a thief, aren't you?' he says. 'You should be able to get out of this.'

As I reach up, feeling along the top edge of the doors, sweat runs rivers down my back. The heat in here is stifling. I feel like it's suffocating me. 'If you'd let us try this before—'

'Enough.' He pokes me in the back with the Glock. 'No more excuses. Get it done.'

Using the flashlight on my cell I squint at the joins. The metal is smooth; it has no obvious stress points and no external screws. There's no lock to unpick. The only way to get the elevator open is to force it. I turn. 'Otis, I need you to go get those knives Anton had.'

'Okay,' says Otis. Standing, he moves away from Mikey and towards the living space.

Cabressa turns the gun towards him.

For a moment I think about trying to disarm him, then I decide my energy is better spent trying to get us out of here. I can deal with Cabressa later. First I need to stop us all from getting dead. 'Hurry,' I urge Otis.

Cabressa is frowning. 'You think I'm an idiot? Stay where you are.'

Otis dithers, looking wide-eyed at the gun.

I take a step towards Cabressa. We don't have time for this. If he's going to act like a dick I'm going to have to try and disarm him, but right now I'd rather work on our escape. I make my voice no-shit tough. 'You want me to open this, then I need tools. Those knives are strong steel, I can use them to lever the doors. If I can't do that, it's game over. Your choice.'

He looks pissed, but seems to realise the logic. 'Fine. Get the knives. But try anything else and you're both dead.'

With his cellphone lighting his path, Otis sprints into the living space. I put a hand against the elevator doors. Try to take a deep breath, but I can't, the air is too thin. My body is starting to ache. The places Cabressa punched me in our fight are throbbing. I grit my teeth. There's no time for pain or feeling sorry for myself. I have to get us out of here.

Otis rushes back into the hallway and hands me two knives. 'This is the best we've got.'

I look at them. Frown. Only one is the size that Anton had, the other is much smaller. 'How so?'

'I couldn't find the other knife.'

'Where'd you get this one?' I say, nodding towards the big one.

'Under the couch.' He gestures to the smaller knife. 'That was all that was left in the knife block. Only had three.'

This is bad. Real bad. 'What about the one Anton stabbed into the table?'

Otis shakes his head. 'Gone.'

Shit. Someone has taken that knife. The little knife isn't big enough for what I need to do. I stare at Otis. Wonder if I can trust him. 'You keeping the other blade for yourself?'

He puts his hands up. 'No way, I just want to be out of here, man.'

I look across at Mikey. He looks awful: his skin is bathed in sweat, his eyes are half closed, there's blood dripping through the scarf tied around his hand, and he's gripping his leg tight with the other. 'Did you get the knife, Mikey?'

'No.' His voice is weaker now. His breath's coming in gasps.

I believe him. But if neither of them have the knife, that means someone in JT's group must. I shudder. Can't afford to think on that right now. With no cell service I can't warn him. I have to focus on getting these doors open.

Crouching down, I lever the biggest knife into the crevice between the door and the frame. It's real tight, and it takes several attempts before the knife slides into the gap almost to the hilt. Hoping that it's far enough in, I stand. My chest is heaving from the effort. I can't catch my breath.

'Get on with it,' says Cabressa. There's fear in his voice now.

I can't answer him, can't act. I double over. Chest heaving. Breathing rapid. I press my hands into my knees. Close my eyes. Try to slow my breaths.

I hear Cabressa moving about behind me. 'We're running out of time. What are you—?'

I open my eyes. Check my watch: seven minutes left.

Damn.

I force myself upright. My vision spins. Blinking, I try to focus. Use the smaller knife to wedge into the gap between the two doors. They resist.

Behind me Otis is telling Mikey to hang in there, to stay with him. He breaks off from speaking and coughs – big, wracking coughs that leave him gasping for air.

'You okay?' I say, not looking around.

'That voice said this place is sealed, airtight,' says Otis, his words slow, almost slurred. 'If that's true we're never going to get into this thing.'

'There's no alternative.' I hope the voice was wrong and try to force the blade into the gap again. It moves a fraction. I push harder. Put all my weight behind it. Gradually, inch by inch, it slots inside.

'Come on,' says Cabressa.

'Not. Helping,' I reply through gritted teeth.

Changing my grip, I put my right, stronger hand on the top of the knife handle, and my left underneath it, and lace my fingers together. I breathe in as best I can. Then, on the exhale, I twist the knife to force the doors apart.

The doors resist. I keep twisting. This has to work. I have to get us free.

There's movement. The doors part, just a fraction.

Then the blade shears away from the handle. The doors snap back into place.

'Goddamn it,' I say. Dropping the broken handle, I smack my fists against the elevator doors. The impact vibrates through me, and I feel like I'm going to vomit. I can't catch my breath.

'We're screwed,' Otis says. He starts praying again.

'Find another way,' says Cabressa, poking me in the side with the Glock's muzzle.

I turn towards him. 'There is no other way. This was it.'

Otis lets out a cry.

I look past Cabressa to him. He's stabbing at the screen of his cell, but the screen is dark.

Otis sees me watching. 'It's dead. The battery's gone.'

I look at my cell. Only twelve percent battery power left. I figure all our cells will be similar. And once our smartphone flash-lights are gone, we'll be blind in here. Given how much air we have left, we'll be dead before that happens.

I glance at Cabressa. His expression is grim. Over by Otis, Mikey looks as if he's passed out.

I check my watch. We've barely five minutes of air left.

My muscles feel on fire. My head's pounding. I taste bile, sour on my tongue. Death is in sight, creeping second by second towards us in the darkness.

I turn back to the elevator. I have to think of something.

38

JT doesn't know if it's the heat or lack of oxygen, or the fear of Lori being out in the lobby, but he's failing. He repositions the picks. Tries again to release the mechanism, but the lock holds fast.

Cussing, he wipes the sweat from his brow to stop it dripping into his eyes.

'You done yet?' Carl growls. 'We're burning up in here.'

'Not yet.' JT bites back the things he wants to say. Knows losing his temper won't help a damn. 'Hold on a bit longer.'

'I'm not sure I can...' Carmella's voice trails off.

JT glances over his shoulder. In the dim light from the phones he can just make out Carmella. Her eyes are still open, as is her mouth. Her chest is rising and falling fast. She's in a bad way.

He turns back to the lock. Tries again.

'This is nonsense,' Carl says. 'We can't carry on like this.'

'Woah, steady,' says Johnny. There's fear in his voice.

'Oh God,' Carmella cries.

The picks slip against the mechanism again.

There's a noise, a scuffle behind him.

JT looks round. Adrenaline fires through him.

Carl's got a knife. Looks like the one from the table, one of the two that Anton had been brandishing earlier. Shit. There isn't time for this.

'Steady, steady,' says Johnny, his hands out towards Carl. 'There's no need to start waving that around.'

'There's every reason. We don't have enough air in here for us all,' Carl shouts. 'We have to prioritise. We can't—'

'Put it down,' says JT, still trying to wrestle with the lock.

'No.' Wild-eyed, Carl points the knife towards Carmella. 'She won't survive anyway. I'm doing what has to be done, what none of you have the balls for. We have to save our...' He launches himself at Johnny. The knife's raised. Carl stabs it towards him.

They fight. It's dark. Johnny drops his cell as he tries to defend himself. The light from Carl's swings around as he lunges over and again. Crouching down, JT scoots over to Carmella and pulls her clear of Carl's reach and over to the second door. He turns off her cell flashlight; making her a harder target. Then reaches for his picks again.

As the men fight, JT battles the lock. He hears grunts and cries. Punches and cuss words. Glancing over his shoulder he can see in the light of Carl's flashlight that Johnny's been slashed across the arms and chest. He's bleeding. But he's fighting Carl for the knife. Carl is older, less fit, but Johnny's been drinking – his coordination isn't good. Both men are weakened from the lack of air.

They cannon into JT. He feels the knife blade dance across his forearm leaving a sting of pain behind. He shoves the men away from him and Carmella and across the small space. Turns back to the lock and reaches for his picks, but they're not there.

JT bellows in rage. Uses his cellphone flashlight to scour the floor, searching for the picks. Behind him he hears Johnny shouting. Carl's snaring like a dog. The men thump into the wall. Cussing. Scrambling. JT sees the picks.

As he grabs them, he turns. In the flashes of light from the moving phone, JT sees Johnny pull the knife from Carl, turning away as he does. Carl throws himself after Johnny. Johnny turns back towards Carl, the knife outstretched.

JT hears the scream as Carl impales himself on the blade. Sees him fall to the floor, the knife still in his flesh. Watches the blood pour from his stomach, thick and dark. There's no coming back from a wound like that. Not here. Not on the outside either. He'll bleed out real fast. There's nothing JT can do.

So he turns away. Leaves Johnny panting, staring down at Carl's crumpled, blood-splattered body, and gets back to work.

There's no time for pity. No time for regret.

If JT can't pick this lock in the next few minutes they're all going to be dead.

39

My head's pounding. Chest is aching. My whole body is drenched in sweat.

I thump on the elevator doors again.

I feel weak, and I hate it. Must fight. Can't let this be the end. Cannot let that happen. I have to get back to my daughter.

'I've seen plans ... for a lot of places like this,' says Mikey. 'All plans submitted to City Hall. I'm on ... new-development committee.'

I turn towards him, find him in the beam of my flashlight. Otis is sitting on the floor beside Mikey, his head in his hands. Mikey himself looks shit – skin flushed and sweaty, body trembling, eyes bloodshot and unfocused – but he's conscious again.

'You got any suggestions?' I ask.

He nods. 'Maybe there's another way to get it open.'

'I'm listening.'

'This elevator is state of the art – no buttons inside – all controlled by the touchpad.'

'Yeah.' I look at the touchpad on the wall to the right of the doors. I press at the screen but nothing happens – just like before, it's dead from lack of power. Has been since the blackout began, and stayed that way even when the back-up generator kicked in. 'The touchpad isn't working.'

'That ... doesn't matter,' says Mikey, forcing out the words. 'Should be ... safety feature to open. In case of malfunction.'

With my flashlight I scan the doors and the touchpad. There's nothing obvious. 'So how do I access it?'

Mikey opens his mouth to speak, but the words catch in his mouth and he starts coughing, wheezing. Sounds real bad.

'Tell her,' says Cabressa, pointing the gun at Mikey.

'Put the damn thing down,' I say. 'It isn't helping none.'

Cabressa ignores me.

Mikey stops coughing and gets his breathing under control. He uses his non-injured hand to gesture weakly towards the left side of the elevator. 'There should be a failsafe button recessed into the frame.'

I shake my head. 'I checked the frame earlier.'

'The outside of the frame ... against the wall – did you check there?' Mikey asks.

'No,' I say, spinning back to the elevator doors. Pressing my fingers tight against the outside of the metal frame where it joins with the wall, I run them down from top to bottom. I feel light-headed, my balance off-kilter, so I put my cellphone with the flashlight app onto the floor and use just my sense of touch.

A half-yard from the bottom I stop. In the darkness I feel a slight ridge under my fingertips. Moving more to my left, I peer at the spot on the frame. There's a small, round circle within the frame, barely the size of a penny. 'I see it.'

Cabressa crowds closer. Shines his cellphone flashlight at the frame. I can feel the warmth of his breath against the skin on my shoulder. I shudder. Try to stay focused.

'Press it,' says Mikey.

Heart pounding, I do as he says.

40

JT's vision goes fuzzy. There's a metallic taste in his mouth.

Slumped against the wall, Carl is gasping, groaning, his blood a dark pool mingling with the shadows across the floor. Johnny is standing over him, watching. There's blood over his clothes and in his beard. He looks like monster, but JT knows it was self-defence. Carl would have killed Carmella for sure.

JT is dying. He knows it. No doubt. There's not enough oxygen left and his body has started shutting down. He can't give up though. Won't. He pictures Lori's face and sticks the picks back into the lock. Slides one into the mechanism. Uses the other to try and stimulate the release. He gets them in position. Black spots dance across his vision. He knows this is his last shot. Takes what breath he can. Exhales. Makes his move.

The mechanism yields. The lock unfastens.

He shoves the door open. Pushes it wide.

Can't speak. Doesn't have enough breath.

Johnny moves past him through the doors and up the stairs towards the roof. JT gasps for breath that won't come. There's no air. He has to get out. Turning, he looks around for Carmella. Sees her lying on the floor. He staggers as he tries to move towards her, and loses his balance, dropping to his knees.

'Carmella?' His voice is a weak whisper.

She doesn't response.

He leans over her. Checks to see if she's still breathing, still alive. He finds her pulse, feels her breath on his skin – faint but there.

Knows he cannot leave her down here.

Summoning everything he's got left, JT picks her up and hoists her over his shoulders. Every muscle in his body is on fire. His lungs are screaming for oxygen. His vision is a haze. But he manages to move through the doorway. He half walks, half crawls up the stairs. He can see the garden room at the top of the stairs and knows from what he saw on the blueprints that from there he can get out onto the roof terrace.

There are seven more stairs to go. He manages one.

JT collapses. He's all out of gas. Carmella slumps onto the stairs beside him.

They're not going to make it.

41

The elevator doors inch open.

The failsafe must be powered by some kind of mechanical winch that doesn't need electricity to operate it. It's slow, but it's working. And for that I'm real thankful.

Twisting round, I grin at Mikey. 'You did it.'

He smiles, but within a second I see the relief on his face turn to horror.

I turn back. Feel my stomach flip.

Cabressa cusses. Otis starts praying again.

The elevator car isn't there.

The shaft is a pitch-black void.

I check my watch. There's less than four minutes before the oxygen reaches a critical level. We have to move. I cannot die here.

Stepping closer to the edge of the shaft, I gaze down into the abyss. We're on the sixty-third floor; it's a hell of a way down. And without light, in this heat and humidity, this is going to be far from easy. I look over my shoulder at the others. Otis's skin glistens with sweat, but his expression is more hopeful than I've seen in a long while. On the floor beside him lies Mikey. His eyes are half closed, and his chest is heaving hard from the effort of breathing. He's bleeding from his hand and his thigh and is looking real bad. I can't see how he's going to make this climb. But we have to try.

I look at Cabressa. There's an odd expression on his face. As our eyes meet, a muscle twitches above his eye and he looks back towards the open-plan area.

My voice is firm and clear as I tell them, 'We're going to have to climb.'

'There's something I need first,' says Cabressa, backing away from the edge. Keeping the gun trained on me, he moves down the hallway to the living space and disappears inside.

I don't know what the hell he's up to, but there's no time to pay it any mind. We need to get gone. Fast. I gesture to Otis and Mikey. 'Come on, we need to start climbing. Oxygen should come up through the elevator shaft. Once you start climbing you'll feel better.'

'I can't,' says Mikey. His voice is weak. He barely opens his eyes. 'Leave me here.'

Otis is shaking his head. He shifts his weight from one foot to the other. 'No, no, no, man. You're coming.' Bending down, he gets his huge arms around Mikey and pulls him onto his shoulders. Mikey groans from the movement. Otis grimaces at the weight. He takes a step towards me, and then another, his legs shaking from the effort of the lift.

I turn back to the shaft. Shine the beam of my flashlight down the sides. The elevator shaft is lined with a metal cage. The struts criss-cross each other. They're close enough to give us hand- and footholds, but I've no idea how Otis can make the climb with Mikey on his back. Mikey's not fat, but he's six foot two, easy, and broad with it. As fit as Otis is from his boxing, I just can't see it working. But I say nothing. It's Otis's choice. Has to be. I see no other way of getting Mikey to safety.

Otis arrives beside me, panting heavily.

Mikey is slung over his shoulder, his eyes half closed. He pokes at Otis's back. 'You can't climb down there with me. Put me down.'

'I told you no,' Otis says, tightening his grip on Mikey.

That's the moment Cabressa returns. In his free hand, he's carrying the wooden box containing the chess pieces and in the other he has the gun. Undoing a few of his shirt buttons, he tucks the wooden box between his vest and shirt, and re-buttons the shirt as far up as he can. Sure that the box is secure, he gestures towards the elevator shaft. 'Time to get out of here.'

Otis tries to step forward to the elevator shaft, but Mikey starts to move, pushing away from his shoulder, trying to detach himself. Cabressa can't get to the shaft. I see the frustration on the mobster's face.

Mikey continues trying to get down from Otis's shoulder, landing ineffective blows against the boxer's muscular back. 'I said leave me here, I'll slow you down.'

'No,' says Otis, clinging onto Mikey. 'I won't leave you while you're still breathing.'

I see the movement out of the corner of my eye. Fast. A blur of metal. I yell, 'No, don't...' But I'm too late.

The shot echoes in the metal shaft.

Otis groans and falls to his knees.

Mikey slumps backwards from Otis's shoulders onto the floor. His eyes are open, his lips are parted, and on his forehead a bloody bullet wound marks his cause of death.

Otis is on all fours, gasping for air. He stares at Mikey's body. 'What the hell? I could have carried him. I could have—'

'He would've slowed us down.' Cabressa's voice has no emotion to it.

I swallow back the regret, the anger at what's happened to Mikey. I hate Cabressa for what he's done, but there's no time for talk right now, not if we want to live. We've barely a minute of oxygen left and even though there must be some oxygen in the shaft I'm not feeling any difference. I kick off my pumps and yank my dress up high enough to allow me full range of movement. Shoving my phone into my bra to try and keep the flashlight focused on the metal struts of the cage, I climb into the elevator shaft. 'Follow me. We have to move.'

I start to climb. My hands are sweaty, and several times I lose my grip and think for a moment that I'm a goner. But I manage to cling on. Find more footholds and handholds. As I descend, the air gets cooler and it feels a little easier to breathe. 'You okay?' I call into the darkness above me.

'Yeah,' says Otis. His voice comes from above to the left of me. It's edged with fear, but there's something firmer to Otis's tone now. The tremble has gone.

'Keep moving,' Cabressa says from somewhere to my right in the darkness. 'And when we're out of here, you're going to take me to where you've hidden the knight.'

Ignoring his instruction I pause for a moment. Grip a metal strut with my left hand and put my other hand up to my hairline. I search the micro camera with my fingers. At first I can't feel it but I try again, slower this time. This time I feel it, still in place, pretty much.

I hope Monroe has seen what's happened on the live feed. I hope he can use it in evidence against this asshole Cabressa.

As I reach down for the next metal strut and continue the descent, I hope to hell there'll be a team of federal agents poised to greet us at the bottom of the shaft. Because I realise now why Cabressa wanted me here with him so bad; he wants the complete chess set, and he's prepared to do anything it takes to get it.

I think of all the people who've died for those chess pieces – from California, to Mexico, to Miami, and now here in Chicago. And in that moment I know the truth. Me and Otis have seen too much of what Cabressa has done, what he's like; how he'll murder someone just to get his way. Tonight he hasn't kept to his usual 'hands off' style of terminating those in his way. Tonight he's been the one shooting the gun, and as soon we're not useful, he'll kill us too.

I think of my baby girl, Dakota, in Florida with Red, waiting on me and JT to come home. If Cabressa gets his way, we'll never see her again.

I clench my fists harder around the metal struts.

I cannot let that happen.

42

JT opens his eyes. The stars are bright above him. He moves his head to the side. Sees that he's in the roof garden. He's breathing. Alive. He doesn't remember how he got here.

He breathes in the sweet night air. City air has never been so good. The memories come to him in a rush.

Slumping onto the stairs. Carmella falling beside him. Johnny nowhere to be seen. The summer house and door to the roof in sight. His vision going. Feeling for Carmella. Pulling her onto his back again. Crawling up the stairs, the concrete steps scrapping at his hands, his knees. Reaching the top. The door to the roof busted open. Dragging himself and Carmella through. Collapsing onto the tiled patio. Letting the nothingness take him.

He turns his head the other way. Sees Carmella. She's curled into the foetal position, her black hair fanned out around her face. He watches her a moment. Checks she's breathing. Exhales with relief when he sees that she is.

Gradually, he pushes himself up to sitting. He feels lightheaded and for a moment thinks he's going to pass out. But he fights the urge away. Takes a few breaths. Wonders where the hell Johnny's gone.

He puts his hand on Carmella's shoulder. Gives her a little shake. 'You need to get up.'

She murmurs and her eyelids flicker open. Looks up at him, confused.

'Take a minute,' he says. His voice is rasping, his throat dry. 'We made it outside. You can breathe okay now, but you're going to feel weird a while.'

'Okay,' she whispers. Slowly she sits up. Blinks. 'I don't feel so great.'

'Like I said, give it a minute.'

She does as he says. Stares out across the roof garden. He follows her gaze. After the pitch-black of the penthouse, it seems lighter out here under the stars. He scans the rooftop. The whole place has been planted like a tropical jungle. There are trees and exotic, brightly coloured flowers, a waterfall feature and a small lagoon. Tiled mosaic paths weave between the planted areas. In the distance, the city of Chicago remains shrouded in darkness.

'The power's still off,' Carmella says.

JT nods. 'Guess it could take a while. We should make our way down. Get to street level.'

Carmella frowns. 'Why? We could just wait here for help.'

That's not a good idea. If Cabressa wants the knight, JT knows that he'll want Lori to take him to it – if they manage to get out of the building. He can't leave her out there on her own. He promised he'd help her on this job, and blackout or none, he's going to make it back to her. 'I don't do waiting.'

Getting up, JT pauses a few seconds to get his balance, then walks across the roof garden, searching for Johnny. He spots him over in the far corner and heads towards him.

'Johnny?'

The retired ball player turns. He looks pale. There's blood splattered across his T-shirt and down his jeans, and over his face and arms. JT knows most of it is Carl's, but there's a bunch of ugly knife wounds across the man's arms, and a nasty gash across one side of his face. The blood has trickled down his face and stained his grey-flecked beard crimson. 'He's dead, dude. I killed him.'

'You did what had to be done.' JT doesn't say Johnny's action nearly killed him and Carmella. That he remembers the man pushing past them on his way to the roof, and that he didn't give them a backward glance. Instead he says, 'It was self-defence.'

Johnny doesn't meet JT's gaze. Looks away, off the roof towards the city below.

JT glances down. There's a dull throb in his forearm and as he sees the knife cut, he remembers what happened. 'Carl would have killed Carmella too. Probably all of us.'

'I guess.'

'You need to snap out of this. Dwelling never does no good.'

Johnny's head jerks up. He looks back at JT. 'Why should I—?'

'Look, I'm getting off this building, and Carmella's coming with me. You can come with us, or you can stay. It's your choice.' JT turns away, starts walking back to get Carmella. It's time to get moving.

'How?' asks Johnny.

JT stops. Turns back around. 'There's an emergency stairway – it's the only route down from the roof. I'm going to find it, and use it to get to street level.'

'And then?'

JT holds Johnny's gaze. Thinks about Cabressa and Lori and the chess piece. Feels a punch to his chest as he dares hope Lori made it out the penthouse alive. He has to get to her, help her. Live up to his promise. He gives Johnny a small smile. Shakes his head. 'Then I'm going to forget all about what happened here tonight and just get the hell out of this city.'

43

And so we climb.

The lower we get the cooler the air becomes. Breathing starts to feel easier, and the pounding in my chest begins to subside. It's only after I've been climbing a few minutes that I catch a glimpse of my watch. It's eight minutes after the air in the suite was rendered unbreathable. So far we've climbed down six storeys and there's no sign of the elevator car. There are fifty-seven more to go.

Above me I see the flashlight that I know belongs to Cabressa flicker and die. Otis's cellphone battery gave out long before we'd left the penthouse. Mine is all we have now. I glance at the cell tucked into my bra. The screen shows me there's one percent battery life remaining. It won't last long enough for us to reach the bottom.

'You okay?' I shout up to Otis.

'Yeah,' he says. I can hear the exhaustion in his voice, and the shock. After what happened to Mikey I wasn't at all sure that he'd even start this climb. But he did, and for that I'm relieved.

'Move faster and shut the hell up,' says Cabressa.

Ignoring Cabressa, I yell, 'Hang in there, Otis.'

'Doing my best,' he says.

I smile at that, despite the ache that's creeping into my hands and fingers from finding and clinging on to the metal struts of the elevator cage. As long as Otis is here it'll be two against one when we reach the bottom. There's hope that between us we can disarm Cabressa. We're younger and we're fitter. And the mobster will be tired after the climb, hopefully more so than us. I have to believe we can get the gun from him. I have to make that my plan.

*

There's no light now. My cellphone battery's died.

I keep climbing. Maintain the same rhythm. Find the footholds with my toes, and the handholds with my fingers. My bare feet are sore; cramp is setting in to my toes. There's no way to tell how far down we are. All we can do is keep climbing until we reach the ground, and so we do.

Minutes pass.

We keep climbing.

My fingers become numb. My biceps and thigh muscles ache like a bitch.

Still we climb.

'How much longer?' calls Otis. He sounds exhausted.

'I don't know,' I reply. I want to give him hope, but we could have four storeys to go or forty. The darkness and the echoing metal tube of the elevator shaft are disorientating. I have no sense now of how far we've climbed.

'Just move it,' growls Cabressa. There's aggression in his tone, but tiredness too.

We keep moving, climbing. It's all we can do.

Cramp turns my fingers into claws. I struggle to grip the struts of the elevator cage. Cuss under my breath and force myself to grip the metal through the pain.

I'm not sure how much longer I can do this.

Keep climbing.

Maintain the same rhythm.

Fight the pain in my fingers, my arms, my legs.

My foot hits something solid. Metal. The sound of it echoes like a thunderclap in the constricted space of the shaft.

'Lori?' Otis calls, fear in his voice.

'What's the hell's that?' Cabressa calls from a way above me to the right. 'Did you reach the ground?'

'I don't think so.' I slide my foot along the metal. Put a little more of my weight onto it and feel it flex beneath me. Remove my foot. The metal vibrates.

'What's going on?' Otis asks. 'You okay?'

I don't reply.

'What's happening?' says Cabressa. He sounds worried.

'It's real hard to tell with no light,' I snap back. 'Give me a minute, will you.'

They both stay silent.

I climb lower, so I'm not stretching to reach the platform, then put one of my feet back onto it. The metal is cold against my bare foot. Slowly I put my weight onto that foot. The metal flexes again, but this time I keep my foot in place until all of my weight is on it. The metal holds. Feels secure. I think it's the roof of an elevator car.

Removing my foot I twist around, changing my position from facing the shaft wall to being side-on to it. Gripping the metal strut with my left hand, I reach my right hand out into the middle of the shaft void. They hit the thick, twisted metal cables that move the elevator cars up and down the shaft. Holding onto the thickest one, I feel my way down it to the platform. The cable is attached to the car via a heavy metal ring.

Stepping off from the struts, I place both feet on the car's roof. The metal flexes like before but holds my weight. Letting go of the cage strut with my left hand, I drop to my knees and run my hands over the metal roof of the car. Searching.

It takes me a minute to find it, but when I do I feel relief flood through me. There's a hatch in the car's roof. If I can get it open, we'll be able to climb down into the elevator car.

'What's going on down there?' says Cabressa.

'It's the elevator car,' I shout up to him. 'I'm trying to open the hatch so we can climb down into it.'

Above me in the darkness I hear Otis praying.

'Quit that, will you,' growls Cabressa.

Otis is quiet for a moment. Then he continues, a little quieter than before.

Personally I'm happy for the prayers. Right now we need every piece of help we can get.

I run my fingers around the rectangular edge of the hatch. It's hinged along one of the long edges. Flattening my palms, I swipe them over the hatch. That's when I feel it – a handle. Gripping it with my right hand, I try to open the hatch.

Nothing happens. The handle is stuck rigid.

I try again. Use both hands around the handle. Twist it left, then right.

Looking up, I yell towards the others, 'I've found the way into the car, but the damn handle won't budge.'

'You want some help?' Otis asks.

'Sure do,' I reply.

In the darkness I hear Otis start to climb down towards me. His progress is slow, and from the sounds of his feet on the struts he was far higher above me than I'd realised.

'Come on, come on,' says Cabressa. 'What's the hold-up?'

Otis doesn't reply. But a moment later I hear his feet strike the elevator car roof, and the metal sheet flexes beneath me.

'Where's the handle?' Otis sounds out of breath from the effort of climbing. From the direction of his voice I figure he's on the other side of the elevator car roof, the other side of the cables from me.

'Move towards me,' I say. 'It's over here. Be careful, the cables are attached in the centre of the roof. Go slowly.'

Up above us, Cabressa tuts.

Otis ignores him, says, 'On my way.'

I hear Otis slide his feet across the roof. The metal flexes beneath his weight, and I hope to hell it'll hold us both. Then I hear the sound of clothes rubbing against the steel cables and smell his fruity cologne mixed with the odour of musky, sour sweat. A moment later he's beside me.

'Let's get this thing open,' Otis says.

'Down here,' I say.

He kneels beside me, and I guide his hands to the handle of the emergency hatch. 'I can't get the damn thing to budge.'

'Okay,' Otis says.

I remove my hands and let him grip the handle. I can't see what he's doing, there's no light – all I can make out of him is a vague shadow – but I hear the effort. He grunts like a weight lifter in a muscle gym. Gasps. 'Jeez it's tight.'

'Yeah,' I say.

'Get it done,' calls Cabressa.

We both ignore him.

I put my hands over Otis's on the handle. 'I'll help.'

'Okay,' he says.

We try again. No movement.

'It's hopeless,' says Otis. He sounds beat, real defeated.

'We can't give up. This is our only way out.' I clench my fingers tighter around his and the handle. 'Again.'

We tug at the handle. I'm leaning back, pulling with all my weight. Otis grunts and groans.

I feel it give a fraction. 'Keep going, it's working.'

Otis is breathing hard. He keeps pulling, so do I.

There's a fraction more movement in the handle, and for a moment I think it's stuck again. Then it slides the rest of the way real fast. I lose my balance and fall back against Otis. We land sideways on the metal sheet. The vibrations from our fall echo through the elevator shaft.

'What the hell's happening?' Cabressa yells.

'You okay?' I ask Otis.

'Yeah,' he replies, still breathless.

I push myself back up onto my knees. Reach for the handle. It clicks, and the hatch opens down into the elevator car. I peer through the hole. There's no light inside the car, but it seems that the trim around the top of the wooden panelling is coated in luminous paint, giving the interior a slightly ghostly glow. After the pitch dark of the elevator shaft it seems almost as good as daylight.

Relief floods through me. We've done it. I look up into the blackness of the shaft and call to Cabressa. 'We're in.'

*

Cabressa insists that he's the one to climb into the elevator car first. I don't argue, and there's no sense in it, but something else is troubling me – whether Otis is going to fit through the emergency hatch.

Otis and me step off the elevator car roof onto the struts of the cage as Cabressa steps down onto the sheet metal roof. I figure we're hitting the maximum load it can hold with the two of us. It's safer this way.

'Go onto your knees first,' I instruct Cabressa. 'Then go feet first into the car. It's a little ways down so keep a grip on the roof until you're straightened up.'

'Got it,' says Cabressa. His tone implying he doesn't need my help.

Fine by me. I'm not sure why I'm even caring.

I stay silent. Listen to the sound of Cabressa's breathing, his feet moving across the sheet metal roof, the grunt of effort as he crawls through the hatch opening. There's a bang as he hits the floor of the elevator car, followed by a stream of cusses.

'You okay?' I call.

There's more cussing. Then he replies, 'My goddamn ankle twisted.'

I don't feel sorry, I feel hope. If he's injured it'll be easier for me and Otis to get free and clear of him once we're out of the elevator.

'You go next, Lori,' Otis says.

Neither of us say it, but I reckon he's thinking the same as me – can he fit through the hatch opening?

'Okay,' I say, stepping down from the cage strut and onto the roof of the elevator car. I move lightly across the metal roof to the hatch. Drop to my knees, and bring my feet around to dangle through the hole. I see now why Cabressa fell – there's nowhere to get a decent handhold. I grip the edge of the hatch real tight. Can't afford to injure myself, not if I'm going to break free of Cabressa.

Taking a deep breath, I swing myself down through the hole into the elevator car.

44

It takes a while for JT and Johnny to find the emergency stairwell. And when they do it's not as JT expected – it's like a modern, sleek take on an old zig-zagging fire escape. He's never seen anything like it on such a tall building. He would've thought it'd be against safety regulations, but here it is. It curves like a chrome lattice around the exterior wall, climbing roses with pink, white and red flowers camouflaging it with a riot of colour, fitting in so well into the garden design that it's practical purpose is almost invisible.

JT stands in the space between the exterior wall and the back of the glass summerhouse structure. The gap is a couple of yards wide and is the point that the chrome lattice morphs from a climbing frame for plants to a climbing frame for humans. There's a break in the exterior wall of just over a yard where a heavy metal gate is fastened into the brickwork – the entrance to the emergency escape route. The chrome lattice, flattened into a thin band, bends around the top of the gate and then broadens as it plunges down below it, taking the form of a tight, zig-zagging staircase.

He looks down. It's steep and the treads of each step are narrow. Johnny's bleeding and still drunk, and Carmella's in a bad way from the lack of oxygen. Getting down from sixty-three storeys to ground level isn't going to be easy.

'We going down that?' Johnny says.

JT nods. 'Only option we've got.'

Johnny grimaces as he moves towards the gate and pulls back the heavy bolt to unfasten it. 'Okay then.'

'We need to get Carmella,' says JT.

Johnny looks around. 'Where is she?'

JT spots her through the glass windows of the summerhouse. She's still in the same place as before, on the other side of the summerhouse, lying on the tiled mosaic floor. It looks as if she's sleeping. He gestures towards her. 'I'll go get her.'

'Whatever, dude,' says Johnny, pulling the gate wide and stepping through it onto the staircase. 'I'm out of here.'

JT's not surprised. It's already clear Johnny's only out for himself. He doesn't reply, instead he hurries around the summerhouse towards Carmella.

She's lying flat out on the mosaic pathway, her body limp, her eyes closed. JT crouches down beside her. Puts his hand on her arm and gives her a small shake. 'Carmella, wake up?'

She wakes with a start. Eyes wide, gasping for breath. 'Help ... I...'

'It's okay, you're safe,' says JT.

As Carmella looks at him her breathing steadies, and the panic in her eyes disappears. 'I thought I was back in the suite. That the air had run out and...'

'We've found the way out of here,' JT says, standing up. 'We need to go.'

Carmella peers through the gloom, looking around. 'Where's Johnny? You said he was here too.'

'He's already gone.'

Carmella says nothing. If she's surprised about Johnny not waiting for them, she doesn't show it. Instead, she silently gets to her feet. As she straightens up, she loses her balance, staggers sideways.

JT grabs for her. Holds her upright. 'Take a moment.'

She nods. Grips his arms, leaning into him for support.

He wonders how she's going to manage on the staircase. 'Wait until you've got your balance back. Your body's still trying to get your oxygen levels up.'

'But you're okay. Why am I still affected?'

He shakes his head. 'Everyone's different. Just be patient.'

She mutters something under her breath. Sounds like, *I don't have time to be patient.*

'What's that?' he asks.

Carmella doesn't repeat it. Instead she lets go of his arms and says, 'Okay, let's go.'

He's concerned she's not ready, but he doesn't argue. Carmella's a grown woman; she can make her own decisions. And he wants to get out of here, to find Lori.

'It's this way,' says JT, leading her along the pathway towards the back of the summerhouse. The starlight seems to glint off the tiny silver pieces of mosaic in the path and the chrome frame of the summerhouse roof. It's kind of beautiful – or it would be in other circumstances.

Johnny's left the gate to the stairwell unfastened and swaying in the breeze. Taking hold of it, JT pulls it open wider and gestures to Carmella to go first. She's looking steadier on her feet now. He hopes she's up to this. 'Watch your step,' he says. 'It's pretty steep.'

She takes a few steps down. Looks unsteady, her pace erratic.

'Hold the hand rail,' JT says, keeping close behind her. The steps are narrow, and the chrome is too polished to give any kind of grip. The zig-zagging staircase might look good, but it's more dangerous than the old iron pull-downs its design seems to be based on.

A few steps later Carmella slips. Cries out.

JT lunges for her. Manages to grab the back of her dress and stop her falling. As he pulls her back a metal clip comes loose from her hair and clatters down the staircase. They watch it fall from step to step. A moment later there's a shout.

'What the fuck?' Johnny's voice comes from somewhere below them, but too far away for them to see him in the gloom. 'You trying to kill me, dude? I almost took a dive.'

'Sorry,' shouts JT. 'It was an accident.'

'Just don't do anything like that again.'

'Yep.' JT turns to Carmella. She's pale and shaken-looking, but there's something else in her expression too. Annoyance. 'You okay?'

'Sure.' She smiles but it doesn't reach her eyes. Looks down the staircase. 'How far down is Johnny?'

'It's hard to say.'

Carmella peers down into the darkness. 'He can't be that far away, a couple of levels at most.' She looks back at JT. 'We should catch up with him.'

Before JT can reply, Carmella starts down the stairs again. She's holding the rail now at least, but she's moving faster. JT hurries behind her, alert for any more slips, but it's hard work. His lungs feel heavy, breathing is more difficult than normal, and Carmella is fast.

'Hey,' she calls down the stairs towards Johnny. 'Wait up.'

45

I catch my hip on the way through the hatch; the metal pulls at the fabric of my dress and scrapes my thigh, but I make it through and land with a clatter on the floor of the elevator car. I manage to stay on my feet. Straighten up. Over in the corner I see Cabressa leaning against the wall. There's a pained expression on his face, and he's favouring his left leg, but when he sees me looking he straightens up. Gets his poker face on. It's too late though; I've seen the weakness.

'Clear,' I shout to Otis.

I hear a thud above me and know that he's stepped back onto the elevator car's metal roof. His footsteps are slow and heavy as he moves over to the hatch. I'm real worried. It's kind of narrow. Cabressa was fine and all, but he isn't a broad guy. Otis is tall and muscular from the boxing. I'm not sure he's going to fit.

I wait. Looking up at the open hatch. Waiting for Otis.

'Taking his time,' growls Cabressa. 'We need to keep going down.'

'No,' I say, my tone firm.

Cabressa scowls but he doesn't push it. I figure he knows that he's physically compromised and that puts him at risk. I could tackle him now, and it could be that I'd get the better of him. But I hold back, just for a little longer. If he was to get a shot off inside the elevator car, the ricochet could kill us all. I'm not willing to take that risk.

There's more movement on the car's roof, and I see Otis's feet appear through the hatch opening.

'Steady,' I call up to him. 'It's quite a drop.'

'Yep.' Otis is breathing heavily. He lowers himself down real slow. Feet, calves, knees; he's almost to mid-thigh through when he stops.

'You okay?' I call.

'I'm caught.' He sounds panicked. His words fast, urgent. 'Can't get through.'

'You want some help?' I say, looking up at the hatch's rectangular opening. He looks wedged. 'How about if I support your weight, can you twist diagonally into the gap, make yourself a little more space?'

'Maybe.' He sounds unsure; the fear from earlier is creeping back into his voice.

'Let's try.' I move closer to his legs. Make my hands into a stirrup and put them under his sneakers. 'Press down on me to give yourself some leverage.'

He does as I say. I brace under his weight. Hold steady. But it doesn't seem to make much of a difference.

'We're wasting time,' Cabressa mutters. 'We need to get going.'

'Keep adjusting,' I say. The muscles in my arms are burning. Sweat's running rivers between my shoulder blades and down my back. 'You have to do this.'

Otis gasps from the effort. Keeps moving within the small space of the hatch, trying to get himself through.

Cabressa continues muttering about it being pointless. I ignore him. Will for Otis to keep trying. Suddenly the pressure releases from my hands as Otis raises himself up through the hatch with a roar. Then he forces himself down and through. It works. He drops through the hatch real fast. The power making him land hard. I stagger sideways as his feet connect with my hip. The glancing blow makes me lose my balance, and I fall to the floor, landing hard on my butt.

Pain vibrates up through my spine from tailbone to skull. I pay it no mind. We don't have time for it right now. The temperature in the cramped space of the elevator car is hot and rising, and I know that Otis is more than a little claustrophobic. I need to find us a way out of here before he starts freaking out.

'You okay?' Otis asks me. He puts his hand out to help me up. I take it. 'Yeah, sure.'

He looks around the elevator car. 'So what now?'

'We get out of here,' I say.

'Finally,' mutters Cabressa.

Otis is staring at the closed doors. 'How? Is there another hatch?'

I shake my head. 'No. We're going to need to open these doors to get out onto whatever storey of the building this is.'

I sound more confident than I am. In truth I've no sense of whether the elevator car stopped between storeys, or if it was stopped on a floor at the time of the blackout. There's only one way to find out.

'Get the hell on with it then,' growls Cabressa.

I glance over at him. In the gloom, I see he's gotten the Glock in his hand, his finger on the trigger guard. I fight the urge to challenge him right now. By my calculation he has three more bullets in the gun; more than enough to do some serious damage in the confines of this metal box. I need to wait until we're out of this space before I tackle him. I just hope that Monroe is getting all of this on the micro camera feed. He's in the building, and his SWAT team are stationed outside in vehicles on the street. Once he knows which floor we're on he should be able to help us. I think about JT and the group that were heading up to the roof garden and emergency fire escape, and hope to hell Monroe's already gotten them help.

'Quit dawdling,' Cabressa says. 'Get us out of this thing.'

I take a breath. Swallow down the anxiety that's threatening to overwhelm me. And step towards the elevator control panel. The only buttons on it are the four penthouses. My breath catches in my throat. I remember now. The design of the elevator means they only service the residential or the hotel floors, not both. This is a residential elevator – if we've climbed down past the floors of privately owned apartments we might not be able to exit the elevator car at all.

At the top of the panel there's a call button for emergencies. I know there's no sense in pressing it – the power outage will have cut all communications – but I try anyways. I flinch – the alarm sounds loud in the small space of the elevator car. But nothing else happens. I lift the emergency phone. The line is dead.

'Well?' Cabressa says.

I shake my head. Think back to the blueprints and the elevator design. I didn't study that section of the plans real close, but there's usually a way to get elevator doors to open manually in the event the electronic mechanism failed. 'We're going to have to do it manually.'

Otis shakes his head. 'How do we—'

'There must be a manual override for the doors.' I scan the control panel. The luminous glow from above the wooden panelling gives me enough light to see there's a small compartment, its access door built into the panel. The sign on it reads: *In case of emergency. Authorised use only.*

I run my fingers down the side of the compartment looking for the release. Turn to look at Otis and Cabressa. 'I think this is it.'

I feel the door release for the compartment and press it. The small door springs open. Inside is a metal lever with an arrow pointing downward. The sign above it reads *Emergency Door Release.*

'Thank God,' says Cabressa.

'Yes, thank him,' Otis says, without a hint of sarcasm.

Gripping the lever I pull it down in the direction of the arrow. There's a clunk as something in the elevator doors disengages, and I see the doors move apart a fraction.

Looking at Otis, I step towards the doors. 'I'm going to need your help with this.'

'Sure.' He moves over to join me.

We push our fingers into the small gap between the doors. He takes the left, and I the right. The elevator car could have stopped anywhere within the shaft – on a floor or between floors. There's only one way to find out.

'You ready?' I say to Otis.

He nods.

I brace my legs. Focus all my energy on the door.

Slowly we start to prise open the doors. They're real heavy and all kinds of stiff.

I grit my teeth. Pull harder. Know that if the elevator car is between storeys then we're stuck here with no way of escape until the blackout ends. Beside me, Otis is murmuring quiet prayers.

As my arm and back muscles start to burn again I join Otis in a silent prayer to a God I don't believe in.

Please, don't let us be trapped.

46

They catch up with Johnny but not because of their speed. He's stopped at level forty-nine according to the large number painted onto the emergency door that leads from the building to the twist of the staircase. Johnny shakes his head as they approach him. 'It's the end of the run, dudes.'

JT sees why. There's a scaffold structure erected around the next flight of stairs – stretching from level forty-nine to forty-eight. He's been conserving the battery of his cell, only using it when he has to. Now he pulls it from his pants pocket, switches on the flashlight and focuses the beam on the steps for a clearer look. A few steps below them the stairs have gone – there's a flight of approximately twenty steps missing before the staircase continues. They must have gotten damaged or some such and been removed for repair or replacement. Whatever the reason, it doesn't help them now. There's no way to jump the distance. They're going to need to find another way down.

Carmella turns to JT. 'What now?'

'We go back up,' says Johnny. He gestures towards the emergency-exit door with the number forty-nine painted on it. 'These exit doors can't be opened from the outside, and there's no lock for this dude to pick.'

'We're not going back,' says JT. He can't give up. Has to get round this. Switching off the flashlight on his cellphone, he checks if the service is back on, thinking he could call someone – Lori, Monroe – try and get help. He cusses. There's still nothing.

'The stairs are gone,' says Carmella. 'We can't just—'

'We'll have to climb.' JT moves past Johnny on the twist of the stairs and steps down to the final remaining step on this level. Taking hold of the closest scaffold pole, he pulls himself up and onto the structure. 'If we climb down through the scaffolding we can reach the steps where they continue below.'

Johnny's shaking his head. 'Are you a crazy person?'

'I'm a person who wants down from this building,' says JT, his tone firm. He glances towards Carmella. 'You coming?'

She looks torn. Glances up through the staircase to the roof, then back down at the gap in the steps. Shakes her head. 'I'm not sure if I can.'

'It's your call,' JT says. 'But this is what I have to do.'

'Johnny?' Carmella looks at the ball player. 'What are you going to do?'

Johnny cusses. Looks real pissed. 'I hate heights, you know. This here is my kind of nightmare.'

'We can go back to the roof,' Carmella says. 'Wait until the blackout's over.'

Johnny shakes his head. 'No, I don't think so. I ain't no pussy.' He moves down onto the final step and reaches for the scaffolding bar. 'And I want to get out of here just as much as this man.'

JT's surprised, but he doesn't say anything. His arms are starting to ache from the effort of holding the scaffolding, and he can feel a tremor in his legs as he braces against the bar below. 'We need to move.'

Carmella bites her lower lip and steps towards the scaffold. 'Okay.'

'Go back up if you want,' says JT. 'We'll make sure someone comes to get you once this is all over.'

She shivers. Hugs her arms around herself. 'I'd rather climb down with you guys than stay up there alone.'

JT's worried she's not up to the climb, but it has to be her decision. 'It's your choice.'

'Yes it is,' she says, moving her gaze from JT to Johnny. She narrows her eyes. Takes a hold of the nearest scaffolding bar, still

looking at Johnny, and pulls herself up onto the scaffold structure.
'And I've made my decision.'

47

The doors open real slow.

Otis and me keep pulling. My arms are shaking from the effort. My dress is drenched with sweat. Opposite me, in the gloom of the elevator car, Otis grimaces as he leans back, putting all his strength against the doors.

Inch by inch they open. The scrape of metal on metal is loud in the elevator car, the sound amplified by the confined space of this metal box. I grit my teeth and redouble my efforts. Hope to hell we're not opening the doors to reveal the side of the elevator shaft.

A few more inches, and the news is good. The elevator car must have stopped abruptly, in motion along the shaft, just past the exit to one of the floors – it's half and half. From waist height the car is level with the wall of the elevator shaft, but waist-down there's an opening into the building.

'Do you know where we are?' Otis says. His breath still laboured from the effort of opening the doors.

Crouching down, I peer out through the gap. It looks like a hallway, but it's hard to tell as there's no main lighting. The dull light there is comes from out of my eye-line – emergency lighting in the ceiling I reckon. Still, wherever we are, our best option is to get out of this elevator car.

Cabressa steps alongside me and squints out through the gap. 'What's out there?'

'Freedom, man,' says Otis, bending down to look.

I nod. 'We're going to need to climb out through the gap. I can't tell exactly how far down it is to the hallway floor, but it's definitely a bit of a drop. I'll go first and then I can—'

'No, I'll go first,' Cabressa says.

I glance over at him. In the murky darkness I see the outline of the Glock. Realising I'm watching, Cabressa taps the barrel against the palm of his other hand.

I'd hoped to get out first then overpower Cabressa while he was off guard during the climb down. I guess he's figured I might have been thinking that, but in this tight, confined space, and with him holding the gun, there's no sense in arguing right now. I step back from the edge. 'Fine, go ahead.'

Cabressa moves first to his knees and then swivels round onto his belly so that he can use the floor of the elevator car for stability. He swings his legs over the edge, and starts to lower himself down into the hallway. It's not fast, and he doesn't make it look easy, especially with the gun in his hand.

'Come on,' says Otis.

I look over at the big boxer. His leg's jigging and he's looking real twitchy again. 'You okay?' I say in a hushed voice.

He nods. 'Yep. Just hate being in this metal coffin. Need to be out, you know?'

'Sure.'

Cabressa lets go of the edge and I hear a thud as he lands in the hallway below. There's a beat, and I wonder what he's doing. Then I hear his voice.

'Come on.'

I want to get out of the elevator car real bad, but I can manage a little longer. I look at Otis. 'You want to go next?'

He nods. Cracks a brief smile. 'Appreciate it.'

I watch him manoeuvre himself into position – facing towards the back of the car on his hands and knees – and then reversing out of the gap feet first. He's faster than Cabressa, and I'm thankful for that. I'm itching to get out of this metal box too.

As Otis drops down through the gap and disappears, I get ready to follow him. As I slide backward out through the gap, and dangle for a brief moment half in and half out of the car, I try not to think about what would happen if the power returned at this moment; how the elevator car would restart its journey along the shaft, and I'd be cut in two. The thought makes me move faster.

My exit isn't elegant, but it's effective. I land on my feet and exhale in relief. The hallway is dark aside from a dim glow from the safety lights that are recessed every few yards into the ceiling, powered, I assume, by the building's back-up generator. We're in a small lobby-type space. There are a couple of couches and a low table with a large flower arrangement in the centre. Opposite us, over on the far side, there's a large floor-to-ceiling window.

Turning to Otis and Cabressa, I ask, 'What floor are we on?'

'Forty-nine,' says Otis.

Hot damn. We climbed down fourteen storeys and have made it through the residential levels to the main hotel. This is good news. Monroe's room is 5209 – just three levels above us. I hope the micro camera is still in place and working so he's getting the feed; the power shouldn't be a problem – it's field equipment, de-signed to run off batteries and track by satellite. If he sees where we are he can come help, or send in the SWAT team he'd have gotten stationed outside the building. I stare at the sign for floor forty-nine to make sure the camera picks it up, and repeat Otis's words. 'We're on floor forty-nine, great.'

'Enough chit-chat,' says Cabressa, gesturing along the hallway with the gun. 'Let's get out of here.'

I need to delay. Give time for Monroe and his people to get to us. Taking a risk, I ignore the old mobster and walk over to the floor-to-ceiling window on the opposite side of the foyer space. I gaze out through the glass. The city is still in darkness. The blackout isn't over.

Glancing over my shoulder I look back at Cabressa. He's scowl-ing. Obviously anxious to get out of here and force me to lead him to the missing chess piece. He doesn't care how many people have died. And he doesn't care how many more die before he gets his way.

But I do.

This isn't over.

48

The scaffold poles are rough from rust and the wear of usage. The air is damp, moisture lining the bars, making them slippery to handle. JT moves steadily along the pole, making sure every move is deft and deliberate. He keeps a tight grip and pushes his weight down into his feet. There's no safety net – a mistake will result in a plummeting, forty-eight-storey fall, and there's no coming back from that. The breeze that seemed gentle on the roof garden is stronger out here on the side of the building, powerful gusts buffeting them as they climb.

JT glances up towards the others. Johnny's doing okay; he's tall like JT so he can reach between the poles and get good holds for his feet and hands. Even with the alcohol in his system, his athleticism means he's navigating the scaffold with relative ease. Carmella's a different story. She's petite and lean, and too short to be able to get secure hand- and footholds at the same time. JT can see she's tiring as she alternates between pulling herself up with her upper body strength, and then resting for a moment, crouched with her weight in her legs. Every movement down is riskier for her, and every drop to the next bar an over-extended stretch. JT can't fathom why she didn't choose to wait on the roof.

As they descend no words are spoken; the silence of the night broken only by the noise of their breathing and the occasional grunt of effort. Through the gaps in the scaffold JT sees the city stretching out below like a sleeping dragon. It looks still, dormant, but he knows that's not true. In a blackout people can lose their perspective, sometimes their humanity. He hates to think what horrors are happening below on those darkened streets. He hopes Lori is staying safe.

He reaches the bottom of the structure. This is the hardest part. The scaffold sticks out over the staircase; to get back onto the steps he needs to manoeuvre himself around the bottom of the poles and a couple of yards back towards the stairs. There's no easy way to do it. He figures the best option is to use the scaffold pole like a gym bar, and use his upper body strength to swing himself along the pole and onto the first step.

JT takes a breath. He plants his hands firmly onto the lowest pole and swings his legs clear so that they're dangling free. Doesn't look down. Can't. Mustn't think about the drop below. Instead he focuses on his breathing, on keeping a steady rhythm – one hand over the other – and pictures Lori and Dakota's faces in his mind. He can't let them down. He won't.

His palms are getting sweaty. His breath is coming in gasps. The muscles in his arms and shoulders are screaming out from the strain of supporting his 220 pounds of bodyweight. He ignores it all – thinks about Lori, about Dakota, and how he will not fail them – keeps going.

Finally he's hanging over the top step. He can't reach it from here, guesses the drop down to it – from his feet to the stairs – must be a little over a yard. Not far in the usual scheme of things, but sixty-eight storeys up, with nothing to catch him if he mis-judges the jump, it feels like a hell of a lot more.

JT lets go of the scaffold.

He's falling. Flying. Making a leap of faith.

Adrenaline races through him. Air rushes past him.

He lands with a thud on the first of the stairs. Helicopters his arms, fighting for his balance. He feels the steps below him move from the sudden addition of his weight. Crouching down, he lowers his centre of gravity, and waits for the stairwell to stop shaking.

He takes a breath. Feels relief flood through him. He's made it.

That's the moment he hears Carmella scream.

49

We move along the hallway in the direction of the hotel's emergency exit. The place seems deserted; there's little light, and no ambient noise. Any hotel guests are either asleep, so unaware of the blackout, or waiting it out quietly behind closed doors. The silence seems unnatural. It's dangerous too. In this environment we'll hear any move Monroe or his team are planning on making before we see them. They can't hope to have the element of surprise.

There's a real danger this will turn into a fire-fight. Cabressa might not have many bullets left, but I'm sure he'll not give himself up easy. I shudder. Need to find a way to stop things happening that way. I know the best option: take Cabressa out of the game myself.

Cabressa stays a few paces ahead as he leads us along the hallway, following the emergency-exit signage. I keep step with Otis. Glance across at him. I'm wondering where his loyalties lie. At the beginning of this evening I'd thought he'd been a friend of Cabressa's, but some of the things he's said, and the way Cabressa has acted towards him and the others, makes me question that. Even so, I need to know he's got my back.

Otis sees me looking at him and gives me a small smile. 'We're nearly out of here, man.'

'Yeah.' I don't smile. I'm wondering how JT is doing. 'But what about the others?'

'Dunno.' He glances upwards. 'What happened in the penthouse, it was all kinds of bad. Feels like a nightmare.'

'It wasn't a nightmare, it was real,' I say, my voice granite hard. 'People died.'

'Yeah, yeah.' Otis looks twitchy. He glances towards Cabressa then back to me. 'It was bad shit.'

I stay silent. Keep walking. Wait to see if he'll say more.

Half a minute passes before Otis turns to me again. His voice is hushed. 'We've got to go to the cops, man, soon as we get out of here. They'll find whoever locked us into the penthouse and unleashed that crazy shit.'

I nod. 'Good idea.'

With Cabressa so close, I can't ask Otis outright if he'll help me, but if he's thinking of going to the cops I'm hoping he'll step in if I tackle Cabressa and get into trouble. The cops do need to know what happened up in the penthouse tonight, but right now we need to fix the immediate threat from Cabressa.

I flick my gaze towards him. He's still facing forward, leading us along the hallway, but there's more tension in his posture – his back is rigid – and I wonder if he's overheard us. I sure hope that he hasn't.

We take a right into another hallway. A little ways ahead I see another emergency-exit sign with an arrow pointing to a set of doors. My heart accelerates. We're almost at the stairs. It's possible Monroe could have chosen this place to ambush Cabressa.

I slow my pace. Otis shortens his stride to keep level with me.

'Move it,' growls Cabressa, putting his hand on the release bar for the door. 'Let's go.'

We maintain our steady pace as we watch Cabressa push open the emergency-exit door and step into the stairwell. I take a breath and get ready to drop to the ground, pulling Otis with me, in case Monroe is waiting inside to ambush us.

Nothing happens.

Otis pushes open the door and walks through. He holds the door for me. Only Cabressa and Otis are on the stairs. Otherwise, the space is empty.

As I walk through the door, I take a brief glance over my shoulder. The corridor is still deserted. There's no sign of Monroe or his SWAT team. I think about what he said, how he'd gotten the team stationed a little way down the street, outside the building, and guess that he's taken the decision to apprehend Cabressa at ground level. I can understand that. But the problem is, that means there's another forty-nine storeys to go before we act against Cabressa.

Personally, I don't want to wait that long.

50

The stairs seem to go on forever.

We spiral down, step after step. It's hot and humid in here. Dark too, with only a narrow strip of low-level emergency lighting giving a dull glow along the curved outer wall. Our footsteps are loud against the concrete stairs. My eyes struggle to focus in the gloom.

To my right, the banister curves downwards. I keep my eyes on the stairs, don't look over the rail into the void. It's shrouded in darkness, but I know the drop continues to the ground floor. The thought of it makes me feel sick to my stomach.

After ten storeys our pace is slowing. Cabressa is breathing heavily and favouring his left leg. Otis is sweating; I am too.

'Do you know where the nearest police precinct is?' Otis asks me. His voice is hushed, but the sound echoes in the stairwell, sounding far louder.

Cabressa looks around sharply. 'We're not going to any cops.'

Otis widens his eyes. 'We have to. The rest of the group could still be trapped on the roof. We have to—'

'I said no.' Cabressa's voice is firm. He doesn't turn around.

Otis looks at me. I give a shake of my head: *Don't pursue it. Not here.*

Right now, we're like fish in a very tall barrel. And Cabressa is the only one with a gun.

So we stay silent and keep going down. My dress is damp with sweat. My thighs burn from the effort, and my feet are starting to feel sore from walking barefoot on the concrete.

A few minutes later, Cabressa falters. He catches the edge of the stair with his toe, misses a step, and makes a grab for the banister. It's not high – more level with his waist than mid-torso – and as his belly hits the rail I think he might fall. I *hope* he might fall. But it doesn't happen.

Me and Otis say nothing. Cabressa continues downwards, acting like nothing's happened. But he's limping more heavily now, and each time he puts weight on his right leg his fingers cling claw-like to the rail to try and keep some of the weight from his leg.

We've travelled another storey down before Cabressa stops and raises his free hand. 'Hold up,' he says. His voice is weaker than before, more breathless.

As he turns back towards us I see that the box of chess pieces has slipped down and is starting to force its way out the bottom of his now half untucked shirt. He fumbles with the buttons, tries to retuck the shirt, but with the Glock in one hand he fails. He shakes his head and sticks the gun into the back of his pants waistband. Uses both hands to take a hold of the box, then tucks it under one arm while he sorts out the shirt.

He's looking down at what he's doing. Not focused on me or Otis anymore.

That's when I make my move.

I take the three steps between us in a rush. One-two-three. Slam my fist into his belly, using my momentum to drive into him harder. He doubles over, but he's not done yet. He's hitting me with his free hand. Forcing his weight against me, his shoulder pushing into my chest, trying to get away down the stairs. I ignore the blows. Stay focused on what I'm after.

I reach for the gun.

Cabressa stops hitting me and lurches sideways, trying to shake me off. I stay with him. Focus on pulling the Glock from his waistband.

My fingers close around the handle.

I don't see the blow coming until it's too late. The wooden box with the chess pieces smacks into my head. I drop to my knees.

Lose my balance and fall forwards, tumbling down a few steps. The concrete bites into my bare legs and arms.

I lunge for the banister to stop myself falling. Grab the bottom rung of the rails and cling on tight to stop my momentum. Halfway up the flight of stairs, Otis stands open mouthed, leg-jigging, watching.

'Otis,' I yell. I need him to back me up.

Cabressa's closing in on me. 'Goddamn bitch,' he shouts, spittle flying from his mouth. He raises the wooden box again.

Just in time I put my arm up to protect myself, and he slams it down onto me.

I'm down, but I can't be done. I have to get up.

'You think you can outwit me?' Cabressa shouts. 'You little cunt.'

The blows keep coming. I have to move.

Using the rail to pull myself up, I propel myself up the stairs towards Cabressa. But I'm too slow and too unbalanced. My vision swims, and I feel like I might vomit. Force myself forward. I can't give up. And Otis seems incapable of helping.

Cabressa hits me across the ribs and the wooden box splinters open. The chess pieces cascade out, showering down the stairs with a clatter. 'What the...?' He shoves me hard, away from the pieces, and I fall backwards.

I land hard against the wall in an awkward position. The breath leaves me. And I feel a sharp pain in my back. I recognise the feeling enough to know that I've busted one of my ribs for sure.

'Look what you've done,' hisses Cabressa. There's fury on his face as he stomps down the steps towards me and reaches into his waistband for the gun.

Biting back the pain, I press my hands against the concrete and get ready to throw myself back into the fight even though I'm out-matched in firepower, and anything I do now is most likely futile.

I try to take a full breath. Grimace from the pain in my back.

Cabressa raises the gun and takes aim at my head.

51

Carmella screams again.

JT squints up through the darkness. He sees Carmella's hanging by one hand from the bottom corner of the scaffold. Her body is swinging back and forth, uncontrolled – in danger. Johnny moves past her around the bottom turn. Ignores Carmella's screams.

'You asshole,' she yells at Johnny, her voice thick with fear. 'You pushed me, you bloody pushed me.'

Johnny doesn't answer, just keeps moving – one hand over the other, his legs swinging free. His focus is on the top stair where JT is standing. It's as if he doesn't even register JT is there.

'Get both hands on the bar,' JT shouts at Carmella. 'Don't stop there.'

Carmella looks down. 'Oh God I...'

'Look at me,' JT yells. 'Carmella, look at me.'

She manages to do as he says.

'Now move this way. Keep going. You've got this.'

As Carmella starts to move along the pole towards him, JT keeps his gaze on hers. 'Look at me, Carmella. Not down, not at Johnny – just at me.'

She holds his gaze. Her jaw is clenched. Her dark hair is falling over her face, sticking to her forehead with sweat.

'Keep your eyes on me,' repeats JT. He sees her eyes widen.

'Watch out.'

Johnny slams into him. The force sends both men tumbling down the steps.

'What the hell?' JT yells. He grabs for the railings on the side of the stairs. Stops himself falling. Shoves Johnny away from him. 'You dumb—'

'Sorry, dude. Sorry.' Johnny puts his hands out towards JT in surrender. The gashes on his arms and face are bleeding again. 'I was losing my grip. Couldn't hang on any longer. You were so set on helping Carmella you didn't see me coming. I didn't have a choice. It wasn't like I wanted to—'

JT doesn't listen to the rest. He's got no time for excuses. Pulling himself up, he scrambles back up the steps. 'You okay?' he shouts to Carmella.

'Yeah,' she replies, slowly moving her hands along the pole. 'You?'

'Yep.' He doesn't say Johnny's actions nearly sent him plunging down the stairs, that he could have broken his neck. He doesn't say that it was in no way an accident. And he doesn't say Johnny just tried to kill both Carmella and him. Instead he says, 'You're nearly done. Half a yard further and you can jump down.'

'I'll try,' she says. Tears of effort and pain are running down her face, mixing with her eye make-up and sending black rivers over her cheeks.

He can see she's tiring, but she's still too far out. 'Come on,' he says. 'Keep going.'

Carmella starts to kick her legs as if she's trying to walk through the air. Her teeth are gritted. Her arms have started to shake from the effort. She begins to cry out, each time she moves her hands along the pole. 'I can't … it's too—'

'You've got this,' JT shouts. 'You're nearly done, just a little further. Keep going. Come on.'

Carmella rushes two more grips, then misses the next, her fingers closing around air rather than the iron bar. For a moment she holds tight, swinging on one arm, like a puppet with all but one string cut.

'Reach back up,' JT calls.

She tries to grab for the scaffold bar, but misses. The movement makes her body swing even more dramatically. She looks down into the blackness – there's nothing between her and the sidewalk forty-eight storeys below.

JT sees her grip start slipping. Storming up to the top step, he lunges for Carmella just as she starts to scream. Manages to get a hold of her dress and one arm, and pull her to safety. JT falls back against the railing. Holds onto her until she stops shaking, then releases her. She takes a step down to the next stair. Holds onto the railing with both hands. Doesn't look at JT as she says, 'Thanks.'

'No problem,' he says, but it's not the truth. Carmella isn't the problem, but he's starting to believe there is one. Because that's the moment JT turns and looks down the stairs to where Johnny is standing looking up at them.

He looks furious.

52

Everything happens real fast.

Otis roars as he charges down the stairs towards us. Cabressa swings the gun from me to Otis.

'No,' I yell. But it's too late for warnings.

Cabressa pulls the trigger as Otis launches himself down the last step. He slumps forward as the bullet rips through his chest, his body slamming into Cabressa and knocking him backward, into the banister. They grapple. Otis looks weaker, his movement less co-ordinated. He's bleeding but he's still alive.

'Otis,' I shout, as I move towards the two men, peering through the gloom, trying to see what's going on more clearly.

Cabressa raises his arm, and I see the gun glint in the soft glow of the emergency lighting. He brings it down hard onto Otis's head. Otis staggers sideways. Collapses onto the banister.

I see Cabressa reach for Otis's shirt. Understand in that moment what he's planning. I shout for him to stop. Throw myself towards them, grasping for Otis, to try and pull him back. But I'm too late. Too weakened. My fingers clasp at the air.

Otis cries out as Cabressa tips him over the rail. He clutches for the banister and for a moment stops his momentum. Then Cabressa pistol whips him again, and he falls, flailing, into the void of the stairwell. His screams fading as he drops the twenty or so storeys to the ground.

I reach the banister. Look over into the dark void. It's too far to the ground to see Otis, but I know he's gone. No one could survive a fall like that.

I turn on Cabressa. Fury making me spit out my words. 'You

asshole! You didn't have to kill him. He was a good man. We'd have died in the penthouse if it hadn't been for—'

'He'd never have kept his mouth shut. All that God stuff; he'd start feel guilty and then start telling people. He's done it before.' Cabressa shakes his head and peers down into the darkness of the stairwell. 'Better to take that burden away from him.'

'This wasn't about him. It was about you.' Wincing, I press my fingers to the cut above my eye. Try to stop the bleeding.

Cabressa shrugs. Then hardens his gaze. 'Maybe I just don't like people challenging me.' He looks down at the chess pieces shattered across the stairs. Gestures towards them with the barrel of the Glock. 'Get them. Don't miss any.'

I stand my ground. Don't move.

He steps closer to me, sandwiching me against the banister. Prods the gun into my side, twisting it against my ribs.

I gasp from the pain.

He increases the pressure against my ribs. Twists the barrel again. 'I said to pick them up.'

I push past him, away from the banister and the gun. I don't want to do as he says, but I'm injured and outgunned. I need to play this smart. Level the playing field. If I can get him to ground level, hopefully Monroe's team will be there ready to apprehend us. I just need to stay alive long enough.

So I crouch down and start collecting up the chess pieces. My body aches. My vision is a little fuzzy. And each time I bend down nausea strikes and I taste sour bile in my throat. But I keep going. Keep playing this mobster's game. Just for a little while longer.

Cabressa moves across the stairs to the outer wall and leans against it. I'm a good five steps down from where Cabressa is now. I figure I could outrun him if I raced down the stairs from here. He's not doing so well, but he's still got the gun. Given his behaviour so far I doubt he'd hesitate to shoot me. He probably wouldn't kill me, not right now, but he'd injure me enough to stop me getting away. Frustrating the hell out of me as it is, I decide not to try to escape. Once Cabressa's out of bullets his advantage will be lost. That's the time I'll need to act.

I move down the steps, searching for the last remaining chess pieces.

'How many more?' Cabressa asks.

'Two.'

'Hurry it up, we need to get moving.'

'Why the rush?'

He doesn't answer the question. 'You know I knew Otis virtually his whole life. My family own the boxing gym he started out in all those years back as a scrawny, nine-year-old kid. I saw he had something right off the bat.' He glances towards the banister. Shakes his head. 'Waste of a talent.'

Cabressa's change of tone takes me by surprise. I straighten up. 'This could stop right now. You could just let me go.'

He meets my gaze, and for a moment I think he's going to agree. Then his expression darkens. 'That's never going to happen, Miss Anderson. I've worked it out. I know who you really are.'

I frown. Don't know what he's getting at. 'Who I really am?'

'That's right,' says Cabressa. 'I know you're Herron.'

53

Johnny takes the lead and goes first down the staircase. JT's glad for it; in front is exactly where he wants the man to be. He doesn't want him behind them, that's for sure. He doesn't want to give him another opportunity to take them out of the game.

He's said nothing to Carmella of his suspicions, but the more he thinks on it, and replays the events that have happened since he picked the locks of the external door from the penthouse, JT is convinced Johnny wants the pair of them dead.

The reason is simple enough. They're witnesses. Carmella and him saw Johnny kill Carl. It might have been in self-defence, but it still seems Johnny wants to clean house. If JT had to guess, he'd say his plan is to make JT and Carmella have an 'accident' and then pin the murder of Carl on him.

JT grimaces. It wouldn't be the first time someone's tried to frame him for murder. He keeps moving down the stairs. Checks the next emergency-exit door they pass – the number painted on the door is thirty-seven. They're getting closer to ground level, and he's glad of it. His breathing is getting laboured, and it feels like there's a vice around his lungs. His legs are like iron from the effort of the steps. He's starting to feel lightheaded.

Carmella is doing better. She's ahead of him, pretty much a whole storey lower, and gaining on Johnny even though there's at least a storey between the two of them still. JT pushes himself harder, tries to speed up his progress – can't let Carmella catch up with Johnny alone.

Black spots dance in front of his eyes. He blinks them away. Feels nausea rising and tastes bile in his throat. Swallows hard. Looks down.

That's when he sees the cut on his forearm is bleeding again; blood is flowing down his arm, dripping off the ends of his fingers. It must have reopened when Johnny crashed into him on the steps. After everything that's already happened, JT knows the blood loss isn't going to do him any favours.

He grips his arm around the cut in his other hand and squeezes to try and stem the flow. Trips on the stairs and only just manages to shoot a hand out to grab the rail before falling.

His head's spinning. He needs to stop.

Sinking down on the step, he sits and raises his injured arm. Grips the flesh around the wound again and adds pressure. He has to stop the bleeding. Needs a moment to get his shit together.

Johnny and Carmella are getting further away. JT hears her calling to Johnny, but Johnny doesn't respond. She speeds up. Within a minute it looks like she's closing in on him.

'I said wait,' Carmella shouts. 'JT needs a breather, we should stop.'

'I'm not stopping,' Johnny yells back.

'He saved you, you ungrateful bastard, the least you could do is—'

JT hears them clattering down the steps. They start shouting again, but he can't make out the words. Forcing himself to his feet, he starts to follow. He's slower though, and the distance between the pair and him is increasing. He manages to make it another level down, then stops. His arm's still bleeding, the blood flooding out of him. If it keeps going this way he's going to be too weak to make it to the bottom. He sinks back down to the step, and leans against the outer railing. Peers down through the gloomy night and tries to make out what's happening.

There's a gust of wind and the sound carries better.

'I said stop,' Carmella shouts again.

Squinting down through the treads of the staircase, JT sees that she's caught Johnny. He sees her reach for the ball player. Johnny pushes her away, and she hits the inside railing with a thud.

'Back the hell off,' Johnny yells. He turns and starts running down the stairs again.

'No,' Carmella shouts as she leaps after him. In the dim light of the stars their silhouettes meld together.

JT watches, trying to get a better view as the pair move across the stairs. He hears Carmella cry out, then a grunt from Johnny. But now they're so close to each other he can't tell the shadowy figures apart. He watches as they slam into the outer railing and the railing beside him vibrates. One of the figures stops the other and pushes them against the rails. The second figure loses balance, tries to shove the other off. The first pushes back, shoving them against the railing until they're leaning out into the darkness. The blacked-out city of Chicago is lying in wait silently beneath them.

The second figure's arms are flailing. They're trying to pull themselves back to safety but they can't. The other figure doesn't let up. They keep pushing.

The wind whips around JT and he hears more words.

'Get the hell off...'

'...this is your fault ... what you did ... deserve what you...'

Gradually the black spots clear from JT's eyes. The urge to vomit has gone. He stands. Knows he needs to get down to the other two. Break up the fight. Stop this craziness. Holding the handrail for support, he starts the descent again.

He makes it down another flight of stairs before he hears it.

There's a scream. The railing vibrates hard and then is still.

Squinting through the darkness, JT can just make out the outline of a body as it topples over the railing and plummets down through the night.

He hears another scream. This time the noise fades away fast into nothing.

Goddammit.

Pushing away from the handrail, JT sprints down the steps as fast as he's able. But no matter how fast he moves, he knows it's not going to be enough. The damage is already done.

Only one silhouette remains standing on the steps two storeys below him.

Another person is dead.

54

In the gloom of the stairwell I stare at Cabressa. I don't move. Don't speak.

'Didn't think I'd figure it out, did you?' he says, shaking his head. 'But you underestimated me.'

'I didn't plan to—'

He holds up his free hand to silence me. 'See, I did my due diligence on you, Miss Anderson. Couldn't quite believe how these chess pieces resurfaced so many years after they were taken, and were in the possession of a thief I'd never heard of. To me, it just didn't add up. But I couldn't put my finger on why.'

Damn. I need to convince him I'm on the level. That I'm not Herron. 'I told you why. I said—'

'I know what you said.' He fixes me with a hard stare. 'And I knew right from the get-go it was a lie, a bullshit cover story, to hide your real affiliations.'

Despite the heat and airlessness of the stairwell, a shiver runs along my spine. If Cabressa knows I'm working with the FBI I'm screwed. Never mind his OCD, he'll shoot me right here as a traitor, the last chess piece be damned. Maybe that was his plan all along – pick off the others until it's just the two of us left, then confront me and kill me.

'What, cat got your tongue now?' he sneers, stroking the grip of the gun like it's some Bond villain's cat. 'Not so smart mouthed when you get called out on the truth.'

I can tell there's no way in hell he'll believe me if I plead. Being straight is the only play I have. I fix him with a hard stare. 'I'm not lying, because I am not Herron.'

'Bullshit.' His tone is getting angrier. The grip on his gun is tighter.

I'm seven stairs down from the spot where he's standing and five more stairs before the next twist; I need to put more distance between us. Sliding my foot along the stair to the edge real slow, I take a step down to the next. 'I'm telling the truth.'

'Why are you running away then?'

I glance down at the stairs. 'I'm not running, I'm searching for your chess pieces, remember?'

'And there's that smart mouth.' Cabressa pushes himself away from the wall and takes a few steps down towards me. He has the Glock aimed in my direction the whole time. 'The whole Herron thing always seemed strange. The rumours, all the things he'd supposedly done, yet no one had ever seen him. That was weird. Not usual in my business. It's normal to claim your triumphs, to make your face known, and feared.'

'From the conversation at the poker game tonight it sounds like Herron is feared, you just don't know the face of the person you're all fearing is all.'

Cabressa takes another two steps down. He narrows his eyes. 'I know Herron – you – is funded by the Miami Mob.'

'That's not true.'

'Isn't it?' Cabressa cocks his head to the side. 'I've played along with your bullshit story about being a thief until now, but I know who you really are. Like I said, I did my due diligence. That blood-bath at the Miami Mob compound last month, Luciano Bonchese getting banged up, and your pal North taking over as leader while Old Man Bonchese convalesces – all that was your doing. You're a bounty hunter who's been turned.'

I can't deny I was there. I won't let him believe I work for the mob though. 'I helped North out of a difficult situation is all. I work for myself.'

'Come on, admit it – you work for the goddamn Miami Mob. You're in bed with North and the Old Man, it's obvious. Hell, your ex-husband was one of their enforcers. You've been connected to them your whole adult life.' He takes a breath. 'Stands to reason you might ask for something someday. My guess is you asked for Chicago.'

I shake my head. 'Like I said, it's not true.'

Cabressa steps down onto the step above mine. Presses the Glock into my temple and snarls, 'And like *I* said, I don't believe you.'

I meet his gaze. Don't flinch away from the gun. If he were going to kill me right now he'd have done it already without these theatrics – just like he did when he killed Mikey and Otis. The fact I'm still here means that at this exact moment he wants the full set of chess pieces intact more than he wants to see me dead. I need to use that to my advantage. It's the only ace I've got left. 'So what are you waiting for?'

His mouth twists into a smile. 'You know what I want.'

'And you know I don't have it here.'

He taps the gun against my head. I don't react. Keep staring at him.

'Then you'd better take me to it.'

He raises the gun again, ready to tap it against my skull again, but I take a step down, away from his reach.

'I'll take you there, and I'll give you the knight,' I say. I make sure my words are clear. Hope to hell that Monroe is listening, and takes action. 'And then we're done.'

Cabressa nods. 'You're right, we will be.'

I don't reply. Instead, I bend down and pick up the final two chess pieces from the stair and hand them to Cabressa. I watch him stuffing them into the inner pockets of his jacket and buttoning the pockets shut. Then he turns and continues down the stairs. If the micro camera has been damaged, and Monroe can't hear or see me, I'm on my own. If that's the case, I've got until I hand over the knight in the hotel room to make my move. Because once I've done that, I know for sure that Cabressa will shoot me dead.

It takes what seems an age to reach ground level. As the floors count down, anxiety starts to gnaw at my stomach. If Monroe has sent in the SWAT team, chances are they'll be lying in wait outside the emergency-exit door. I need to make sure Cabressa exits first. Don't want to get caught in a firestorm.

Know that I need to act cool. Not give anything away.

Can't help but hope that Monroe has come through for me.

'Why are you slowing?' Cabressa growls, poking me in the back with the Glock.

'I'm tired,' I snap back.

He prods the gun against my ribs, and I clench my jaw as the pain vibrates through me. Move faster around the twist and down the last flight of stairs.

We reach the bottom. Ahead is a white security door with a green *Emergency Exit* sign across it. I hesitate, waiting for Cabressa to take the lead.

But he shakes his head. Gestures with the Glock towards the door. 'Ladies first,' he smiles.

Damn.

I step towards the door. Put my hand onto the metal bar that releases it. My heart's beating thunder loud. My breathing quickens. If the SWAT team are outside I'm about to step into their direct line of fire.

'Move it,' growls Cabressa.

I can't put it off anymore. Have to get it done.

Hoping Monroe is listening and feeding information to the SWAT team, I turn to Cabressa and say, 'Fine, I'm opening the door now, okay?'

Then I push the release. Push the door open. And step out into the night.

55

The lone figure is leaning over the railing, staring down into the blackness; it turns as JT draws closer. There are tears in her eyes, but could be that's due to the wind.

'Carmella?' JT can't hide the surprise in his voice. He'd been sure Johnny would be the one he'd find down here. Carmella's gym fit and toned and all, but he'd have put money on Johnny, with the strength of a professional athlete, being the victor.

She peers down over the railing. Shakes her head. 'He didn't care.'

'So you pushed him?' JT stops, a few stairs above her.

Carmella turns back to JT. Her stare is hard, her voice flat, emotionless. 'After everything he's done, he wasn't even sorry.'

That's when JT sees the device in her hand. It's much smaller than Lori's X26, and it's clear that the black weapon is a domestic Taser rather than weapons grade, but the voltage would still be enough to disrupt a person's nervous system. He realises now how she managed to overcome Johnny. 'How did you get that?'

'You both left me alone while you looked for the emergency fire escape. You thought I was passed out, or asleep or whatever, but I wasn't. I'd remembered the knife used to kill Carl, but couldn't remember if Johnny still had it. I didn't trust him, with or without the knife.' She taps her finger against the Taser. 'So while you weren't watching me, I removed this. I always wear it under my clothes at a game – just in case. Although we check players for weapons on arrival you can never be sure what might happen if someone on a losing streak gets desperate. I thought it might come in handy.' She glances out over the railing where Johnny had fallen. Looks back at JT. 'I was right.'

JT stays where he is. He'd never had figured Carmella for the murdering kind, but now he's witnessed it with his own eyes he's wary, feels it's wise to keep his distance.

'It was self-defence, you know,' Carmella says. She looks down at the Taser in her hand. 'It looks bad, but he came at me. I just defended myself.'

JT says nothing. He'd believed Johnny wanted to get rid of him and Carmella because they were witnesses to him killing Carl, so it's not a stretch to believe that Johnny was the aggressor. But the Taser bothers him.

'You don't believe me?' The wind picks up. Carmella's black hair whips around her face. 'I told you, it was self-defence. He was a threat.'

She's right, JT doesn't believe her. She's holding something back. 'And me, am I a threat too?'

She looks towards him, but can't meet his gaze.

That's all he needs to know.

When she launches herself at him, he's ready. Unlike Johnny, he knows she's got the Taser. He feigns left, and moves right. Avoiding the firing pins, he thrusts his shoulder into her chest as she connects with him, and knocks her backwards. She loses her balance, mis-judges the step and falls sideways, grabbing for the handrail with her free hand. He follows. As she clings to the rail to stop herself falling further, he grabs her. Pulls her backwards towards him. Grabbing her Taser-free hand he wrenches her arms up behind her back and holds her still with his arm around her throat. She's cussing, trying to zap at him with the Taser. He hears the electric charge crackling, but the angle is wrong. She can't connect it to him.

He needs her to stop. Doesn't like having to restrain a woman. Never has. But he'll do what's necessary to stay safe and get back to Lori. He uses the smallest amount of force necessary. Carmella might have killed Johnny, but he doesn't want to hurt her. There's something else going on here, something he doesn't know, and he wants to find out what.

Carmella struggles against the hold. Tries to lash out at him, bite him. 'You're just like the rest. You're selfish, evil. You deserve to die the same as them.'

JT holds her still. 'The rest?'

'Cabressa, Johnny, Carl and the others – all those men at the game; they deserve everything they got tonight.' She spits the names. Glares at JT. 'It's taken months to engineer that game, with those players, and then Cabressa insists that woman Lori plays tonight, and the pair of you stroll in and almost ruin everything.'

'Ruin what?' asks JT. But as he asks the question he already knows the answer. 'The lockdown, the recorded message and de-contamination protocol – that was you?'

Carmella shakes her head. Doesn't answer. But she's smiling – grinning. That's enough, JT thinks. She did this. 'Why?'

'I told you. They don't deserve to live. After what they did … and you and the woman, Lori, are part of their world too, so you're just as bad as them.'

'But you and Thomas, you were inside the penthouse. We were all running out of air.'

Carmella tries to jerk away from him. Fails. Speaks through gritted teeth. 'Thomas was stealing from me. He deserved what he got.'

JT remembers Carmella's distress when Thomas was injured and then killed. How she cried and looked beaten. He realises she's one hell of an actress. 'There was no guarantee you'd get out alive.'

'What happened to me wasn't important. I wanted those men to die in the penthouse. As long as that happened I'd have achieved my aim.'

Everything that happened inside the penthouse suite was pre-planned. JT looks into Carmella's eyes. She looks calm, totally rational. 'Why would you want that?'

She shakes her head.

He feels her body tense.

'Enough questions,' she says. She kicks back against him.

Throws herself to the right, trying to wrench herself from his grasp.

It doesn't work. JT holds her firm. 'You're wrong about us. Lori's with the FBI.'

'No,' says Carmella, shaking her head. 'You're lying.'

'It's the truth,' JT says. Adjusting his grasp so he can hold Carmella in place and reach a hand into his pocket, he pulls out the crumpled sheet of paper that Monroe had them sign before the night started. He shakes it open so that the FBI logo is clear in the centre of the page, and holds it in front of Carmella. 'I've got proof.'

Carmella reads it. As she does, her stance softens. She drops the Taser. Looks at JT. 'You're not part of Cabressa's organisation?'

'Never have been.'

'Then how did you get Cabressa to insist you were invited to the poker game?'

'A confidential informer to the FBI got us a meeting, vouched for us. From there it was set up. The first time we met Cabressa was tonight.'

Carmella's shaking her head. 'I didn't know, I didn't want to hurt any innocent people, it wasn't supposed to—'

'There's no reason you should have. It was a sting operation. The FBI have a hard-on for Cabressa. The plan was to get proof of him handling stolen goods linked to a multiple homicide. Those chess pieces were the bait. Once he was in custody a whole bunch of people were ready to testify about the rest of his criminal activities. All we had to do was get him off the street.'

Carmella narrows her eyes. Looks doubtful.

'A lot of people have died for those pieces over the past few years, and a lot of lives have been ruined because of them. Lori nearly lost her life. So did I.' JT rubs his hand over his jaw. 'Cabressa needed to pay for what he'd done.'

'Getting arrested isn't justice for that man.' Carmella scowls. 'It doesn't come halfway near it.'

'It's the right thing.'

Carmella shakes her head. 'You don't know what he's done, what he's capable of. Even death is too good for him.'

'Is that why you removed the oxygen from the penthouse. You wanted him to suffer?'

Carmella meets his gaze. Holds it. Says nothing.

JT shakes his head. 'Look, I've been around mobsters before. I know what they—'

'No, you don't know.' Carmella's voice is louder now, passionate. 'You don't know about Cabressa. He's evil. The things he's done are...'

'You're right, I don't know,' says JT. He takes a step down, closer to Carmella. His eyes are on her, but he keeps the Taser in his peripheral vision. 'So tell me what he did.'

56

There are no guns, no spotlights, no SWAT team. No sign of Monroe. The back exit of the building is deserted.

I swallow back my frustration. Try to act normal, or as normal as is possible when there's a mobster holding a gun to your back.

'Which way's the hotel?' Cabressa asks.

I scan our surroundings. We've come out onto a narrow concrete path that seems to follow the outside perimeter of the building. Ahead of us is a high metal fence with razor wire at the top of it. Through the slats of the fence I see more buildings – apartment blocks and hotels, I'm guessing from their design. All of them are cloaked in darkness.

I don't recognise this area. We must have come out around back. I turn to Cabressa. 'I need to get to the front of the building, I know my way from there.'

Cabressa cusses under his breath. Prods me with the gun. 'Move then.'

I do as he says. Follow the narrow path around the building.

In the distance I hear the wail of a police siren, shouts and screams, and the sound of glass shattering. There's an unmistakable smell of burning in the air. I can imagine what's happening – there'll be looting and riots, and worse. The power outage has brought out the crazy in the people of Chicago. Blackouts always do.

We reach the front of the building. Earlier, when me and JT arrived, the place was lit up with spotlights. Now the metal-and-glass frontage looks dull and uninviting. I peer into the lobby. There's no one inside.

I turn at the entrance to the lobby and go down the steps to the street. I scan the area for a van that could have the SWAT team in, but I see nothing. There's no one here. The unlit sidewalks are empty. The buildings all around us are shrouded in darkness. The street has a desolate feel to it, like we've stepped onto the set of a post-apocalyptic movie. As we walk in the direction of my hotel the burning smell grows stronger, and the screams and yells louder. I look back at Cabressa. 'I think this is a bad idea.'

He scowls. He's walking fast, but with a strong limp. 'This is my city, I'll go where I want in it.'

'I don't think we should—'

'Enough talking,' he says, pushing me in the back with the gun. 'Take me to the hotel.'

I keep walking. Listen out for the shouting, the smashing and the cheering. Try to weave a path through the streets to avoid them.

We travel a few blocks, dodging into smaller alleys, taking short cuts between the larger buildings, avoiding the main streets. Cabressa pushes us faster. He might talk a good-enough talk, but I can tell from his expression that he's worried. We're alone out here and our phones are dead. He doesn't have the protection of his security and his generals. All he has right now is me.

And I, for sure, do not have his back.

Keeping low, we hurry along the sidewalk towards the river. I look back at Cabressa. 'We have to get across.'

He nods. Grim-faced.

I follow his gaze. See the problem.

There's a burning mass forming a makeshift barricade across the bridge. I slow my pace and squint towards it, trying to work out what it is. The closer we get, the more the stench of petrol fills my nostrils. The fire crackles and pops, and through the flames I see the burning shells of two cars that have been flipped onto their sides and set alight. The city is in chaos, and we are in the thick of it.

Left with little choice, I hang a left at the end of the block, start down the main drag alongside the river. The skyscrapers lining the water stand in the darkness like silent sentinels witnessing the city as it loses its mind.

This isn't where I wanted us to be. It's too exposed. Too damn dangerous.

Up ahead I see shadows moving in the darkness. Further still, the reflections of the blue lights of police cars kaleidoscope in the mirrored glass of the building's windows.

I break into a run. Clutch my arm around my ribs, trying to stop the worst of the pain. It doesn't help much. But I grit my teeth. Push forward. Cabressa follows, and as I glance back over my shoulder at him, I notice his limp is more pronounced at the faster speed.

'We need to find a way to cross,' I tell him. 'There's a footbridge a little way along this street I think.'

'Few hundred yards,' he says. 'We need to get onto the other side of the street.'

I nod and dart across the empty road. Cabressa stays with me. We sprint along the sidewalk, then hang a right at the sign for the footbridge and follow the narrow path between buildings to the river. We emerge from the path at the water's edge and halt. Ahead is the footbridge. It looks deserted – no burning cars, no human-shaped shadows. I glance at Cabressa. 'You ready?'

He nods.

'Okay then,' I say. Then I start running across the narrow bridge.

The wind is stronger on the bridge. The stillness of the streets replaced with persistent gusts. I pump my arms faster. Keep running. Behind me Cabressa does the same.

We make it to the middle of the bridge before our luck runs out.

57

They stand on the twist of the stairs, the wind gusting around them, sending Carmella's long black hair swirling around her face. JT doesn't think she's a threat to him, but he wants to know more about what she planned and why she did it. He wants them to keep moving too. Needs to get to Lori. He lets go of Carmella, gestures towards the stairs. 'I need to get going.'

He steps down onto the next flight and Carmella follows. They climb down in silence for a few levels. Then, as they pass the thirty-third floor, he looks back over his shoulder. 'You say I don't know how evil Cabressa is, why he deserved everything that's happened tonight. Tell me; help me understand.'

Carmella doesn't reply at first. Their footsteps clank on the metal treads. The wind gusts around them. Minutes pass, and JT figures she's not going to tell him. Then she starts to speak.

'I was young when it happened. It was three days after my four-teenth birthday.'

JT slows his pace, letting her catch up with him. Nods.

'I was telling the truth earlier when I said that I'd lied to the players about where I grew up. I never lived in New Jersey. I was born here in Chicago. Carmella isn't my real name either. I changed it a long time ago. After everything that happened back then, and before I started preparing for what *would* happen.'

'Back in the penthouse you said you ran away from home at fourteen – was that true?' JT's wondering if Carmella had fallen in with the wrong people – easy to do if you're living on the street and desperate. She could have been pulled into working for

Cabressa through one of his seedy businesses. Maybe that's why she holds the mobster responsible.

Her expression darkens. 'My home was destroyed when I was fourteen, and my family was too. I didn't run away – there was nothing left here for me.'

JT keeps his voice soft. Tries to coax the story from her. 'Did you need money. Did the mob find you and force you to work for them?'

Carmella stops partway down the flight of stairs. She spits out the words like they're poison. 'I'd never, ever work for Cabressa … that bastard's the reason I lost everything.'

JT wants them to keep moving, but he needs to know why Carmella wanted to kill the men in the penthouse too. He stops and turns back to face her. 'What did he do?'

'My papa was a good man. He'd worked construction his whole life, and helped our community in his free time. Everybody loved him. One of the things he did was run the residents' group for our apartment building.' Her expression hardens. 'And it got him killed.'

JT stays silent. Waits for her to tell him more.

'When the city issued the compulsory-purchase orders he knew something wasn't right. They said our building was riddled with rot and the brickwork was crumbling. That it couldn't be saved. But Papa had worked construction over thirty years and he knew that wasn't true. He understood how things worked, and so when he went to City Hall and looked up the plans for our neighbourhood – the site of our apartment block – he realised things weren't right. The more he investigated, the more he spotted discrepancies that others had missed. He tried to make appointments to see the city planners and the development syndicate who'd be awarded the contracts for redeveloping our block, but they avoided him. He looked up the people who'd signed the paperwork on the syndicate's behalf but they refused to meet.' She shakes her head. 'So he lodged complaints. Got the other residents behind him to fight the development syndicate. Started to talk to the press. And so they had him killed.'

'Over a real-estate project?'

Carmella nods. 'It was a multi-million-dollar development that made all its investors a lot of money.'

JT leans back against the railing. 'And you know for sure they killed him?'

'I found his body.' Carmella takes a breath. Closes her eyes. 'The charred remains of it, anyway. They'd taken him on his way home from work. Forced him down into the basement of our apartment building, put a tyre around his neck and filled it with gas before setting it on fire.' She opens her eyes. Blinks back tears. Glares at JT. 'He would have died in agony.'

JT's heard of the practice – it was in Monroe's briefing notes on Cabressa. He knows it's a way of getting rid of enemies that the Cabressa crime family picked up from the cartels. 'I'm sorry.'

'Yeah, me too,' says Carmella. She looks away. Wipes her eyes. When she turns back to JT her expression has hardened. 'That's why every person in the development syndicate had to die. They ordered his murder, or they stood by and did nothing. They let their desire for money overrule any decency they might have once had. After Papa died the residents group gave in. There were threats of more violence if we didn't comply. We had to move away. People did the best they could, but my mom never re-covered. She hung herself from the bathroom door the day before the enforcement order was to take effect.'

'That's real tough. I'm sorry.'

'So you said. But sorry isn't enough. For years I tried to forget, to put what had happened behind me, but I never truly could. I needed closure, and the only thing that could come close to that was to get revenge. So I made that my mission. I went through all of Papa's papers and researched the development syndicate and the person in the mayor's office who signed off the compulsory purchase order. It took over a year but I found out each and every one of their names. I found out their flaws and weaknesses, their dirty little secrets, and thought about how I could make them my advantage. Take Cabressa and Mikey, for example, they've had a special arrangement going between the mayor's office and the mob for years, but they know they're getting older, and challenges are likely to be made for their kingdom. So I used their paranoia about young-blood threats and created Herron – a gangster set on taking over the city. But he never actually existed. It wasn't hard: myth and rumour spread fast in worlds like Cabressa's. Anytime a stash house got raided, or some mob guys got beat on, I put the word around that it was Herron. Pretty soon the rumour took on a life of its own.'

'I don't understand how you could have known about this,' JT says, pointing over the railing, towards the city in darkness.

'I didn't just know about it. I caused it.'

'How the hell did you—'

'I wasn't alone when I found Papa's body. There were five of us kids hanging out that evening. My nickname was Hawk back then, because I always led the way. That evening we all went down into the basement. All of us saw what was done to Papa, what the development syndicate did. We don't know for sure who carried out the hit on him, but from the way they killed Papa we all knew it was Cabressa who gave the order. Necklacing – that's his signature move. Everyone in the neighbourhood knew that. After Papa was murdered and the residents' group fell apart everyone was forced out, my friend's families included. They never got the full compensation they were promised – the compulsory purchase price was way below the market – but they were running scared, afraid if they complained they'd end up the same as my papa.' She shakes her head. 'Those apartments had been home to their families for generations.'

'I don't get how that caused the blackout and everything,' says JT. 'The security must be—'

'I never forgot what happened. And I made a vow that I would avenge my family.' She meets JT's gaze. 'It took years of planning and a hell of a lot of money. One by one I got the people with the skills I needed on board. I used our shared history to persuade a couple of the most bitter people from my old neighbourhood to help me. To get the rest of the help, and the access I needed, I bribed the people who worked the right jobs. It wasn't cheap: over half a million dollars for an engineer to sabotage the power; a few hundred thousand to alter the alarm system. I paid a couple of gangbangers to say they'd heard a new boss – Herron – had come to the city.' She smiles ruefully. 'It's lucky that running poker games has been so lucrative, because I needed a lot of cash to pull tonight off.' Her expression and voice harden. 'And it was worth every penny to see the people responsible for my parents' deaths suffer.'

JT nods as he takes it in. A kid whose life was ruined by the greed of already-rich men, driven in adulthood to take revenge. 'You plotted to murder all those responsible for what happened.'

'At first I wanted to get the development syndicate into a room and confront them, but the more I studied these men, I knew they didn't care about others. Otis and Mikey might have put on a good penitent act, but the rest would've probably laughed. They knew what they did. They were all complicit in murder. So I wanted them to murder each other. And those left – the ones who did the killing – they'd be arrested and jailed for homicide.'

'But the lack of oxygen would have killed us all if we hadn't escaped.'

Carmella shakes her head. 'No it wouldn't. The oxygen level would have run down to a level low enough for everyone to pass out, but not so low to kill them. I'm not a murderer.' She meets his gaze. 'Or, at least I never meant to be.'

JT stares at her. She set a chain of events in motion to intentionally cause the deaths of nine people, including him. 'You killed those people as surely as you would have done if you'd pulled the trigger.'

'I guess I'll have to live with that.'

JT studies her expression but she's got one hell of a poker face. Her story is sad, real sad, but what she's saying about tonight isn't consistent; first she said she wanted to kill them all and was happy to die to make that happen, in the next breath she's saying the oxygen wouldn't have run out completely. He doesn't know what to believe, but he's sure he can't trust her.

58

We're halfway across the bridge as the looters start across from the opposite side. Flaming torches held aloft, baseball bats and already-looted products in their hands, they look like the cast of *The Purge*. Their march is purposeful, their posture threatening. These people are out to get whatever they can.

'Stay close,' I say to Cabressa.

There's fear in his expression. Panic in his eyes. I'm guessing that all of a sudden he doesn't feel so safe here in the city he controls.

We keep moving along the bridge. Keep to one side. Watch the mob of looters advancing towards us.

They're shouting, yelling. Some have carryalls filled with loot slung over their shoulders. Baseball bats slam down onto the metal railings of the bridge. *Bang. Bang. Bang.*

Next to me Cabressa flinches. Starts to slow.

'Keep moving,' I say. 'Make yourself look non-threatening. No eye contact.'

He does as I say. Unpuffs his chest. Looks at the ground.

That's when the crowd spot us. Catcalling and whistles.

'Where you going?'

'You running the wrong way.'

'The best stores are back the way you came.'

'Got nothing to say?'

They swarm around us. Blackouts are when all the usual bets get voided. Law enforcement can't cope. And in the darkness simmering frustrations boil over into anarchy. These people are a pack; they move as one, think as one. Determined to take whatever they can for as long as the lights stay off.

Someone pulls me into the crowd. The fug of sweat and adrenaline feels like it's suffocating me. My vision blurs, and I trip and fall against a big guy in a Chicago Bulls shirt. Get spun around. Lose sight of Cabressa.

The looters keep moving. I try to fight my way forward, but the surge of people is too strong and I find myself pulled back along the bridge the way we've come. Again I try to turn back around, but the crowd is too tightly packed. Scanning the bridge behind us I see more looters behind this group. We're not going to be able to get to the other side, to the hotel. There's no room. A stick is thrust into my back. A carryall filled with electronics equipment hits me in the side of the head.

Gasping from the pain, I turn and scan the faces in the crowd for Cabressa. I spot him a little ways off, sandwiched between two muscular guys who are carrying a huge flatscreen television. If I want to run, this is my chance. I weigh up my options. Try to decide whether to attempt to get away and leave Cabressa.

Much as I want to run, to get clear of Cabressa and everything that's gone down tonight, I can't. If I let Cabressa out of my sight, law enforcement might never get this chance again. I need to finish this job, end my alliance with Monroe. And Cabressa needs to pay for all that's gone down tonight; all the people he's killed. I can't allow him to disappear in the wind. So I change tack, and push sideways through the looters towards Cabressa.

As I reach him the shouting starts behind us. A second group of looters have caught up with this one. They're pulling carryalls from the first group's hands. Trying to wrestle the flatscreen televisions away from the people who have them.

I look at Cabressa. 'This is going to turn nasty. Come with me.'

For a moment he looks confused. But as fighting between the two looter groups breaks out around us there isn't time to explain. I turn and yell to Cabressa, 'Run!'

We sprint to the side of the bridge.

Grabbing Cabressa's arm I pull him towards the railings. 'Climb,' I shout.

'What?'

'They're fighting. We need out.' I climb the railing fast as I can. Put my leg over the top rail, straddle it. Ready. 'Come on.'

He takes another look at the two groups of looters clashing over their stolen goods and climbs over the railing. 'What now?'

I put my other leg over the rail. Take hold of his arm. 'Take a deep breath.'

As he opens his mouth, I jump. Pulling him with me.

We fall, straight and fast. Disappear into the water's inky blackness.

59

He can't trust Carmella with Cabressa, but JT doesn't believe she's a threat to him or Lori. Her motive is vengeance, pure and simple. What he's struggling with is his own ethics. She's a killer, or she meant to be, no matter the technicalities. He should hand her over to the authorities, he knows that, but something is holding him back. 'Tell me: how did the poker come into it?'

'I didn't get to go to college. Instead I spent my time trying to survive. Like I said before, I did a lot of things, but one guy I met taught me how to play poker. I was a natural, best he'd taught, and for a long time we travelled from place to place and played in underground clubs and private games. All the while I was researching who was behind the enforced purchase of my parent's apartment building – I wanted every single person involved to pay for what they did. And as I studied them, I realised they were just like the people I played at the poker tables – people prepared to gamble far more than is decent, on odds that are often against them, for the chance of winning big. It was my way in to their world. But first I had to reinvent myself, give myself a new name and a new backstory. Then I was ready to set up my own games.' She takes a breath. Shakes her head. 'It was easier than I thought. Men like that, they're all egos and bravado. As soon as I started making a name for myself they came crawling out the woodwork, and once you've got one big name – Cabressa in my case – all the others clamour for a seat at the table. After that it was just a question of getting all the members of the development syndicate in the room at the same time. That time was tonight.'

'One thing I don't get,' JT says, 'is how the recorded voice knew

I was in the penthouse. I shouldn't have been, I was an extra person because Lori had to make that call. You couldn't have predicted that.'

'I didn't predict it. Just after the blackout happened, when we realised the cell service and wi-fi was out, and I went to the study to see if the landline was working so I could call the concierge – that was when I changed the recorded message and added you in. I used auxiliary battery power to keep it running, and had the controller in my pocket once I'd changed the messages. Whoever they'd said was Herron would never have been right. I just played the appropriate message – I'd pre-recorded one for every eventuality. It was easy enough to do without being seen, what with all the drama going on. The whole point was to turn them against each other.'

Smart.

'What about your security detail in the room downstairs, and the players' close protection?'

'We fitted gas canisters in the air vents. Nothing lethal, just something to make them sleep the rest of the night.' She holds his gaze. 'You missed out on that by just a few minutes.'

JT keeps the eye contact. He can't tell from her expression whether she regrets that he escaped the gas or not.

'So now you know the truth, what now?' Carmella says.

JT looks down the emergency stairs. They've still a lot of floors to go and time is ticking. He understands why Carmella staged tonight. What happened to her papa and her mom was horrific, he gets that she'd crave revenge. But laws have been broken, and a lot of people have died. JT knows he should cuff her and hand her over to the cops, or the FBI. But he doesn't. He feels oddly conflicted, and anyways, he can't stop and divert now. He needs to get to Lori.

'Those men, they all deserved it.' Carmella's voice cuts into his thoughts.

'And me and Lori?'

'That was a mistake. I didn't—'

'If Lori got them out of the penthouse, Cabressa will try and force her to get the last chess piece for him. I know where it is. I have to help Lori.'

'I put you both at risk,' Carmella says. 'I'll help you stop him.'

He runs his hand across his stubble. 'You can't attack Cabressa. The FBI have to arrest him. That's the only way this'll work.'

Carmella holds his gaze. Frowns. 'Okay.'

JT stares at her a long moment. Thinking. She wants revenge, that hasn't changed, so he knows he can't trust her. But if Cabressa fights back she could be useful to have onside. He makes his decision. Nods. 'Come on then.'

60

The frigid water punches the air clean out of me. It closes around my head, dragging me down into its icy depths, twisting and turning me over within its clutches.

I try to hold on to Cabressa, but the water forces us apart. Opening my eyes I try to look for him, but the river is dark and murky, and I can barely even see my own hands in front of my face. There's no light. No way to tell which way is up.

My lungs start to burn. I need air. Thrash against the water, turning, searching for a sign of life, light.

High above me I think I see the looter's torches. My heart races as I kick hard, forcing myself up towards the light. Hope it's not a trick; my oxygen-desperate mind playing games with me. Keep kicking.

My head breaks the surface, and I gulp down the cool, fresh air. On the bridge, high overhead, the looters are still fighting. Ignoring them, I scan the surface of the river for Cabressa.

There's no sign of him. Damn.

Taking a breath, I dive down beneath the surface. See nothing. It's too dark, and the river too dirty. Bob back up. Swim a little ways. Try again. Still nothing.

I can't have lost Cabressa. He can't get away with what he's done that easily.

Swimming a few more strokes, I search again. Then I swim a little further. Try again. Keep trying.

It takes me over a minute to find him. My stomach flips. He's floating face down just below the surface, ten yards or so from where we jumped. I swim to him. Turn him over. His eyes are closed. It doesn't look like he's breathing.

Shit.

I feel his neck for a pulse. There's a faint one, real weak. I have to get him breathing. Hate having to touch the murderous bastard, but this death is too good for him, too easy. He has to pay for what he's done.

Fighting back the revulsion, I pinch his nostrils closed and blow two breaths into his mouth. It's not easy in the water, but I can't leave it until we get to the shore. I wait a long moment, then repeat the process. Then I watch his face, but he doesn't respond. I try again. Wait. And have another attempt.

Still nothing.

The cold is leeching into my bones. I feel stiff, my fingers and toes are turning numb. I need to move, we need to move. I inhale again and breathe two breaths into Cabressa. His eyelids flutter and he coughs, hard, wracking coughs that make it sound as if he's choking.

'Cabressa?' I say. 'You back with me?'

He splutters. Pushes me away. Then flails against the water, too weak to stay afloat. 'What the fuck did you...'

So much for a thank-you. I grimace, and look up towards the bridge. The crowd has moved on, marching across the bridge in the direction of the Skyland Tower. We're safe from them at least. I point towards the far side of the river, in the direction of the hotel, and say, 'We need to swim.'

He glares at me. He's struggling to tread water. And angry, for sure.

Ignoring the look, I start swimming. My feet and hands are numb. My face feels weird, kind of rubbery. I need to get out of this water. Warm up.

Suddenly the far bank of the river seems a hell of a long way off.

I push on. Grit my teeth against the cold. Try to keep to a steady rhythm. Every few strokes I glance back over my shoulder and check on Cabressa. So far he seems able to keep up.

We keep swimming.

The cold in my bones intensifies. I fight to catch my breath. Have to keep going.

We're a few hundred yards from the bank when Cabressa cries out. Stopping, I turn back and see him floundering. As I start back towards him, he disappears beneath the surface.

'Cabressa?' I yell.

He doesn't resurface. Shit.

I dive down, scanning the murky water for him. See him struggling against the water – he's kicking with his legs, but his arms are wrapped around his body. I swim towards him, grab him around the shoulder and heave upwards, kicking my legs to try and propel us both back to the surface. He doesn't help. Let me do the work.

We break the surface. 'What the hell?' I yell at him.

'The chess pieces,' Cabressa shouts. Still clutching his jacket to him. 'I can't lose them.'

I realise then, he's trying to stop the pieces emptying out of his pockets. He sinks beneath the surface again, and I have to fight to pull him back up. The choppy water splashes over my face, and I swallow a mouthful of water. Coughing, I spit out the water. 'Swim, goddammit, or you're going to drown.'

He either doesn't hear me or doesn't listen. Keeps his arms wrapped around himself, using only his legs to try and stay afloat. It doesn't work, and he sinks beneath the water again. Cussing under my breath, I put my arm around him and swim towards the bank, pulling him after me. Monroe had better give me a goddamn medal for this.

The swim to the bank takes what feels like an age. I reach it, panting and exhausted. Take a few deep breaths, then heave myself onto the concrete platform at the base of the bridge, before turning to haul Cabressa up after me. He's still breathing, still alive. I am too. And for that I'm real thankful.

Then I collapse onto the ground. I'm freezing. Soaked through.

My arms and legs feel as heavy as iron set in concrete. Every bit of me aches.

'You dead?' Cabressa asks.

'No.' I open my eyes. See him sitting a few paces from me. Watching. 'Nor are you, thanks to me.'

He doesn't acknowledge what I've said. 'We should get moving.'

There's no thank-you, no apology for his behaviour, just an instruction. I clench my jaw. Anger blooms in my chest. 'I need a minute.'

Cabressa pushes himself up to standing. 'A minute, sure. Don't make it longer.'

Ignoring him I do a mental check of my body. Everything seems okay, moving still, but I'm cold. So very cold. Much as I hate to admit it, moving is no doubt the best thing for me to do right now. I need to get warm, put on dry clothes.

I push myself up to sitting. Look at my feet and grimace. The soles are red raw and covered in cuts from running along the blacktop and sidewalks. I need bandages and shoes. None of which we've gotten here.

'You ready?' says Cabressa. There's no trace of empathy on his face. No gratitude.

I glare at him. The asshole. And wish I'd left him in the river to die.

He looks away first, fiddling with his jacket. When he turns back towards me the gun is in his hand.

I stare at the weapon. 'Why didn't you use that on the bridge?'

He holds my gaze. 'There were a lot more of them than I've got bullets.'

I don't know how many bullets he has left, but the Glock 21 holds ten so he must be almost out. 'A warning shot would have scared them. They weren't hardened criminals, just people going a little crazy in the anarchy of the blackout.'

Cabressa shrugs. 'Maybe so. But I wanted to save these bullets.'

He cocks his head to one side. 'Can't go giving up my advantage over you now, can I?'

I frown. 'You could have died on the bridge, or in the water.'

He smiles – a sickly sweet grin, fake as sweetener in tea. 'I've learned enough about you to know you wouldn't let me die.'

'Why's that?'

His smile widens. 'Because then you wouldn't get to try and kill me yourself, Herron.'

'Like I told you, I'm not Herron.'

'Yet here we still are.'

I push my hair out of my face, and that's when I realise it's gone – the micro camera. It must have gotten loose in the river and washed away.

My heart starts to race. That means Monroe doesn't have eyes and ears on me for sure. I'm alone now – alone with a gun-toting, murderous mobster. It's not the first time, but that's of no comfort right now.

'Come on,' says Cabressa, gesturing up the bank with the barrel of the Glock. 'Let's get to the hotel.'

I nod, and make like I'm wringing the water out of my dress. Cabressa looks twitchy, moving his weight from foot to foot, and I see that he's still favouring the left leg over the right, although he's doing his best to hide the fact.

There's things whirring about in my mind. When did the micro camera stop transmitting? What was the last thing Monroe witnessed? And, if Monroe saw us surrounded by the fighting looters – knew that we were in danger – and then watched as I plummeted down from the bridge into the river with Cabressa, why the hell didn't he send a team to come pull us out?

Unable to put it off any longer, I start to move. I climb up the concrete steps behind Cabressa, trying not to wince each time my injured feet hit the ground. I can't afford to show weakness. Not now. Not when I don't know for sure if Monroe knows where I am and where we're going.

There are four blocks to my hotel, and I have to be prepared for the fact that Monroe might not know what's happening; the micro camera could have stopped transmitting at any point after my call with him back at the moment of the blackout. If that's the case, I've gotten the time it takes for us to travel four blocks to think on a plan.

Of one thing I'm real sure – there's no way I'm going to give Cabressa the last chess piece and let him kill me.

61

It takes them another ten minutes to reach the ground. By the time they do, JT's thigh muscles are cramping and Carmella is struggling to breathe. The lack of oxygen is still affecting her, JT notices. He looks at her, concerned. If she's coming with him to find Lori and Cabressa he hopes she'll be able to keep up.

Carmella sees him looking. 'It's my asthma, okay? Just give me a minute. I don't have my inhaler.'

JT nods. Scans their surroundings through the darkness but doesn't recognise the area. Tall buildings loom over them, ghostly without light. From what he's seen he figures they've come down around back. He needs to get to the front entrance of the Skyland Tower to get his bearings and work out the fastest way to the hotel where Lori and him have been staying. He glances back at Carmella. She's doubled over with her hands on her knees. Her long black hair is hanging over her face, obscuring her expression.

In the distance he hears the wail of cop car sirens. He can't wait any longer.

'Come on,' he says to Carmella. 'We need to go.'

Straightening up, she follows him around the building towards the front. He stays alert, keeps scouring their surroundings for threats as they head down the steps and onto the sidewalk.

Carmella halts. Sniffs the air. 'What's that?'

There's a burning smell, like rubber and gasoline. Next moment there's a crash and the sound of glass shattering. It's not real close, but close enough. JT grimaces. 'Looters.'

'But the smell, it's like...' Wide-eyed and shaky, her previous cool is gone. Carmella doesn't need to finish the sentence for JT to understand.

He guesses what it reminds her of – the most traumatic thing in her life, and the discovery that kick-started the chain of events that led to this moment; her papa being burned alive. 'We need to keep moving. Are you able to do that?'

Carmella nods. JT hopes she's right.

They move through the streets towards the river. Stick close to the buildings. Stay deep in the shadows.

Windows have been smashed. Vehicles battered and set alight. Couches have been pulled from buildings and destroyed. Debris is scattered over the blacktop. Up ahead looters run from building to building. Some carry flaming torches, others have armfuls of stolen items.

'Jeez,' says JT. 'We have to get away from here.'

Carmella doesn't speak. She stands stock-still. Wide-eyed. Non-responsive.

'Come on,' JT says, his tone urgent. Grabbing Carmella's hand, he pulls her into a run. Forces her to keep moving. Can't afford to hang around.

They keep running until they reach the river.

Then they have to stop because of the flames.

62

We travel the four blocks in silence. The streets are deserted this side of the river, but they bear the scars of the angry crowds that have passed through them – vehicles lie upturned and burning, stores with shattered windows sit ransacked, their goods strewn across the sidewalks and streets. Debris and glass crunches beneath Cabressa's shoes as we walk. A little ways behind him, I pick my way through it, trying not to injure my bare feet more. The pain is getting worse, but I keep on going. Heading back towards my and JT's hotel.

JT. My heart lurches as I think of him – of how I had to stay with Cabressa to save Otis, even though it was futile in the end. JT's expression as I stepped away from the door and he realised I wasn't going with him – like I'd betrayed him – it makes me shudder. I wonder where he is now, if he's safe and clear of the penthouse. Can't think on the alternative. Have to believe he'll be okay. Have to believe we'll be reunited soon.

My fear for JT's safety fires my hatred for Cabressa. Cabressa and Monroe. Two men who've used me in their game like one of the gold pawns in the chess set – a disposable player in the game.

A few blocks ahead I see a cop car speed across the intersection, blue light flashing but siren turned off. There's no other traffic on the streets. No people. The post-apocalyptic feeling is back. The quiet seems eerie and unnatural.

'We nearly there?' growls Cabressa, his voice loud in the silence.

'The hotel's another block away,' I say. I keep my voice low. Don't want to attract attention if there are people around here, lurking in the darkness.

'You kept them in your hotel room? Jesus!' Cabressa shakes his head as he keeps trudging along the sidewalk. 'I thought our intelligence was complete. Guess I should have had you watched.'

I don't reply. We're both exhausted, but he's the one with the gun – the advantage. I need to think on a way to get the upper hand. I could escape, sure, but that isn't enough. I need to have Cabressa taken into custody. He cannot be allowed to get away with the things he's done tonight – all the people he's killed.

As I walk, I think. My Taser is back in the Skyland Tower – confiscated by Carmella's security when I entered the penthouse and then taken down to the floor below for safekeeping. JT's weapon is there too. Lost to me, at least for now. I think on what else I brought with me. Remember the pepper spray I always keep in my purse, and the plasticuffs too. It's not much, but it's something more than nothing. If I can get to the pepper spray, use it on Cabressa, it could give me enough time to snatch the gun.

We reach the end of the block. As we turn the corner I see the hotel looming up ahead. Like the other buildings around us, it's shrouded in darkness. The fountains out front are silent; the water lying still like a dark pool. I point towards the entrance to the foyer. 'This is it,' I say.

Cabressa nods. 'Good.'

As we move closer I see faint glows from some of the windows. It's people using flashlights and candles I'm guessing. I glance at Cabressa. The fact I know there are people in the hotel is no kind of comfort – if he fires the gun a stray bullet could injure someone. I cannot allow that to happen.

Stepping to the entrance I take hold of the door and pull. It doesn't open. Stays wedged shut. I scan the entrance. See the door release and press it. Nothing happens. 'It needs power.'

'Goddammit.' Cabressa pushes past me and grabs the door handle. He grunts as he yanks it hard, forcing the heavy door open. He steps through and then looks back at me. 'What are you waiting for?'

This is it, the moment of reckoning. I take one last look at the desolate street – searching for help that I now know isn't coming – then look up at the sky. My watch stopped working after we hit the river, but we must still be hours from dawn. There's no moon, no stars – nothing and no one to bear witness to the events of this deep dark night.

No one, except me.

63

The bridge is on fire. Flames leap and crackle into the air. Their orange, red and gold colours reflect in the water below, like two fires instead of one.

'Jeez.' JT clenches his jaw. Wonders how the hell he's going to get to Lori.

Beside him, Carmella stares at the flaming barricade on the bridge. She's shaking her head. Her lower lip quivers. 'This is all my fault. I only thought about revenge on the men in the penthouse. I didn't imagine what would happen on the streets after the blackout.'

JT agrees; it is her fault, but there's no sense in having that conversation here and now. 'We need another way across. We can't continue along the main street or we'll get caught up in that crowd.' He steps to the edge of the sidewalk, bordering the river, and scans along the water to his right and left. Every bridge has been lit up. 'And there's no way across from here anyways.' He clenches his fists. Doesn't want to admit defeat, but he's got nothing. Turns to Carmella. 'With all the bridges out, how the hell can we get to the other hotel?'

Carmella thinks for a moment, then turns back towards the direction they've just come. 'I know a way that might work. Follow me.'

They run through the streets, zig-zagging through the blocks, with Carmella in the lead. When they see groups of people up ahead, they divert. When they pass flaming debris and vehicles, Carmella turns her head away.

They keep running.

Minutes pass.

To JT it seems as if they're moving away from the river.

It's another few minutes before Carmella stops. Bending over, coughing, she struggles to catch her breath. When she straightens up, wheezing, she looks real pale.

JT looks around at their surroundings. They're on the corner of some block; he can't read the street names because of the lack of light.

'Does your cell still have juice?' Carmella asks.

JT pulls the phone from his pocket and checks the screen. 'Juice but no service.'

Carmella smiles. 'We won't need service where we're going – just light.'

He doesn't know what she means. Frowns. 'Okay.'

'This way,' says Carmella, heading around the corner.

JT follows. A few steps onto the next street Carmella points towards a building a little ways ahead, and he gets what she's planning.

He smiles at her. Nods. 'Good call.'

'The tunnels go under the river. With the power off, we should be able to run through them.'

It's a smart play. He hopes, unlike the bridges, the tunnels have been unscathed by the looting mobs.

Carmella pushes open the door and leads him across the foyer. She turns, and announces through the gloom, 'Welcome to the L.'

JT switches on the flashlight app of his phone, illuminating the subway station's foyer. It's deserted now. Only discarded food wrappers and newspapers, and the sickly-sweet smell of fresh sweat indicate that there've been people here recently. He spots the ticket machines over on the wall, turnstiles up ahead and beyond them the stairs that lead down towards the platforms.

There's no sign of fire. No sign of trouble.

Hurrying across the foyer to the stiles, JT grabs the barrier with one hand and vaults over. Turning back towards Carmella, he gestures for her to do the same.

Together they run down the stairs and towards the subway tunnels.

64

I can hear them in the darkness, the people in the rooms along this hallway. Hear their hushed voices from behind the closed doors. See the soft glow under some of the doors. The people here are hiding out until the blackout is over or the sunlight returns. I wish I was one of them, but I don't have that luxury. What I have is Cabressa breathing down my neck, and the barrel of his gun in my back.

We take the stairs to the fifth floor. My thigh muscles burn from the climb. Every step sends vibrations through my body, making the pain in my ribs worse. Cabressa's limp is more pronounced, but aside from that he's in good shape. Better shape than me, anyways.

We hustle along the hallway. After the fanciness of the Skyland Tower, this hotel seems plain and basic. Bland cream walls and beige-carpeted halls, no art or mirrors, no lighting either, aside from a green-tinged emergency lamp recessed into the wall at the end of each hallway.

It seems quieter up here, and for that I'm thankful. If I'm right, and Cabressa means to kill me once he has the final chess piece, he won't want any witnesses. I hope to hell the guests on this floor stay in their rooms. Don't want him to have any excuse to kill again.

He prods me with the gun. 'Move it.'

I hadn't realised I'd slowed my pace, but I guess I had. Subconsciously trying to delay us reaching the room. I lengthen my stride. Move a little faster. We reach the end of this hallway and turn into the next. I can see my and JT's room a little ways ahead. There's no sign of Monroe. No sign of the SWAT team.

My stomach flips. I'm alone. And I'm running out of time.

I stop outside the room. Removing my water-sodden phone from my bra, I take the hotel room keycard from the pouch on the back and hold it against the sensor. I know it's pointless with the blackout, but I'm trying to buy some time. As predicted, nothing happens.

Cabressa frowns. 'You got the right room? You trying to fool me.'

'There's no power, that's why it isn't working.'

He prods the gun harder into my ribs. 'Get us in.'

I bite back a gasp. Won't let him see the pain he's so casually inflicting on me. 'I'm doing my best.'

I try the handle and the door opens. Weird. It was locked when me and JT left earlier. The power outage must have caused all the doors to unlock. I think of the looters who'd clashed on the bridge, and of the smashed storefronts and stolen goods, and hope none of them realised hotel rooms were easy targets too.

Pushing the door open, I lead Cabressa into the room.

'Where is it?' he growls.

I don't answer. The room is just as JT and me left it. My go-bag on the floor by my side of the king bed, his on the armchair in the corner. The table we used to practise poker, the deck of cards sitting on the corner, the stacks of coloured chips lined up like soldiers alongside them. There's still the faint tang of JT's cologne in the air – a zesty lemon freshness mixed with a hint of his smokes.

It makes me think of the moment I left him in the penthouse.

My breath catches in the back of my throat. I feel emotion start to build inside me, and I push it away. JT is savvy and skilled and I cannot think on the possibility of him not making it. I have to believe that he's fine. And if I want to survive this, I have to keep my head in the game.

I glance across at the central air vent in the corner of the room. There's no sign of the knight through the slats of the vent – no light to reflect against its gold body – but still I fancy that I can see it.

'Where is it then?' repeats Cabressa. 'You said you left it in here.'

'I did,' I say.

I walk across the room. Pick up the chair, just as I did before, and position it under the vent. Taking a screwdriver from my go-bag I climb onto the chair and undo each of the screws that hold the grill in place.

As the final screw comes loose, and I prepare to lift the grill away from the wall, Cabressa moves closer to me. I glance down at him.

He pokes the gun into my calf. 'What are you waiting for?'

I don't answer. I know he's most likely going to kill me once he's got the knight. If I'm going to act, it has to be now. And I sure as hell am going to act.

As I slowly remove the grill, I rehearse my next moves in my mind: step down from the chair; step clear of the chair, in front of Cabressa with his back to the wall; make like I'm handing him the knight, and as his focus shifts to taking it from me, punch him in the gut and grab the gun.

I drop the grill onto the floor. Take the knight out of the vent.

'Set it down on the table,' says Cabressa.

I look down at him. This isn't part of the plan. 'What?'

He's moving away from the chair, from me. Backing across the room. He gestures towards the table with the gun. 'Put it on there, then stand by the wall.'

Damn. He's out of range. If I make a move now he'll shoot me before I reach him. By my calculation he's gotten two bullets left. At this range he'll only need one.

I move real slow. Try to think of another way to turn this situation upside down. Come up with nothing.

'The table, now,' Cabressa says. He's looking twitchy, shifting his weight from foot to foot.

I take my time. Step down from the chair. Move to put the knight onto the table. Watch Cabressa, waiting for him to look at the chess piece, to lower his guard and give me a chance to make a move. But he keeps his eyes on me, doesn't look at the knight, even when I set it down and let go.

'Turn around and face the wall, Herron,' Cabressa says.

My heart accelerates. I know what this means, how it goes. And how it goes is real bad. I shake my head. 'I'm not Herron.'

'Another lie,' he says. 'I said, turn around.'

I stay where I am. Play the only move I've got – a last chance all-in bluff. 'You want me to face the wall because you can't even look me in the eye as you shoot me.' I shake my head. Act like I'm disgusted. 'What kind of a man are you?'

'This is the kind of man I am, Miss Anderson,' he says, jabbing the barrel of the gun into my side. 'I'm the man who's neutralising the Miami Mob's attempt to take over my city. Your body will send a message to Old Man Bonchese and Carlton North that Chicago is my city, and if I find anyone from Miami trying to take over my business I will eliminate them.' He thrusts the gun into my side again. Pushes me back against the wall.

Pain spikes through me, but I don't let him see. Like a cow horse on a dude ranch, I've had enough of getting dug in the ribs. It's time Cabressa got him some manners. Instead of moving away, I grab the gun and pull it hard towards me. Wrong-footed, Cabressa loses his balance and steps towards me.

Keeping hold of the gun I step to the side and swing my other elbow, jabbing it hard into his nose. He reels away from the blow, but keeps hold of the gun. I move with him. Lock both hands over his and try to turn the gun away from me, towards him.

Fail.

Keep trying.

Beneath my hands, I feel his fingers move.

The gun bucks beneath my grasp. The noise of the shot is real loud.

I feel it like a punch to the stomach.

I hunch over, the breath knocked out of me.

The heat spreads through my hands. I smell the cordite.

But I don't let go. Won't let go. Cannot give up.

I launch myself at Cabressa, slamming my head into his nose. Feel the impact; bone on bone. Hear a crack, and he cries out in pain. He loosens his grip on the gun, and I snatch it away. Aim it at him. Grab some plasticuffs from my go-bag. 'Turn around. Hands behind your back.'

'You're going to regret this, you—'

'Shut the hell up,' I say, jamming the barrel of the gun into his ribs, just like he's done so many times to me. I get no pleasure in it though. The asshole deserves a hell of a lot worse. I imagine how it would feel to put the gun to *his* head. To press it against *his* skull. And pull the trigger. I remember all the people he's killed tonight and figure it'd feel pretty good to serve a rough kind of justice. But I don't. Because then I think of JT, and how he'd look at me if I shot an unarmed man, and the disappointment I know he'd feel that I let this mob boss take the easy way out. And he'd be right. Cabressa needs to pay for his crimes. A bullet in the head is too good for him.

I repeat the command, slow and firm. 'Put. Your hands. Behind. Your back.'

Cabressa doesn't respond. Doesn't move.

I brace myself. Get ready for him to fight back. 'I'm the one with the gun now. Don't *you* make me use it.'

He's silent for a long moment, then he cusses, a stream of bile and anger, calling me all kinds of names. He smacks his hand against the table, and the knight jumps, toppling over and falling. It hits the ground and rolls across the carpet, disappearing under the table.

If it was an attempt at diversion, it doesn't work. I keep the gun pointed at him. Slowly he turns around and puts his hands behind his back.

I snap the plasticuffs into place. I'm not gentle. Sharp pain shoots through my ribs, joined with another throbbing, deeper pain in my side from the movement, but I pay it no mind, stay focused on the job in hand. When it's done, I take a step back, keeping the gun pointed at Cabressa, and say, 'Turn back around.'

As he starts to move my vision swims and he becomes blurry. All of a sudden I feel real lightheaded. The pain is getting worse, the throbbing intensifying. I put my hand against my side and wince. Feel dampness.

Fighting back the urge to throw up, I look down.

That's when I realise I'm bleeding.

65

They run from the L station. JT doesn't know how long it takes – five minutes, ten, more – it doesn't matter. His lungs are heavy, his stride faltering, but he will not rest until he's found Lori.

Carmella's right beside him as he throws the door to the hotel open and hurries inside. They sprint along the dark corridor with only the ghostly green-tinged emergency lighting to guide them. JT navigates the familiar layout and heads to the stairwell.

He takes the stairs two at a time. Carmella's breathing is laboured, the wheeze of her inhale becoming more pronounced. JT doesn't slow down; he can't wait for her now. They're too close to stop. He has to get to Lori.

Carmella's still a flight of stairs behind when he reaches the fifth floor. He pushes open the door. Calls over his shoulder, 'Room 514.'

'I'll find you.'

He sprints down the hallway. Stays light on his feet, keeping his footfalls muffled. Makes it back to the room he'd left hours earlier, at the start of the night, and stops.

The door's closed. There's no noise from inside.

He shoulders the door. Puts all his bulk into the movement. It flies open and he lurches into the room. Behind him, back in the hallway, he can hear Carmella's footsteps getting closer.

He stops inside. Sees Cabressa, half turned against the wall. His hands are cuffed and he's cussing a stream of obscenities as he wrestles against the cuffs. Lori has a gun pointed at the mobster's head. 'I said turn around.'

'Lori.' JT feels relief flooding through him. She's okay, she's alive, and she's gotten Cabressa restrained. Everything is good.

Then she turns towards him.

Lori smiles, but her eyes are dazed, unfocused. Her gun-free hand is pressed against her side. It's covered in blood, and there's a gash in her dress, the skin beneath is stained crimson.

'Lori, oh Jeez.'

'JT?' She drops the gun. Raises her bloody hand towards her face. 'I feel so...'

He races to her. Tries to grab her as she loses consciousness but fails to reach her in time. She falls. Her head hits the edge of the table on the way down.

In the doorway, Carmella whispers a prayer.

There's a click as the bathroom door unlocks. Special Agent Monroe – all cockatoo hair and gangly limbs – hurries out; he's got his gun in one hand, his badge in the other. 'FBI, everyone stay where you are.'

Cabressa cusses again. Wrestles harder against the cuffs.

JT wrenches his gaze from Lori to Monroe. Frowns. Doesn't understand. 'You were here? What the hell happened?'

'He wasn't here,' says Cabressa. 'I've never seen him.'

'Shut up,' Monroe says to Cabressa. 'Eyes to the wall.'

JT notices movement by the door.

It's Carmella reversing away from the room. There are tears on her cheeks. Sorrow in her eyes. As she meets JT's gaze she mouths the words, 'Forgive me.'

And then she's gone.

66

I wake up on the floor. The carpet is prickly against my face, and the room seems to be moving, revolving. My vision's blurred, but ahead of me, underneath the table, I can make out the golden colour and shape of the knight. It comes back to me then – Cabressa, the gunshot – and immediately a throbbing pain explodes in my side. It takes my breath away, and I gasp, try to turn over, to see where Cabressa is, whether he's going to shoot me again.

'It's okay, Lori. I've got you.' It's JT's voice, strong and gravelly and all kinds of soothing. I can't see him but it feels good to know that he's there.

'Cabressa?' I croak the name, the word scratchy in my throat. 'Did he...?'

'You got him.' There's pride in JT's voice, but it's mixed with something else I can't place. 'Monroe's read him his rights. He's going into custody.'

My mind feels mushy, like I'm on go-slow. I try to think on what happened, but my memory's fragmented, like a movie that's skipping scenes. I remember removing the vent, Cabressa taking the knight, and wrestling him for the gun, but nothing more. 'I don't remember.'

'It doesn't matter.' I feel JT's hand on my shoulder. He slides his fingers upward until he's caressing the back of my neck. 'None of it matters.'

I try to turn towards him, wanting to see his face, but the pain kicks into my side harder, like a bucking horse on a last hurrah. I cry out. Can't help it.

'Medics are on the way,' JT says, his voice more urgent. 'They're taking longer because of the chaos, but they'll be here real soon.'

'Then we can go home to Dakota.'

'Yes we can.' I hear it now, the fear laced into his voice.

That's when I know I should be worried.

'How's she doing?' It's Monroe's voice, more distant – seems like he's a million miles away to me.

JT's voice is hushed. Harder to make out, but I catch some of the words. '...lot of blood ... where the hell ... if I lose her you'll never...'

My memory starts to return; the last twelve hours replaying on fast forward across my mind's eye. Playing poker, the blackout, the electronic voice saying one of us in the penthouse was Herron, and the decontamination procedure – all the people who died. Then I remember the micro camera and the SWAT team that never came. All the chances I gave Monroe to find us, to help us; and the fact that no help arrived. Anger courses through my body. I want to know why he didn't come. Why he abandoned us. 'Monroe...'

'He's here too.'

I try to shake my head, but can't get it to move.

'It's okay, just lie still,' says JT.

I want to hold his hand, but again my body won't obey me. My teeth start to chatter. Coldness spreads through me – my skin, my flesh, my bones – and I feel tired, so very tired. 'JT?' I say. My voice sounds weak, alien.

'I'm right here.'

'I feel ... weird.'

'You just need to rest,' he says. His voice cracks. I feel his fingers leave my neck. Sense that he's moving away. Then I hear his voice again, further from me now; a fast, angry whisper. 'Monroe, get the medics here, now. She's going into shock.'

'They're on their way.' Monroe's drawl seems laid back, relaxed, compared to JT's. 'Things are tricky out—'

'You said that before. Get them here *now*. Use a chopper. Anything.' JT's tone is granite hard and laced with fury. There's a bang, like a fist connecting with a wall. Then JT growls, 'I won't lose her.'

That's when I know something's wrong for sure. JT never panics. He never loses his cool.

'JT?' The word is hard to force out. My throat's dry. My lips cracked. The weakness of my voice makes it sound as if it belongs to someone else.

Footsteps hurry towards me. I feel his hand on my shoulder again, and the warmth of his body next to mine. 'I'm right here.'

I smile. Even that seems like an effort. 'I'm tired.'

'I know, baby.' He takes my hand in his. Strokes my palm.

'Tell me it'll be okay.'

He squeezes my hand. Doesn't hesitate. 'It's going to all be okay.'

'Thank you,' I say, my voice barely a whisper. And I mean it.

His words give me comfort, even though I know they can't be true.

67

He won't lose her. Can't lose her. She's slumped in his arms. Unconscious. Her pulse is barely there. He knows that without medical attention she's not going to last much longer.

'How far out are they?' JT yells at Monroe. 'Tell me that.'

Monroe barks something into his sat phone. Gets a rapid answer back. 'Five minutes, could be ten,' he says to JT.

'Wrong answer.' JT looks down at Lori. She's so pale she looks dead already. 'She doesn't have that long.'

He hears Monroe barking more instructions into the sat phone. Tunes out from the conversation – concentrates on Lori. He checks her pulse again. It's getting slower. Pulls off his jacket and puts it over her. Needs to try and stop her falling too deep into shock.

'Five minutes,' Monroe shouts. 'They can make it in five.'

JT can't bite back the anger any longer. He wants to grab the scrawny asshole and give him a beating he'd never forget. But he doesn't. He can't. He cannot leave Lori's side.

'It'll be okay,' says Monroe.

JT glances over at him. He's standing over Cabressa, who's now lying face down on the carpet. The mobster's hands are still cuffed behind his back, and Monroe's added ankle cuffs to be sure. He looks like one of those bastard big-game hunters with their trophy kill. Except in this case he didn't even bag the trophy. Lori did. And it's gotten her killed.

JT scowls at Monroe. 'You did this.'

'She was perfectly fine. In control the whole way, I was watching on the micro camera feed and I could—'

'Where were you before I arrived?' JT's voice is getting louder, his fury rising higher. 'Hiding in the goddamn bathroom, that's where. You could have stepped in. You should have stopped this—'

There's a flurry of words from the sat phone. Monroe turns away. 'Yes. Yes. We will.'

'They're landing on the street out front. They won't be able to stay there long – it's crazy out there. We need to hurry.'

'Okay.'

Monroe lunges towards him. Grips his arm. 'Don't tell anyone what happened here, okay? You let me do the talking. Stay quiet.'

JT stares at Monroe. Can't believe even he could sink so low. Shakes off his hand.

Monroe acts like it's no big deal. He moves towards the door, pushing Cabressa, shuffling, in front of him. Monroe turns. 'They'll be landing any minute. Are you coming?'

'Yes.' JT scoops Lori's limp body into his arms and gently lifts her. Cradling her head against his chest, he strides to the door. Glares at Monroe. 'But know this: if Lori dies, I will hunt you down and I will kill you.'

68

I wake up to the sound of beeping. It's cold in here, and the air smells of antiseptic and bleach. My eyelids feel heavy, and my mouth is real dry. Every bit of me aches.

I can guess where I am. These sounds and smells are familiar from all the treatment Dakota had to endure. But things were different then. I wasn't the one in the bed. I force open my eyes. They feel scratchy, itchy. And I see that I was right.

I'm in a hospital bed, hooked up to machines; there's a heart-rate monitor, an IV pump, and some other thing I don't recognise. It's bright in here – it seems unnaturally so – with the white walls and floors, and the lights on full.

Lights. They could be from a back-up generator, I guess, but maybe the blackout is over.

JT is slumped in a chair to the side of my bed, his head is bowed, and his stubble-covered chin rests part on his shoulder and part on the headrest. He's asleep. I watch the rhythmic rise and fall of his breathing. Notice the cuts and bruises on his face, his arms and his knuckles. He's frowning in his sleep, and every few moments his eyelids flicker and his fists clench. I wonder what he's dreaming about.

There's a dull throbbing in my side. I try to sit up, to see what's going on down there. I've only moved a fraction when the pain spikes deep inside me. I gasp. Drop back down to the pillows. Fight back the urge to be sick.

'Lori?' There's concern in JT's voice. Relief too. He rubs the sleep from his eyes. 'You're back.'

'Sure am.' I manage a small smile. My face feels odd, rubbery somehow. I glance down at my body. 'I was trying to check out the damage.'

'Ah.' From the look on his face I can tell he doesn't think that's a good idea.

'You going to help me?'

'Sure.' Getting up, he steps over to the bed and gently pulls back the covers.

Although all I'm able to do without pain is raise my head a little, it's enough. I see the thick white compression bandage wrapped around my torso, and I know things are serious. 'What happened?'

JT shakes his head. 'That asshole Cabressa shot you.'

I try to remember. Everything seems hazy, like I'm seeing the memories of last night play on a movie screen covered in a dark veil. I close my eyes. Focus harder – trying to cut through the drugs that are dulling my senses. But I can't recall what happened. I keep my eyes closed. Keep trying. After what seems like forever the veil drops and I remember everything, as if in HD.

Opening my eyes, I meet JT's gaze. 'We both had the gun. I was trying to disarm him. He pulled the trigger.'

'You got him though. You must have fought back even after you were shot. When I came into the room you'd gotten him cuffed.'

'I wasn't going to let him get away with what he did. He killed Anton and Mikey. Otis and Thomas, too.' My voice is rasping against my parched throat. There's a tippy cup on the side table. 'Could you pass me the water?'

'Sure.'

He does and I take a sip. The water feels like liquid needles against my raw throat.

'You should know...' JT exhales hard. 'Anton, Mikey and Otis weren't the only ones who died last night.'

I stare at him. Wait for him to continue.

He runs a hand over the stubble on his chin. 'Johnny and Carl didn't make it.'

'What happened?'

The question hangs in the space between us. The machines beep on.

JT says nothing. Looks real conflicted.

I break the stalemate. 'Where's Carmella?'

He shakes his head. 'She's gone. In the wind.'

'I don't understand—'

He glances over his shoulder towards the closed door. Moves closer to me, crouching down so he can whisper in my ear. 'It was her. She got that specific group of men together for a reason; she orchestrated the power outage, she set up the electronic voice and the penthouse lockdown, and initiated the decontamination process. The voice recordings implied one of them was Herron for a reason – she knew they'd fight, that none of them would want to reveal their secrets or lose face. She meant for those men to either kill each other or be arrested and jailed for killing.'

It doesn't make sense. 'Why?'

'Because those men were all part of a development project that destroyed her family. Her father was leading the residents' group against the development – so they had him killed. Her mother hung herself a little while after. Carmella was just a teenager, a few years older than Dakota is. She ended up on the street.' JT shakes his head. 'It doesn't make it right, but she wanted to destroy those men – to make them pay for what they did to her family.'

I give a slight nod, as much as I can manage. I can understand why Carmella did what she did. I've felt those feelings of revenge myself. I know how powerful a motivator they are, but also that they're a false promise. I know from experience how empty you feel after you've gotten revenge. How it doesn't make the loss you've experienced any easier to bear. 'Shit.'

'Yeah.'

'But she didn't try to kill you?'

'Not once she knew the truth. She'd assumed we were mob, because Cabressa was so insistent you came to the game. She hadn't wanted anyone in the penthouse except for the men in-volved in the property syndicate, but she couldn't refuse Cabressa and risk alienating him, and it was too late to call off the game. So she went ahead. Figured that you were mob so if you got taken out then it was collateral damage she could live with. I wouldn't have been in the penthouse at all if Cabressa hadn't insisted you made the call to get the knight delivered to the suite. She had to change the electronic recording when the lockdown happened and I was inside. Everyone had to have a secret revealed, so she made up a secret for me. Each person had a secret – but only one was Herron.'

'So Carmella was Herron?'

'As far as anyone ever was, yes. See, Herron was a myth – just a part of the set-up. She paid a lot of bribes to people with the skills she needed to make the plan work, and used the same tactic to get Herron's name whispered whenever things went wrong on the street. When attacks and thefts went unclaimed, the rumours started that it was Herron's doing. It didn't take long for people to believe them.'

'You felt sorry for her, so you let her go. Even though she was responsible for people dying?'

He doesn't speak, but I can see from his expression that I'm right.

'She was in the hotel last night. I saw her.'

'Yeah,' says JT. 'And now she's gone.'

'You tell Monroe about her?'

He shakes his head. Grimaces. 'You know how I feel about that guy.'

'Yeah.' Me and him both.

'Shit, Lori. This...' JT gestures to the hospital room, my wounds. 'It's real bad.'

I fake a smile. Try to lighten the mood. 'You should have seen the other guy.'

'I did.'

'Then you know I didn't let him get off so lightly.'

'I thought you weren't going to make it.' He takes my hand. Squeezes it. 'You almost didn't. If that had happened, I couldn't have ... Dakota would have...'

'I know.'

There's nothing I can say to change the situation; JT's speaking the truth. I've been shot twice in the last three jobs I've done. That's double the number of gunshot wounds I've gotten in the rest of my career before that. And there's a common factor in both. His name's Special Agent Alex Monroe.

I meet JT's gaze. 'Something needs to change.'

69

Monroe keeps jawing on, but I don't hear a word he says. Instead, all I can hear is the voice in my head screaming at him: *Liar, liar, liar*.

I hold up my hand to stop him. Even through the morphine the small movement hurts like a bitch. 'Why are you here?'

He frowns. Looks real confused. 'Like I've been saying, we've got him. It's a watertight case. All the evidence we've got, your testimony – he's going to jail, no way to dodge it this time.'

'How much did you get on camera?'

'All of it, Lori, we got the whole damn thing.'

'Really?' There's doubt in my voice. Enough, I hope, to get Monroe to talk me through the detail of what the micro camera captured.

He takes the bait. 'We've got it from the moment you stepped into that elevator and went up to the penthouse suite, until you cuffed him in your hotel room. We've got what he said, what he did, and what he planned to do. It's multiple homicide, clear and simple. There's no wriggle room.'

'So the micro camera kept working even after I jumped into the river?'

He nods. 'They're robust little suckers.'

'Huh. I thought I'd lost it.'

'After the medics did their thing, my tech team checked you out and retrieved it. It'd dislodged from the original spot in your hairline, ended up down near your ear, so the picture angle in the last section of footage is sort of wonky, but the audio's good.' He looks real pleased with himself.

I muster my strength. Fix Monroe with a hard stare. 'So you knew the whole time I was out on the street, and in my hotel room with him, that Cabressa meant to kill me?'

Monroe glances away. Doesn't reply.

'You didn't step in when he put the gun to my head, even though you were right there in the bathroom?' My voice sounds stronger now; the anger overcoming the weakness of before. 'And don't deny you were in the bathroom. I saw you. As I started to fall, I saw you open the bathroom door.'

Monroe runs his hand through his hair, pulling at the unruly tufts. 'It wasn't like—'

'Save the bullshit.' I look from him to the machines, and back again. 'All this here,' I say. 'You're paying for it.'

It's not a question.

Monroe nods. 'Least I can do.'

I narrow my eyes. 'Yeah. It is. Totally the least you can do. Because you could have stopped this happening.'

He looks away. Fiddles with the cuff of his suit jacket.

'So why didn't you?'

'Things aren't always black and white, Lori.'

'Next you'll be telling me there's a line that gets blurry.'

'Well—'

I glare at him. 'You were watching the feed. You saw what he did. Heard what he intended to do.'

'I needed the case to be strong. The more evidence I had that—'

'So, what: you wanted him to kill me? For me to be another homicide added to his tally. A lot of people died last night. They didn't need to. You could have—'

'Hold up.' Monroe puts his hands up in surrender. 'I didn't want it to get that far.'

'Sure, you say that now, but you could have stepped in at anytime. You had the SWAT team in position, you had yourself, but you chose to stand by and not intervene.' I stare at him. Frown. 'You disgust me.'

'Look, if it helps, I'm sorry.'

He doesn't look sorry. And his half-assed apology is nothing more than a crock of shit. From my silence he seems to realise I'm not buying it.

'Look I really am sorry,' he says. 'I messed up, okay? I get that. I got caught up in the high of finally having the evidence to convict the bastard. I've been after him for so many years, gotten so close but never made anything stick.' He shakes his head, and points towards me. 'You've changed all that, Lori. Together we've put a monster away. We should be proud.'

I don't reply. I don't deny Cabressa needed to go to jail. I just don't think I should've had to nearly die to make it happen. The machines around me beep and click. The bright white room feels claustrophobic with Monroe inside it.

He steps closer to the bed. 'We make a good partnership. We get stuff done, important stuff. We're a team now, Lori, we make a difference, we owe it to—'

'No.' I stop him mid-flow. Can't listen to any more of his delusions. 'It doesn't work for me. I could have been killed, and you would have stood back, stayed in the bathroom hiding, and let it happen.'

'I wouldn't have done that. Like I said, if I really thought you couldn't get out of the situation I'd have stormed in and—'

'Like I told you, I don't believe you.'

He shrugs. 'Well, I guess it is what it is then.'

'Yeah,' I say. Fixing him with a hard stare. 'And what it is, is done.'

Monroe shakes his head. He smiles, but there's no joy in it. 'It's done when I say so.'

The anger flares inside me. 'You don't own me. I've paid back the debt for your help. We're even. And we're done.'

He's shaking his head. 'If you think I'm going to just walk away from—'

'I do think that. And I will not work with you again.' I hold

Monroe's gaze, and make my voice firm, strong. 'So this is the situation: You're an asshole. My debt is paid. And, like I said, this here between us – it's done.'

We glare at each other.

After a long moment, he nods once. 'Well then, I guess this is goodbye.'

I'm all talked out. I've got nothing left to say to him. So I just stare back at him, my expression emotionless, until eventually he turns and leaves the room.

As the door closes behind him I sink back down against the pillows.

Take a deep breath.

And hope to hell my alliance with Monroe *is* finally over.

70

They insist on wheeling me out to the parking lot in a wheelchair. I argue that if I'm well enough to be discharged, I'm well enough to walk, but the medical staff won't allow it. They quote hospital protocol, health-and-safety guidelines, or some such nonsense. In the end I give in and sit in the damn chair. Figure I'll get the hell out of there faster if I do.

JT walks alongside me, carrying the bag with my stuff inside. It feels strange being back outside in the daylight with the sun on my skin. My room in the hospital didn't have a window, and my last memories of the outside world are the darkness of the black-out. It kind of feels like, having been removed from the real world, I'm now getting released back into the wild. It's a good feeling, freedom. Even though I'm under stern instructions to take things easy and rest up, give my body time to heal.

The orderly – an older guy with slicked-back salt-and-pepper hair and a kindly manner – wheels me all the way up to our rental car, then bends down and applies the chair's brakes. 'Here we are.'

JT unlocks the white SUV. Opening the passenger door, he slings my bag onto the backseat, then turns to face me. 'You ready?'

'Sure am.' I push myself out of the chair and turn stiffly to look at the orderly. My vision swims a little from the movement, and it takes me a moment to get my balance back. Now that I'm upright, I feel kind of wobbly. Maybe the chair was a good idea after all. I meet the orderly's gaze and smile. 'Thanks so much, Frank.'

'Anytime,' he says with a smile. 'Get home safe, you hear?' He nods goodbye to JT, then releases the wheelchair's brakes.

I watch Frank push the chair back to the hospital building, then turn to look at JT. He looks real fine leaning against the SUV; faded denim jeans, grey tee, deep tan and those remarkable blue eyes of his, the exact same colour as our baby girl's, only slightly hidden by the dirty-blond hair that flops down over his forehead. I look up at him and meet his gaze.

'Hey,' JT says. He moves towards me. Cups my face in his hand. Kisses me on the mouth.

Even through the bruising and the pain my body responds to him; love and lust mingling as one. I kiss him back. Don't want to ever stop. The taste of him is like home.

When we pull apart he's smiling, but there's still worry in his big old blues.

'Hey yourself,' I say, smiling back. 'It's damn good to be out.'

He laughs then, a proper belly laugh. 'It was only four days.'

'Felt like four years to me.'

'You never did like to stay still.'

'True that.' I rest my head against his chest. Listen to his heart-beat. Feel his warmth as he puts his arms around me, real gentle, and strokes my hair.

We stay like that for a while, wrapped up in each other, standing in the hospital parking lot.

Then he kisses the top of my head. Releases me from his embrace and nods towards the car. 'You all set?'

'Sure am.' I take a step closer to the SUV. My body still aches, the pain meds they've given me take the edge off, but the bruising and stitches make my skin feel too tight, and every movement is an effort. I tire easy, right now. I hate feeling sub-optimal, health compromised, but I'm grateful too – I know how close I was to not getting out of that penthouse, and then the hotel room, alive.

'You need a hand?' JT asks.

I look at the passenger seat. Now that I have to climb inside it, the rental SUV seems higher off the ground than usual. 'Maybe a boost.'

He smiles. 'I can handle that.' Moving behind me, he puts his hands on my hips. 'Is this okay, not hurting?'

'It's fine.' I grit my teeth. Don't tell him that everything hurts. He's not pressing on the gunshot wound, that's the main thing.

He supports me as I grip the passenger seat and the handle over the doorway, and start to ease myself into the vehicle. I'm halfway in when my cell starts vibrating in my pants pocket. I ignore it. Whoever it is, they'll have to wait.

The twist is the worse. Pain stabs into my side and I gasp.

'Okay?' JT says, concern in his voice, and on his face. 'Did I—?'

'It's fine,' I say. I keep my breathing shallow and my body as still as possible. Give myself a moment to get the pain under control. Then I put my hand on JT's arm. 'I'm good.'

He smiles, but the worry is still there in the lines around his eyes. He helps me with my seatbelt, then closes the passenger door and heads around the SUV to the driver's side.

As he climbs into the vehicle I check my cellphone. I inhale sharply when I see the caller ID. Bite my lip.

'Problem?' says JT.

I show him the screen. 'Monroe called me. He's left a voicemail.'

JT frowns. 'What are you going to do about it?'

I put the cell on my lap and try to get comfortable in the seat. However I sit, the stitches in my side seem to pull. I shake my head. 'I don't know.'

'I think you do.' JT's sitting real still, his focus totally on me.

I swallow hard. Know that he's right. 'Yeah, I guess I do.'

Calling my answer service, I wait for the connection, then listen as the service takes me to Monroe's message.

'Lori? It's Monroe.' His Kentucky drawl is even faster than usual. 'I guess you don't want to talk.' He pauses again, like he's hoping I'll pick up or something. A few seconds later he continues. 'Well, look, I thought you should know, we're taking Cabressa to trial. The DA's real hot for the case, so it's getting expedited, which is good news – great news – but, you know, like I said, they're going to want you to give evidence against him. Tell it like it happened that night. Be someone, a victim – survivor if you like – that the jury can make a human connection with, you know.' He takes a breath. 'So you're going to need to be there, at the trial. I don't have a date to give you yet, but, I thought you should know.'

I stare out of the windshield, across the parking lot. Watch a young child and her mother walking along the path towards the hospital building. See the cars arriving into the lot, and others leaving. Feel the freedom I felt just minutes ago drifting away from me. The thought of going to Cabressa's trial makes me feel sick. I want to get out of this city and not come back for a real long time. And I sure as shit don't want to testify.

I end the call. Won't call Monroe back. If they want me to give evidence they're going to have to subpoena me.

'Everything okay?' JT meets my eye. The happiness I saw on his face a few moments ago is now eclipsed by worry.

I force a smile. Don't want to get into things now. 'Monroe says they're expediting Cabressa's trial.'

'Thought they might.' He turns in his seat. Frowns. 'You don't have to be there do you?'

'He wants me there.'

JT nods. 'And what do you want?'

I shake my head. 'I don't want to go. Not if I can help it, that's for sure.'

'Good.' JT looks all kinds of relieved. 'A trial like that, Cabressa's people ... they won't want witnesses taking the stand.'

'I know.' And I do. In trials against mob bosses, the witnesses for the prosecution have a real nasty habit of ending up dead.

We both flinch as my phone starts to vibrate again. I look at the caller ID – it says Monroe again. 'Goddammit.'

'Answer it,' says JT. 'He'll not give us a moment of peace otherwise.'

Knowing JT's right, I stab the screen and answer the call. 'What?'

'Nice greeting. Hello to you too.'

I don't respond. Wait for Monroe to get on with it.

He sighs. 'I assume you've listened to my message?'

'Yep.'

'Well I missed something out. The chess pieces have been delivered back to their original owner – the one Cabressa had them stolen from, several years ago, before Patrick Walker, the man who was transporting them to Chicago, got murdered and the chess pieces were stolen again. So way back before you got involved in all this.'

'Okay.' I'm confused and I have no idea how this relates to me.

'Well, as you can imagine they're very grateful to have got them back.'

'I'm sure,' I say. 'Well, if that's all—'

'Hold up, I'm getting to the good bit.' Monroe pauses.

'And?' I can't keep the irritation out of my tone.

'There's a finder's fee. They offered it way back, a week or so after the pieces first disappeared, hoping that the thief would return them and take the money rather than try to fence stolen goods that were all over the papers. I told the bureau you found the pieces, because ... well, you did.'

I frown. 'Okay?'

'The owner's accountant is sending you a cheque. It's for two hundred thousand dollars.'

My jaw goes slack. I say nothing.

'Did you hear me, Lori? They're sending the two hundred-thousand-dollar reward money direct to you. I thought it might go a ways to making up for what happened.'

I pause. Monroe having me receive this kind of money – it raises all my suspicions. Monroe only does things to benefit him. If he's having the reward money sent to me, it's part of a bigger plan that's for sure. 'What's the catch?'

I wait, thinking this is the moment he'll tell me about a new job he wants me to work. JT's looking at me. He raises an eyebrow. Wondering what's going on, I reckon.

'Look, there's no catch, Lori.' Monroe sounds sincere. 'This is just about you getting what you're due.'

I narrow my eyes, real suspicious. About me getting what I'm due? That's never been on Monroe's agenda before. 'Sure.'

'Been good working with you,' Monroe says. His voice cracks halfway through the sentence. The bravado of the last time we spoke has gone. Now it's replaced by a kind of neediness.

I don't fall for it. Don't reply.

Monroe gives an awkward laugh. 'Don't be a stranger, Lori.'

The line goes dead. I stare at the phone. Monroe's always been Jekyll and Hyde. He's teetered back and forth across the line between lawful and lawless, but, until this job, even his unlawful acts have been motivated by his passion to catch the worst criminals and get justice. This time though, he strayed too far over the line in the wrong direction. Six people died. I was nearly the seventh. Most of those deaths could have been avoided if Monroe had given the command and sent in our back-up. I shake my head. I can't forget that, no matter how much he'd like me too. No matter how much money he's having sent my way.

'What did he say?' JT asks.

'There's a reward, a finder's fee from the owners of the chess pieces. Monroe told them I was the person who located them. They're sending me a cheque.'

'Sounds fair.'

'Yeah.' I meet JT's gaze. 'The reward's two hundred thousand dollars.'

He lets out a long whistle. 'That's some serious money. We could do a lot of things with that kind of cash. We could start that business you were talking about, or ship out and find us a place somewhere else – a new start – as a family.'

'We could.' I nod. My head's full of possibilities, but I don't want to make a hasty decision. 'We should think real careful about it.'

'For sure.' He slips his hand into mine. Caresses my palm. 'So what now?'

I smile at him. Interlace my fingers with his and hold them tight. 'Right now, I just want to go home.'

71

A home isn't a place or a building. It's a feeling – a connection – one made through relationships with family and with friends. JT is my home, Dakota too. And there's one other person who completes the group. A man who's become an essential confidante, friend, and family member to us all. And someone who's saved our skins a good few times as well. Tonight we're going to visit with him.

It's been three weeks since me and JT got back from Chicago. Dakota's real excited.

'Come on,' she calls as she races along the floating walkway, leading us towards the spot where Red's houseboat is moored.

JT and me stroll along behind her at a steadier pace, holding hands.

I watch Dakota reach the end of the pontoon. Stop by the dark-green and gold liveried houseboat and shout, 'You in there, Mr Red?'

A few moments later Red steps out on deck. Fit, rugged, with a deep tan and silver-streaked hair. He raises his hand in a wave.

Dakota glances back to check JT and me are coming, then scrambles under the pontoon ropes and jumps from the walkway to the boat.

'Hello Little Fish.' Red laughs, and ruffles her hair. 'Full of beans as ever I see.'

She beams up at him. Pulling her Miley Cyrus rucksack off her back, she thrusts it towards Red. 'Can I swim before dinner? I've got my swimsuit and all.'

'Well that depends on what your momma says,' replies Red, looking over at me.

'Momma, please,' says Dakota, her blue eyes wide and pleading. 'Can I show you my diving?'

I smile. Nod at Dakota, then look at Red. 'Sure, if you don't mind?'

He smiles. 'It's all good with me.' He looks at Dakota. 'Why don't you go get changed into your suit while I fetch your momma and JT a drink?'

'Sure.'

As Dakota scoots off into the houseboat to get changed, JT steps aboard, then turns back and helps me. Stepping across the gap between boat and mooring, and making the step up to the deck is still a bit of an effort. I'm doing better – the aches are reducing, and the pain is minimal, but I'm not up to full strength just yet.

'Sit, take a load off,' says Red, gesturing to the cushioned seating around the outside of the deck. 'What can I get you – sweet tea, a glass of wine, a beer?'

'Beer sounds good,' I say.

JT nods. 'For me too.'

Red takes three beers from the cooler under the middle bunk, twists off the caps and hands us each a bottle. He raises his. 'To safe returns.'

'I'll drink to that,' says JT, and clinks his bottle against Red's.

I do the same. 'I'm just glad we made it back.'

'Amen to that,' says Red. He glances towards the cabin. 'How's she been?'

'Okay, I think,' I say. 'She's back at school, doing real well according to her teacher, and seems to be enjoying it too.'

'She wants us around more, I'd say,' JT adds. 'Doesn't like it if one of us goes out, prefers us all being together.'

'I guess that's normal,' I say. Although as soon as I've said it I think how stupid it sounds; nothing has been normal about Dakota's home life, not for the past six months or so. She's been kidnapped and taken hostage; we got her back; and then she was on the boat with Red and JT when Miami Mob enforcers tried to sink them. Then she's had to cope while me and JT went to Chicago on a job and ended up being away a week longer than intended. Then she's seen me returning after a hospital stay and nearly getting dead. These are all things no ten-year-old kid should have to deal with.

There's more, as well. She's gotten to know JT, and she knows me and him go way back, but we've not told her that he's her dad. We need to do that, I know we do. And we will. Real soon. Just as soon as we've gotten things a little more settled. 'Normal, considering what she's been through, anyways,' I add.

Red nods. Looks at me real direct. 'And you, Miss Lori, how are you coping?'

I take a gulp of beer. Avoiding the question.

JT steps in to answer for me. 'She's getting stronger each day.'

Red looks thoughtful. Takes a sip of his beer then sets it down on the small table between the bench seats. 'Where's your head at, with the job an' all?'

I exhale hard. Shake my head. 'I've not gone back to work yet, if that's what you're asking.'

He holds my gaze. 'You know that it's not.'

None of us speak. Red's concerned about me, I get that. He knows I was having doubts before the Chicago job. That the three-way mob shootout in the Bonchese Miami compound last month shook me in a way that I hadn't experienced before. He knows I didn't want to go to Chicago, and that JT came with me because I was having nightmares about the Bonchese massacre.

I open my mouth to reply.

'Here I go…' Dakota flies out through the door to the cabin wearing her pink-and-gold swimsuit. As the door swings open I catch the aroma of Red's speciality dish – shrimp gumbo – cooking in the galley, and my stomach rumbles.

Dakota hurtles past us across the deck, and climbs up onto the railing. She pauses, getting her balance, then, with the agility of a cat, stands straight. 'Watch this,' she says. Next moment she leaps into the air and executes a perfect dive.

'Wow,' I say, clapping my hands. I look at Red, grinning. 'You taught her to do that?'

'I helped a little,' he says. 'Gave her a few pointers. But the girl's a natural. Swims like a fish.'

'I'm a mermaid,' says Dakota, her head and shoulders appearing out of the ocean as she treads water. 'Aren't I, Mr Red?'

Red laughs. 'You sure are, Little Fish.'

'I'm going to have a swim around,' she says, disappearing back under the water with a splash. She resurfaces a moment later. 'It's so cool in here,' she calls. 'You should come in too, Momma.'

'I don't have my swimsuit,' I say. 'Maybe next time.'

'Okay,' Dakota calls.

Leaning over the side of the boat, I watch her swimming around in the bay. She stays close. Is watchful for boats and jet-skis and the like. Red's taught her well.

'JT? You want to swim with me?' calls Dakota.

He looks at me and shrugs. 'Okay, kiddo. You're on.'

JT takes off his tee, revealing his tanned, toned chest, and removes his jeans and sliders. 'Here I come,' he says, as he climbs over the rail, and dives into the water beside Dakota. She giggles with delight. I watch the pair of them swim out a little further from the mooring. Smile at the delight on both their faces.

Red clears his throat. 'So, Miss Lori, you going to answer my question?'

I look back at him. Shrug. 'I'm okay, I guess.'

'Okay, you guess?' Red raises an eyebrow. 'One thing I admire about you is how you've always known and spoken your own mind, even when you know that your choices will be problematic. What's stopping you now?'

'I've been taken away from Dakota too many times this summer.' I shake my head. 'And then after the job with North and Old Man Bonchese – the shootout at the compound in Miami –

and now everything that happened in Chicago. It's like I've gotten away from what I am, who I am, and been pulled into this world of federal agents and escaped fugitives and mobsters.'

'You've done good work.'

'And a lot of people have died. Some of them good people, honest citizens.' I exhale hard. 'I didn't sign up for that.'

'What did you sign up for?'

I look out across the water. On the horizon, the sun is sinking lower in the sky, colouring the sea a burning gold. 'Justice, I signed up to help serve that. To get those who'd done bad deeds to face what they'd done and atone.' I look back at Red. 'To atone myself for not preventing the murder of my friend, and for shooting the man who killed her.'

'And now?'

'I still want that. But I want a family life with my child.' I look back out over the water to where JT and Dakota are swimming alongside each other. 'And with JT.'

'Sounds fair to me.' Red follows my gaze. 'She's a good kid – smart, bold, and as determined as her momma when she puts her mind to things.'

I laugh. 'Very true.'

'JT's a good man too.'

I nod. Watch JT pretending to be a shark and chasing Dakota through the water. See her laughing and kicking her legs real hard in the water, showering him with spray. I smile. 'He is that.' I meet Red's gaze. 'And so are you.'

He puts his fingers to his forehead in a mock salute. 'I'm happy to help out, Miss Lori. You know that.'

'I appreciate it.'

Red nods. Knocks his beer bottle against mine. 'Anytime.'

'Momma, did you see us?' Dakota pulls herself up over the rails and flops down onto the nearest seat.

'I did. You're fast.'

'Faster than JT,' Dakota says, real proud.

'*Almost* faster than JT,' says JT, climbing back onto the deck.

'Whatever,' says Dakota, rolling her eyes. '*Almost* faster.'

JT shakes his head. The damp from his hair sending water over us all, like a wet dog shaking itself dry.'

I shriek. Laugh. Keep laughing until I can't stop. It feels like I haven't laughed like this in forever. It feels good. Dakota joins in. Then JT and Red. And for a few moments we're laughing, and JT shakes again, and Dakota joins in, and we're wet and laughing and it's perfect. This is what's important – moments like this – happiness and being together.

'Is dinner ready, Mr Red?' Dakota asks.

'Real soon,' Red says. 'You best go get washed up and ready to eat.'

'I'll be fast,' says Dakota, rushing across the deck and disappearing through the door into the cabin. She calls over her shoulder, 'Don't start without me.'

Red reaches into one of the storage compartments under the bench seats and takes out a striped towel. Throws it to JT. 'You want a dry pair of shorts?'

JT uses the towel to dry his hair. Pats down his body. 'I'm good. It's so warm out, these'll dry in no time.'

'Alrighty then.' Red stands, and ambles towards the cabin. 'I best go get the gumbo ready to serve.'

'Just hold up a moment,' I say.

Stopping, Red turns back and squints towards me, shielding his eyes from the setting sun. 'What's going on?'

I clear my throat. Feel my heart rate accelerate. 'You know how you said you were always happy to help out?'

Red nods. 'Surely do.'

I pause, and glance at JT. Make sure he's ready for this; that the plan we've been working on these past couple of weeks is totally what he wants.

JT smiles. Gives me a nod. And suddenly I know that everything is going to be just fine. We've figured out how we're going to use the two-hundred-thousand-dollar reward for finding the chess pieces. Now all we have to do is persuade Red.

Taking a deep breath, I look back at Red.

This is it, the moment of truth. Yes or no.

I smile to hide my nerves. Hope things go the way we hope. 'The thing is, Red, we've got a proposition for you.'

Acknowledgements

I first visited Chicago just over ten years ago and was awed by the soaring skyscrapers, stunning parks and wide waterways of the city. For Lori Anderson's fourth adventure I wanted to do something a little different to the chase stories of the first three books; something more contained, like a locked room mystery. So when I had the idea for this story I immediately thought Chicago would be the perfect setting – so thank you Chicago for being such a fabulous muse.

Although it's the writer's name on the cover, many people contribute to getting a story from idea to finished book – it's a real team effort. First a massive shout-out to my brilliant agent and all-round great guy, Oli Munson, for his wise advice, expert guidance and tireless enthusiasm. A huge thank-you to my wonderful editor and publisher, Karen Sullivan and to the fabulously eagle-eyed editor, West Camel, who both help me refine the story and polish it into the final version, and to proofreader extraordinaire, Victoria Goldman. And big thanks to the whole of Team Orenda – including the tirelessly working Cole Sullivan, Megan Robinson, Mark Swan, Sophie Goodfellow and Anne Cater.

I'd like to thank the brilliant cheerleaders who are #TeamLori, and all of the bloggers, reviewers and readers who've read, enjoyed and reviewed the books so far – I hope you like this one too!

To my family and friends for being so supportive and encouraging, a massive thank-you for always being so fabulous, with a special shout-out to the wonderful Andy, Susi, Helen, Marie, Caroline and Kirsten for listening to me banging on about ideas, plots and characters for hour after hour – thank you a million times; you guys rock!
Other titles in the Lori Anderson Series

STEPH BROADRIBB

'Fast, confident
and suspenseful'
LEE CHILD

Deep
Down
THE LORI ANDERSON SERIES
Dead

STEPH BROADRIBB

'Like *Midnight Run*, but much darker ... really, really good'
IAN RANKIN

Deep Blue Trouble

THE LORI ANDERSON SERIES

STEPH BROADRIBB

'A real cracker ...
Broadribb kicks ass,
as does her ace
protagonist'
**MARK
BILLINGHAM**

MOTEL

THE LORI ANDERSON SERIES

Deep
Dirty
Truth